PRAISE

"Geneva Lee convinces with fluid writing that's full of drama, ups and downs..."

— PEOPLE MAGAZINE

"Romance and drama...when it comes to dirty talk, the British heir to the throne can hardly be topped..."

— THE HUFFINGTON POST

"Sexy, sinful, and downright delightful! Geneva Lee is the queen of writing drama and angst. .

— CORA CARMACK, NEW YORK TIMES BESTSELLER

"A royal tale unlike any other. Heart-stopping, mesmerizing...I only wanted more."

— AUDREY CARLAN, #1 NEW YORK TIMES BESTSELLER

ALSO BY GENEVA LEE

THE ROYALS SAGA

Command Me

Conquer Me

Crown Me

Crave Me

Covet Me

Capture Me

Complete Me

THE ROYAL WORLD™

Cross Me

Claim Me

Consume Me

STANDALONE

The Sins That Bind Us

Two Week Turnaround

CROSS ME

Ivy Estate Publishing

www.GenevaLee.com

First published, 2019.

Ebook ISBN: 978-1-945163-30-2

Cover design © Date Book Designs.

Image © vasyl/Adobe Stock.

THE ROYAL WORLD: ONE

CROSS ME

GENEVA LEE

IVY ESTATE
SEATTLE

To Audrey,
For turning on the light

CHAPTER ONE

ALEXANDER

W hoever said it was good to be King had clearly never had the pleasure.

The Royal family has come under increasing scrutiny the last two years due to the controversial actions of Alexander, who recently succeeded his father to the throne. Alexander's decision to marry a half-American was the subject of contentious public debate. The crown seemed intent on making an even bigger statement with Alexander's recent approval of Prince Edward's marriage to Scottish man David McClane. Vocal minorities and religious organizations throughout the world have attacked the king's support for the union. The Catholic Church issued a statement condemning the act and it's been the source of much media speculation in America. Other activist groups, however, applauded the Crown's

*progressive stance, stating that Alexander and his
family are breathing fresh life into stale Royal
traditions. Will public opinion swing in favor of
the king's choices, or is Alexander threatening the
stability of the Crown? Only time will tell, but—*

The television snapped off and I glanced over my
shoulder to find my wife leaning against the bathroom's doorframe. "It's too early for bad news, X."

She had voiced opposition to mounting a television in the bathroom, but given that I was expected to
be up on world news and that I had very little time in
the day to catch up on what the media was saying, I
had overlooked her concerns. I reached behind me
and took the remote, flipping the television back on,
but changed the channel to a cable sports station. "I
was just checking the times."

"Since when are you into racing?" She was
calling my bluff, but what my wife didn't know was
that I had recently become much more interested in
racing. When I didn't answer, she hit me with, "You
don't even like driving."

"I like driving you."

"Driving me crazy maybe."

I continued to shave, which was a dangerous
proposition because my eyes kept drifting from my
own reflection to hers. The dawn light had begun to
filter into the bedroom, haloing her in a soft glow that
accentuated her luscious curves and made her look
like God's gift to man. She was certainly God's gift to

me. Her dark hair cascaded over creamy shoulders. Last night I'd pressed my lips to them as I rocked her to two climaxes. In the mirror, her own lips twisted into a knowing smirk as if she knew exactly what I was thinking. As I was usually thinking about finding a way to get her naked—something I had never kept secret from her—the smugness was warranted.

She moved towards the counter, hips swaying slightly. Her smile slipped as she studied herself. In the harsher artificial light of the bathroom, I could see what was making her frown. Faint blue smudges circled her eyes and she looked even more pale than normal.

"Have you considered the houses I found for Edward?" she asked.

I'd looked at my wife's list yesterday. She'd been obsessing over his wedding present since we'd returned from the holidays and he'd left on his honeymoon. "I'd like him closer."

"Windsor is close," she gurgled as she brushed her teeth.

"Windsor Castle is a bit extravagant for everyday use, Poppet."

She shot me a look. "Have you seen our house? There's a smaller house in Windsor that sounds perfect and its only half an hour from the city."

"That place?" I shook my head. "It's unacceptable. Practically falling down."

"You need to make a decision soon or they'll never come home from Seychelles."

I wouldn't if I were my brother. I kept this to myself. It would be taken care of, but for now I had more pressing concerns.

"Are you feeling all right? I heard you up earlier this morning." I tried to keep the concern in my voice to a reasonable level, but it was a struggle.

"I'm fine," she said, but it did little to reassure me. At the moment, my wife's moods swung between angelic calm and hysterical rage. I had learned the hard way not to get up and join her when morning sickness hit. I didn't want to allow her to go through it alone, but since my presence seemed to upset her even more, I'd had to keep a restless vigil from the bedroom.

I found other ways to manage her care, though, waking our daughter and doing my best to help Clara get extra rest. That was the hardest, because it usually meant keeping my hands to myself, even when I wanted to spend a few quiet moments together before the rest of the household intruded on our lives.

"Did you get enough sleep?"

"Sure," she said noncommittally as she glared at her reflection. "I look terrible and I have the Child Watch Symposium this afternoon."

She turned the faucet on in the marble sink and bent forward to splash cold water on her face. I took the interruption to quickly wipe remnants of shaving cream from my jaw.

"You know, maybe that's a sign you should stay

home," I said, stepping behind her. I stopped my arms around her slender torso, one hand resting over the tiny bump that only we knew about, while the other took a slightly less sentimental path up to her breast. My thumb circled its furl through the thin satin of her nightgown. Clara responded with a soft moan.

"Are you trying to distract me?" Although, even as she pretended to be annoyed, she leaned into me, allowing better access. I slid my hand under the flimsy nightgown and continued my gentle assault. "Because you aren't going to convince me not to go."

We'd been having this argument for some time. After I'd proposed, Clara had struggled with her decision to leave her career behind. When I'd asked her to marry me she had known that one day I would become the King of England. It was inevitable. Before our wedding, I'd promised her plenty of opportunities to continue working on the social programs she'd overseen for Peters & Clarkwell. None of that had gone according to plan. I'd still convinced her to marry me, but both of us had taken on new responsibilities so quickly we might have suffered whiplash. My father's assassination had backed me into a corner, forcing me to ascend to the throne years before I had expected. Clara's discovery that she was pregnant had pushed us both into parenthood, something I'd always thought I didn't want. For the last year and a half, we had been adjusting. I'd had Clara exactly where I wanted her— by my side, in my bed, and, most importantly, home, where I could keep an eye on her personally. Now, despite being pregnant again, she was determined to finally rise to her public responsibilities as Queen. No amount of charm could dissuade her.

"I can think of much better ways for you to spend your day." My other hand abandoned its protective vigil and slid to the hollow between her thighs, working its way past the fabric to the wet heat there.

"You have meetings all day," she breathed. I couldn't help but detect a note of challenge. The message was clear: if I wanted her to abandon her plans for the day I would have to do the same, something we both knew was impossible.

"My meetings are all going to be here." I coaxed her legs farther apart with my knee to give me better access to the prize I was ready to claim. I earned a soft shudder accompanied by a moan of approval as my thumb found its target. "I'm here and you're here. Other people can wait."

My lips whispered temptations as they trailed along the soft skin behind her ear and down to the freckles I'd been fantasizing about only moments ago. I drank in the sight of her languorous body in my arms, the mirror reflecting exactly what I wanted out of life: to possess her completely until she knew nothing but the safety and security I'd promised her.

Clara opened one eyelid, lazily meeting my greedy gaze. "So in this scenario, I'm here waiting naked in your bed—right, X?"

She didn't sound as annoyed about this prospect

as she usually might. Of course, I was actively lowering her defenses.

"Something like that," I said silkily.

"No way in hell." She turned her head, though, allowing her face to come a breath away from my own. "But I don't mind if you keep trying to convince me."

"Challenge accepted, Poppet." And then my mouth closed over hers.

Two discussions later and I'd failed to persuade her to stay home. She said goodbye to me, glowing like a lightbulb, which would no doubt contribute to speculation that she was with child again. If she was going to insist on going out in public, we would have to confirm this pregnancy sooner rather than later. It would be easier if she would just stay here. But her defiance was what had first drawn me to Clara Bishop. I'd never take that away from her. I would never want to. Still, it made things more complicated.

My fingers raked through my hair as I buried my head in my hands, wondering what a simple life looked like. What was it like to be a normal guy whose pregnant wife went off to work? I'd never know. Not for the first time I wished I could trade my birthright in for a less regal model.

"Alexander?" A deep voice interrupted my thoughts. I didn't have to look up to know it was my old friend and longtime personal guard, Norris, because he was the only person on my payroll who didn't constantly address me as Sir.

If he was here, that meant my day was about to start. Then again, Norris shouldn't be here. I frowned, not bothering to hide the reproach written all over my face. "I thought you were going with her."

"The Prime Minister's visit today. The household team had to split duty. Brexton is with her."

My frown deepened. It wasn't that I didn't trust my old friend and Royal Air Force buddy, it was simply that I trusted Norris more. If I couldn't be with Clara, I always felt better when he was there. Norris didn't look like a bodyguard. With his thinning blond hair and average build, he blended in, looking more the part of the fatherly advisor than the trained killer. He was lethal and he wouldn't hesitate to protect her. "I'd prefer these decisions were run by me first."

"Her Majesty was quite determined on the point." His lips pressed into a thin line, recalling an unpleasant memory. "She said I fuss over her too much."

My eyebrow cocked at this bit of information. Perhaps my attempts to persuade her this morning had backfired. Now, not only had she gone out, she had sent a defiant message as well. Clara knew that I preferred for Norris to be with her, so sending him away in favor of a team led by Brex was her way of telling me to back off. "I'll discuss this with her later."

"If you don't mind me saying so." Norris finally stepped into the room, his hands behind his back and his expression unreadable. I had no idea what he wanted to say to me, but I suspected I was about to get a lecture. "Clara seems a trifle emotional these days. Perhaps you can trust her to make her own plans. I think she would prefer that."

"Which one of us is the politician?" I grumbled. Norris had chosen his words carefully, but the meaning was clear. I hadn't confided the news of her pregnancy to him yet. She had wanted to keep it private and only begin to tell people once it was confirmed by the doctor later this week. Norris had clearly guessed what was going on. "I don't know why I try to keep secrets from you."

"Well, Alexander, you have been strutting around here like a prize stud for the last week," he said dryly. "She's out to teach you a lesson. I caught her crying twice last week. We've been here before."

I did take an inordinate amount of pride in knowing Clara was carrying my child again. Watching her body transform with the proof of our love and knowing that she had chosen me was a massage for my ego, admittedly.

"Plus," Norris continued, "there's the matter of you both acting like damned fools."

"Excuse me?" His criticism broke me away from thoughts of my wife. It wasn't that he couldn't speak to me that way. It was that he rarely did.

"She's obviously making a point that she won't be

told what to do and where she can go, which makes me suspect that you tried to tell her what to do and where to go this morning."

I held my hands up in surrender. "I tried to convince her."

"Are you certain you didn't try to command her?" Norris had been privy to many of our premarital arguments. He'd witnessed the few moments where I'd almost lost her because of my controlling nature. He was well aware of my tendency toward possessiveness.

"I asked. Nicely."

He didn't have to know what I meant by nicely. Clara, however, had obviously seen this morning differently. I reminded myself that my wife was pregnant and therefore prone to mood swings, but despite that, my palm twitched. I had to fight my urge to dominate her outside of the bedroom. If my best efforts were going to be rewarded with passive aggressive actions meant to test me, it would be harder to maintain that boundary.

"It's none of my business," he said with the air of somebody who felt it was very much his business. Norris was like a father to me. Because of the terrible relationship I'd had with my real father, I usually appreciated Norris' insight. Today, with the prospect of a morning meeting with the Prime Minister and briefings all afternoon, I wasn't in the mood.

"Anything else? Are we prepared for Prime

Minister Clark's arrival?" My tone shifted to cool business.

His eyes narrowed. He understood when he was being dismissed, but unlike most of the people who worked around me, Norris wasn't prone to sycophancy. Still, he seemed to sense I was on edge.

"Everything is in place and the arrangements for Queen Mary's quarters at Kensington Palace have been made."

Suddenly, I was ready to take my daily meetings. Anything was better than dealing with the family. The Prime Minister wanted to discuss the budget and climate change initiatives, topics I usually found mind-numbingly boring, especially since Parliament was likely to enact whatever budget or legislation they saw fit. The reminder that my grandmother and uncle had decided to return to London was another piece of bad news. Issues of national politics felt positively tame compared to the tangle of family politics that would soon capture me.

"They've chosen Kensington?" I couldn't help but be surprised. I'd expected there to be a fight over Clarence House, the first home I'd occupied with Clara after our marriage. It seemed like the choice my grandmother would make, if only to spite me.

"I believe they were told that Clarence House had potential occupants."

This was news to me. I sat back in my office chair and waited, wondering if it was too early for Scotch.

"It's not official," Norris said. "I thought it

prudent to reserve the premises given your brother's new marital status."

"Good thinking. Clara had pitched Windsmoor."

"I assume you told her it was—"

"Falling apart," I finished. "I think she meant to give them more privacy than London might afford them."

Norris and I hadn't had the opportunity to discuss Edward's wedding present, but it was customary for the reigning monarch to gift a residence to close members of the family. I'd been avoiding the conversation, excusing myself from it by reminding anyone who asked, mostly Clara, that Edward and David were still on their honeymoon. Still, I couldn't avoid it forever. I feared my brother would prefer a country estate. It would make sense. It was the choice I would have made had I not been forced to keep a permanent residence in London. Keeping Clarence House open and offering it to Edward felt right. I wanted my brother nearby. He was the only blood relation I trusted and a friend and advisor.

"Will that be all?" Norris's eyes twinkled as he spoke. He was testing me, calling me out for trying to be dismissive earlier.

I leaned back in my seat, crossing my arms behind my head. "I don't suppose I could convince you to go to that symposium."

He levelled an incredulous stare in my direction.

"Given Clara's condition, it would be better not to upset her."

"I wish you were with her." This time I wasn't teasing. I was deadly serious. But he had a point. Clara had made her desires known and undermining her would only cause a fight. While I liked making up with her after an argument, I also wanted to see that she was healthy. None of that meant I had to do nothing.

"Keep an eye on the situation," I ordered him. "I want to know if there's someone with so much as a sniffle around her."

Norris opened his mouth as if to respond but then thought better of it. He shook his head as he turned to look into it, but as he crossed the threshold of my office, I could swear I heard him mutter, "Stubborn arse."

THE PRIME MINISTER REMINDED ME OF MY father, which was to say he looked like most Englishmen of a certain age: light hair and skin creased with wrinkles from years of apologetic gymnastics, usually wearing tweed. Next to each other, the two of us looked like night and day. Despite spending most of my time in cabinet meetings and offices, I had my mother's rich olive skin tone. I was suddenly grateful to my mother's Greek heritage for the influx of fresh genes.

Prime Minister Clark was unfailingly gracious

and forgiving of the fact I was obviously distracted. With my thoughts on Clara and her event, he'd had to repeat himself several times, making the meeting drag on. We'd taken armchairs by the fireplace in my private office. He was the only politician I met with in closed quarters. No one, not even Norris, attended these meetings. It was meant to encourage a spirit of cooperation. Not for the first time, I wondered if the meetings were even necessary. He had his business and I had mine. We were both busy running very different aspects of the United Kingdom. As he informed me about the latest news on a climate change initiative, I wondered what he would think if he knew the concerns preoccupying me.

"My family stance on climate change is well documented," I reminded him.

"Not everyone will be thrilled with the sanctions," he warned me.

"Do I look overly concerned with my popularity?"

Clark tipped his head, something like a laugh escaping his lips. "The press is crucifying you."

"When I was young, I couldn't do anything right. Now that I'm older, I still can't."

"Welcome to being a politician."

"Isn't that your job?" I only wished it were true. Most of Britain's politics filtered through Parliament and I was expected to simply support or criticize legislation, have a stance on issues affecting my people, and to be up-to-date on all major discussions before Parliament. The government had throttled some of the Crown's powers over the last few years and the monarchy had been turning more and more responsibility over to His Majesty's Government for the last few centuries. That didn't absolve my obligations to my position.

"I should warn you that there are some minority factions in the House of Lords who are questioning the choice to allow Edward to remain in the line of succession."

"That's not really for them to be concerned about." My fist clenching as I imagined getting my hands on one of the dissenters.

"I suppose the authority rests with you—"

"There is no suppose about it. The authority does rest with me. Not that it should be a question at all. I thought Britain was in the twenty-first century."

"It's more about perception. It might strain our relationships with our more conservative allies."

"Sod them." I couldn't help myself. It was my duty to play nice—to act the part of the benevolent king—but I never had much luck hiding my protective streak when it came to my family. That we were still having this argument, even after a year of letting people warm up to the idea of my brother's wedding, pissed me off.

"I'm not sure that should be the Crown's official stance," he said.

"I wasn't planning on releasing a statement to that effect." My lip curled at the thought. The press would have a field day with it, and although there was a time when I would've enjoyed delivering a 'screw you' to anyone who thought they should have a say in my private affairs, I didn't have that luxury any longer.

"Anonymity and freedom from criticism are two expectations only afforded to private citizens." His words were gentle. Not for the first time I suspected the Prime Minister felt a paternalistic responsibility to me, probably owing to the death of my father. He might not feel so inclined if he knew how little I respected my father's advice before his death. I didn't need lectures about the difficulties of being a member of the Royal family. I'd dealt with the media circus for as long as I could remember. My own marriage had been dissected by the tabloids. More than once, my wife's life had been put in danger by overeager leeches who believed exactly what the prime minister had just said: there was no privacy afforded to royals. Of course I knew that, it was why I had been the one to accept the crown. It might've been easier to reject my birthright and make a life on my own. I would never know. The only thing I remained certain of was that my position afforded me the ability to grant some bit of security to those I loved. It also meant bearing the brunt of criticism for my progressive stances.

"Perhaps you could consider another option."

"Which is?" I asked.

"Bring someone in. A publicist of sorts," he

suggested. "Someone you can trust to help you maneuver the stickier situations."

"I'll keep it under advisement," I said through gritted teeth. There were actual matters of state to discuss. Instead we were sitting here worrying about public perception. That was the difference—I realized something. There was a difference between a man who climbed to political office and one who was born to lead. I'd never had a choice of life. In a way, that was turning out to be more freeing. No one could challenge my birthright. No one could vote me out. If anyone had qualms over my choices, it wasn't going to endanger my political career. I would still be King.

No, it would take far more sinister machinations to remove my power. Taking the crown was a much bloodier affair than an election. I had survived my first assassination attempt. My father had not been so lucky. I had no idea how many he'd survived before the one that claimed his life. I suspected that I myself had survived on more occasions than I knew. But those attempts hadn't come from people or journalists or other countries. None of the forces with which the Prime Minister felt so concerned were at play in any of those events. It had been the poison underbelly of Parliament itself. I reminded myself every week, while the Prime Minister sat across from me with a fatherly smile on his face: politicians couldn't be trusted. One member of Parliament had already been arrested in connection with my father's assassination, and despite our best efforts, we still had not discovered how far the plot reached.

Still, perhaps he was right. Maybe I needed someone to handle the public announcements. It would be a load off. If only I could find someone to attend these meetings.

I glanced at the clock, my thoughts slipping away to much more important items on my agenda. I wanted an update on Clara. The longer this meeting continued, the longer I would wait for one.

"There's one final matter I'd like to discuss. The funding for the Sovereign Games."

I grimaced. That had not been on my agenda. "That was my father's pet project."

As far as I was concerned that was the end of that. I'd spent the better part of the last year removing all vestiges of my father's reign from this office. I wasn't about to continue his hobbies.

"It was one of your father's most popular programs. Furthermore, Parliament has approved its half of the funding. There seems to be a general consensus that Britain is feeling more divided than usual." He was choosing his words carefully. It wasn't just the country that felt divided, it was the entire world. Some of my own choices had certainly fractured the unity of the people here, but I didn't see how that mattered in this instance.

"I wasn't even aware the games were moving forward."

"Your grandmother has been quite persistent in—"

"Of course she has." It was starting to make sense. My grandmother, Queen Mary, had left residence here after the death of her son. We weren't exactly on speaking terms. Mostly, because she had called my wife a whore. "So, this has become her baby."

"I suppose in a way. She feels strongly that Albert's memory should be kept alive."

"Doesn't everyone?" I might be the only person content to let my father's memory remain at rest. In his final moments, he had sacrificed himself for me. But while in the end he had granted me acceptance, he had denied it to me for most of my life. His final choices didn't erase the nearly thirty years of disapproval and mistrust between us.

A knock broke the mounting tension in the room, but before I could call the person in, Norris stuck his head through the door. "I apologize for the interruption but I need to speak with you immediately."

"Not a problem." The Prime Minister stood, smoothing wrinkles from his suit. "I need to check in with my secretary. I'll see you this afternoon?"

As if I had a choice.

"I'm looking forward to it," I said in a flat voice.

Norris closed the door behind him and I began to shuffle through the day's agenda, looking to see what unsavory briefing was next on my plate. "Thanks for the save."

But he didn't smile.

"There's been a development. I must warn you that this is likely nothing," he began.

My blood ran cold. It dawned on me too late. Norris wasn't the type to interrupt a meeting with the Prime Minister because I was bored. That was something Brex would do. But Brex was with Clara. If Norris had abandoned his sense of propriety to interrupt a private discussion, something must be terribly wrong.

"This isn't confirmed," he continued, his voice remaining suspiciously even, "but we did receive a message."

He held out his mobile phone and I scanned the screen as the weight of what I read settled onto my chest like a boulder. I couldn't quite digest it—words like bomb and faction and symposium. It didn't matter if there was confirmation. It didn't matter what my wife wanted anymore. It didn't matter if there was only a shred of possibility that what I was reading could be true. "We need to find Clara."

"Alexander, I will handle this."

I was already out of my seat and making my way down the hall. Norris knew better than to try to stop me. Not after I'd received this piece of intel. Not with the threat of an attack on the symposium.

Not before I reached my wife.

CHAPTER TWO

CLARA

I t was proving to be the longest car ride of my life. My plan to send X a clear message—that I wasn't going to be sitting at home gestating for the next eight months—had backfired. Now, instead of a peaceful ride with Norris, who knew the value of solitude, I was stuck listening to incessant bickering.

Brexton Miles was an old army friend of my husband's and one of the few men Alexander trusted. But he wasn't assigned to my personal security team. Alexander had made it clear that Norris was the only acceptable escort for public outings. I intended to make it clear that I could make that decision on my own. Except I hadn't counted on Brex bringing along his partner? Girlfriend? Colleague? It was impossible to tell. Not girlfriend, I decided. There was far too much tension in the front seat, and it was clearly of the haven't-slept-together-yet variety. It was perfectly obvious to anyone with eyes or ears that they wanted to shag.

I couldn't imagine what was stopping them. Brexton was good-looking by anyone's standards—tall and well-built with a quick smile and chocolate brown eyes. He was also too charming for his own good. Perhaps that was what had put Georgia Kincaid off him. She seemed the type to hold something innocuous, like charm, against a man. I could see why Brex was obviously into her. She was gorgeous in a way that stoked my inner inferiority complex. She'd had a relationship of sorts with Alexander once. I wondered, not for the first time, if Brex knew that or if he would even care.

We'd taken the Range Rover, mostly because I used it as a family car. I'd never grown accustomed to the veritable stable of luxury vehicles that came with my title. Unfortunately, my choice of vehicles meant I had very little distance between me and the brewing conflict between them.

My phone rang, and I exhaled a silent sigh of relief.

"You're saving my life," I said as I answered my best friend's call.

Belle laughed, but it sounded off, as though she was trying to force it. "Don't you have a team to do that?"

"I do," I whispered. "That's the problem. They won't stop fighting. What's up?"

"Nothing,' she said, and I knew she was fibbing.

Belle, who'd spent the last year deeply immersed in her honeymoon phase, rarely called without a reason. It was one of the ways our relationship had changed dramatically since we'd both gotten married. "I shouldn't bother you."

"Anything is better than continuing to listen to them debate the benefits of entering through the front or back of the building," I whispered. "Maybe they should stop arguing and enter as quickly as possible."

"I get the impression we're not discussing security arrangements," Belle said.

"I get the impression they aren't, either."

From the front seat, Georgia shot me a look over her shoulder. Maybe I should be having this conversation over text.

"Don't you have a doctor's appointment today?" I asked Belle, remembering I wasn't the only one who had plans for the day. That was why she sounded strange. My heart seemed to lurch to a stop. Had she already been? I couldn't bring myself to ask more. Instead, I waited for her to continue.

"Of course, I do. Why do you think I'm calling you?"

I breathed a sigh of relief. She hadn't been yet. I mentally began rearranging my life to see if I could be there for her. "Isn't Smith coming with you?"

"He is," Belle jumped in before I could get too far in my theoretical rescheduling. "But he's just so confident."

"And you're not?" I guessed softly.

Belle lowered her voice as though Smith could hear through multiple walls. "He's so excited. I don't want him to know I'm scared. We don't know why we lost the first baby. What...what if something's wrong with me?"

"I'm not going tell you all of the statistics again. I'm sure you've looked them all up anyway," I said. "There's no reason to think that's the case. Plus, the sooner you go, the sooner you'll know."

"You're probably right," Belle admitted.

I knew it wasn't enough to alleviate her concerns. I wished I was there to help her get her mind off things.

"I'm always right, except for when I'm wrong, which is very rare," I said. This earned a genuine laugh. "I have that symposium today, but call me as soon as you hear anything. I'll have my phone with me. I'll check my messages."

"I completely forgot about that." It sounded like she was banging her head against the wall. I didn't bother urging her to calm down. I knew how stressful early pregnancy was. "Why am I bothering you with this?"

"Because you're my best friend and because it's not a bother at all. No matter what happens I'm here for you. You're my family."

"I know. I love you," Belle said.

"I love you, too. Look, we're almost there. Make sure you call Edward. I know he's wondering," I reminded her. Edward, my husband's brother and our mutual best friend, had begun his own bump watch since Belle had discovered she was expecting over the holidays.

"He's on his honeymoon." She was stalling, creating excuses so she wouldn't have to face the doctor.

"Well, you shouldn't have told him then," I teased her.

"Obviously, I have no self-control when it comes to secrets."

I paused, momentarily uncertain how to respond. We'd both kept secrets from each other over the last few years. This was different, though. She needed to see that. "Happy news shouldn't be kept secret."

"I just need a little longer to get used to the idea," she admitted.

That was something I could relate to. "Promise to call me."

"I will. I better go before Smith takes a battering ram to the door. He's even more unbearably protective now. Talk later."

The call ended and I dropped the phone into my lap, my mind on my best friend. I wished I could be there with her. I wished that I had known the right thing to say to comfort her. I wished Belle wasn't scared at all. Belle had been by my side during my first sonogram when Alexander couldn't be. I felt like I was letting her down with my absence. With more and more demands on my time, I felt that way a lot lately.

But our lives were different now, and I reminded myself Smith would be by Belle's side for the entire appointment. That wasn't what was really bothering me, though. I had yet to tell my best friends about my own pregnancy. After Belle's miscarriage, I'd always worried about what would happen when one of us got pregnant again. If I did and Belle didn't? How could I comfort her? How could she stand to be around me? I didn't want to lose her. That was the real reason I'd made Alexander promise to keep it a secret.

Then again, I hadn't even seen a doctor yet. We'd been out of town when I'd realized I was pregnant and I'd put it off when we came home. There were patronages to catch up on and emails that needed a response. The baby wouldn't be here for months. It was silly to stress about it. Still, it wasn't as if I could hide what was happening to my own body much longer. Every day since my wedding—and a little bit before that—photographers had taken photos of me, posting them to tabloid websites that speculated on the size of my stomach. It had taken me a long time to get used to it, especially given the eating disorder I'd battled since my teen years. Most of the time I felt perfectly healthy, no doubt owing to Alexander's unconditional love. However, it was a little harder to maintain mental peace and self-care when people noticed if I was bloated from eating too much pizza.

Now I had another reason to worry about the gossip rags. I definitely didn't want Belle to find out that way. The sooner my best friend got the good news that I was praying she would, the better. I couldn't even consider the other outcome.

"Everything okay?" Brex watched me from the rear view mirror, his warm brown eyes filled with concern. Of course, he'd been listening. It was his job to know everything going on around him. It didn't change how strange it was to know how few of my conversations were private anymore. Sometimes even when I was alone, it felt like the walls were watching me. I supposed it was normal. I had traded an average life to be married to one of the most powerful men in the world. I just wished it were different. At least Norris pretended he didn't overhear personal matters.

"Everything is fine," I reassured him.

"How is Belle?" Georgia twisted in her seat, her glossy, black hair swinging over her shoulder like a shampoo commercial. Once again, I wondered why she'd had to come along. Given the sordid past she shared with my husband—a dark mark on Alexander's history that we rarely talked about—no one could blame me for not wanting the woman around. The fact she was gorgeous and confident and a former assassin only made matters worse.

"Why do you care?" I snapped, instantly feeling regret. Given my wildly swinging hormones, it was a little harder to remind myself not to jump to conclusions.

"She is married to my oldest friend." Georgia's scarlet-painted lips twisted into a pained smile. It seemed like she was trying to be friendly and finding it rather difficult.

I forced myself to do the same. There was no need to add any more tension to the car. Brex and Georgia had enough simmering between them.

"She was just checking in." Regardless of Georgia's intentions, it wasn't my place to spill my best friend's news, especially given Georgia's relationship with Smith. He'd probably want to tell her himself. It was strange knowing that these two people I knew so very little about—Smith and Georgia— had such deep connections to the most important people in my life.

Her dark eyes scanned me for a moment as if she didn't believe a word I was saying. But if she wanted to challenge me, she thought better of it. She turned in her seat and began to bicker with Brex over the radio. So it was back to this.

"I don't want it on," he explained. "I need to hear what's going on around me."

That's why we couldn't listen to music? Was this going to be my whole life? Was I going to spend every day being driven from place to place in total silence while everyone around me worried that any moment someone might jump out and grab me? It was a bit much to swallow. Alexander had warned me.

It was hard to believe that only a few years ago I was just a university student trying to dodge being set up on a blind date with Belle's older brother. Instead, that day had brought Alexander and his complicated world into my life. I wouldn't trade him nor any of it. Not for freedom. Not to be able to listen to radio stations. Not for a life without bodyguards over-hearing my phone calls. I wouldn't give him up for anything.

I only wished Alexander would relax a little. There had been no security incidents I knew of for months now. They had even arrested someone recently in conjunction with his father's assassination. But my husband had a long memory. I knew that from how he held onto grudges that stretched to a time before I knew him. He held on to control even more tightly. Even my presence at the symposium today had gone unannounced—a decision from the security team. The council had rolled with it, deciding to make it a surprise. It was a tip of the hat to my life before I'd married the King of England, to back when I'd worked on charity campaigns.

Georgia's voice pitched up an octave and I did my best to block out the now heated argument coming from the front of the SUV. Picking up my phone, I began to scroll through the headlines. I liked to think it was part of my job to be up on current affairs, even if I didn't want to listen to the news in the bathroom. More and more, though, it felt like it was just part of Alexander's job. At one time, I'd expected to talk about treaties and legislation and the rising cost of oil, amongst other things. Instead, I had spent the last year tucked safely behind castle walls with our daughter. I reminded myself that I wouldn't trade anything for my family. No matter how frustrating I found my position at times.

I paused and tapped on a story about the upcoming Sovereign Games. It had been a few years since the UK had hosted the national sporting event. I hadn't thought about it in ages. My world had been different then. I'd only had a passing interest in the games. Now I saw them in a whole new light. Skimming the article sparked a few things I didn't recall. The games had been an initiative introduced by King Albert. According to the story, there had been a lot of speculation as to whether or not Alexander would continue and step into the role of host. But what had really caught my attention was that a member of the Royal family had confirmed the games would proceed. Alexander hadn't said anything to me about them. Then again, there were a lot of things he didn't discuss with me lately.

The event, which is an invitation-only competition in a number of popular sports, draws large crowds to various venues throughout Great Britain. Although no invitations have been formally presented, a few names stand out as likely candidates. Among them is Anderson Stone, the 25-year-old racing superstar ranked among the top three competitors in the world. Mr. Stone, if chosen to compete, makes it a safe bet that one of this year's events will take place at Silverstone.

I skipped the rest of the article. *This* was why Alexander had been checking racing scores this morning. At the time I'd thought I was going crazy. Never once had he mentioned enjoying car racing. Considering how his sister had died and that he'd avoided driving for years, it had seemed weird. But why wouldn't he just tell me why he was suddenly interested? It didn't matter. It wasn't that he kept the games a secret so much as it was beginning to feel like my life with him was divided down the middle. I loved him. He loved me. We were happy. Neither of us complained about the sex. But then there was another side to our relationship, or rather, another side to Alexander. It seemed as if he had systematically cut me out of the duties and responsibilities I had agreed to take on. There were supposed to be a lot more days like today—days where I was out raising awareness and supporting charity programs. When I tried to do more, to be more active, to take on more of my responsibilities, Alexander stopped me at every turn. I hadn't minded as much when I was pregnant, or even when our daughter was a baby. It felt more important to stay home then. Now that I was pregnant again less than two years after our first child had been born, I had to face facts. I suspected we would continue to fill more rooms in the castle.

We couldn't keep our hands off each other—and I wanted to have his children. I just didn't think I should stay home with my feet up waiting for a baby the whole time.

We arrived behind the motorcade. I knew the drill and waited in the car while Brex confirmed security sweeps had taken place. Georgia remained in the car with me, the silence between us saying more than any words we could share. But it wasn't just the atmosphere in the car. The air felt heavy. Wrong somehow. I didn't know if it was the presence of Georgia and her stony demeanor or if Alexander had simply infected me with his own brand of paranoia. When Brex opened my car door, I breathed a sigh of relief. Getting out carefully, I arranged my Givenchy coat to cover the tiny baby bump that showed at the right angle, even with my dress's flowing skirt. If I could keep that secret a little longer...

All around me photographers snapped pictures, rearranging their own bodies in strange ways to get every vantage point possible. I wondered if one of them had caught sight of me adjusting the coat. That would be a subject of gossip. It was ridiculous how obsessed they were with the status of my womb. Brex kept his body close to mine, shielding me as much as possible while Georgia joined and flanked my other side. It never felt quite right to be this close to someone other than Alexander. I would never admit that to my husband. His ego didn't need the boost.

He wouldn't be able to fit it inside Buckingham Palace if it got any bigger.

The symposium was being held at a renovated school in East London. Usually, I found myself in grand ballrooms or at the theater, Alexander by my side. The simple school was a breath of fresh air compared to those places. Children's art had been framed, lining the corridor that Brex led me through. We were met at the end of the cramped hall by a beaming woman in a lilac dress suit. She dipped into a slight curtsy and I felt my cheeks grow hot.

I'd learned to expect this. Liaisons and MPs and community leaders were always advised on Royal protocol before a member of the family greeted them. Despite being married to Alexander, I didn't really feel like the Queen and would never get used to it. My husband had confided in me once that he didn't like it either. But not liking it was different than feeling embarrassed by it. At times I felt like an imposter in my own life: a fake playing a role who would be found out at any moment.

"Your Majesty, it is an honor to have you in attendance today. I'm Mrs. March. I spoke with your team."

"Of course," I said, torn between trying to sound casual or benevolent—and achieving neither. When exactly would I get good at this?

"If you'll follow me, they're almost ready for you. The keynote is about to wrap up." Mrs. March started to lead us toward a door marked backstage.

That wasn't in the schedule I'd been given when I was asked to do this event. "I'm sorry. Did you say the keynote is wrapping up?"

"Yes," Miss March said with a nod, "and then you will be presenting the award. That reminds me. I have some notes for you. We can't tell you what a thrill it is to have you here to do the honors."

She passed a couple of index cards to me and my spirits plummeted.

"I thought I was asked to participate in the symposium." I wished my brain would catch up with my mouth, which seemed to be running away with itself. Did it really matter what they'd asked me to do? Yes, said a little voice I tried to ignore. I'd wanted to be included. I'd wanted to contribute more than a quick public appearance.

"We would never expect such an intrusion on your time." Miss March seemed horrified at the thought. Next to her, it looked like Georgia was trying to bite back a smirk. We'd gotten all dressed up, dragged two dozen guards through London traffic, and we were here to give out a trophy. Georgia was probably enjoying this.

"It was just a miscommunication," I said, glancing around for a momentary out. My turbulent emotional state threatened to get the best of me and I wasn't going to give Georgia the satisfaction of seeing me crack. "Is there any way I could use the loo?"

"It's right this way." Miss March started to take

me in the opposite direction, but Georgia stepped between us.

"I'll take her," she said sweetly.

I wondered if she was fooling anyone. Miss March stepped away, looking possibly mortified that she'd presumed to help me. I sighed, knowing this was my life now.

If I had hoped for a moment alone, I should have known better. Usually when Norris was with me, he stood outside the door, giving me space to panic or cry or touch up my lipstick. Georgia escorted me inside.

"This really isn't necessary," I said.

"That's why you're not the bodyguard," Georgia pointed out. "Alexander was quite specific with his instructions when he discovered you'd rearranged his security assignments. We're not to let you out of our sight."

The petulant streak in me wanted to remind her that they'd sat with their backs turned to me in the car. Then, I realized one of them had probably watched me in the mirror the whole time. I gritted my teeth and opened my purse, digging inside for lipstick. I reapplied it halfheartedly, not really needing to. I had asked to come in here and now I had to make it look like it had been for reasons other than to quiet my nerves. I didn't trust myself to use the toilet without breaking into tears. I definitely didn't want Georgia reporting to Alexander that I'd been crying in the loo.

"What shade is that?" Georgia asked, eyeing the tube in my hand.

Was she for real? She wasn't really the type for idle chit-chat. Unlike me, Georgia seemed to have a knack for speaking in an offhanded manner. I didn't believe for a second she was interested in swapping make-up tips or braiding each other's hair. "It's *Fuck-Off-Red* from the *Let's-Not-Pretend-We're-Friends* collection."

Georgia didn't so much as blink. Instead, she shrugged. "You're right. We're not friends. I was being nice. I promised Brex I would be less of a bitch."

"But you're so good at it," I said.

"Only compared to some." Georgia leaned against the sink, folding her arms over her black fitted jacket. "Are you ready?"

So much for collecting my thoughts. I dropped the lipstick back into my bag and nodded. It wasn't really my fault she rubbed me the wrong way. No warm-blooded woman would be able to look at her husband's former submissive without getting a little jealous. I had once thought that Alexander's playboy past would be the hardest thing for me to overcome. Now I still questioned if I was enough for him. I could blame Georgia for that.

Before I was married, she had warned me that Alexander needed things—physically, emotionally— that I would never be able to give him. Was I failing him? Was that why he was so possessive of me now?

He promised me he didn't need that in our relationship. But every time I offered him my submission, he had taken it. Maybe Georgia had been right all along. Maybe that was why he controlled my outings so strictly. The thought made my stomach turn. Given that I was only ever a few hours from morning sickness, it wasn't a welcome sensation.

We returned to the others, and I did my best to tuck my thoughts away. None of that was why I was here. Once we were shown into the wings, I excused myself to look over the notes they'd given me. There wasn't much to do. Everything had been written out for me. Everything had been planned. I was simply a player in someone else's game.

CHAPTER THREE

CLARA

The speech was taking forever. Since I wasn't going to participate, I wanted to get my part over with. I peeked between the curtains that kept the audience from seeing backstage. The auditorium was completely full, packed with people who shared something in common with me. They had all come here because they wanted to change the world. The Child Watch Initiative was a relatively new coalition aimed at everything from increasing access to education, to promoting STEM courses for girls, to putting a stop to child trafficking. They were out there learning what they could do to impact children's lives while I waited in the wings to present an award. My role was ceremonial, just like my life was becoming.

"They're almost ready for you," Brex said, coming up beside me.

"Great," I said flatly.

He stole a glance at me, no doubt picking up on my tone. "Not what you thought?"

"Someone has to give the empty speeches." That's what it felt like, at least. The speaker currently on stage was outlining what sounded like an ambitious plan to make certain that children living in poverty received adequate nutrition. The speech they had passed to me with all the pertinent information would take me less than three minutes. It had taken longer to put on my stockings this morning. Maybe no one remembered I'd once helped execute campaigns to raise social awareness. Maybe they didn't care.

"Alexander once told me he went to war because he grew tired of being trotted out like a prize stallion." Brex's words were filled with sympathy.

"Before or after you got stuck with babysitting duty?" I asked. When they'd first met, Brex had expected to waste his time protecting the Royal heir.

A good-natured smile lit up his face at the memory. "After. It takes him a while to open up."

I cringed slightly at the implication. How much had he overheard between Alexander and I?

Despite how his relationship with my husband had started, I knew that he sympathized with the position his friend was in. Brex also knew what Alexander was capable of—more than most. Neither of them spoke often about their time at war, but I had watched the two of them together and I knew the kind of respect that Brex gave my husband wasn't given out of obligation. Alexander had earned it from him. I had never asked why. For whatever reason, Brex seemed to extend this respect to me. Sometimes, he seemed more upfront with me than Alexander.

It was the last thing I wanted to obsess over before giving a public speech. Any other topic would be a welcome change of subject. Only one came to mind.

"So you and Georgia?" I tipped my head in the direction of the woman, who was a few meters away scanning the audience.

"That's a favorite question from your family."

So I wasn't the only one to notice. Had Alexander picked up on it, too?

"That isn't an answer," I pointed out.

"I like keeping it a mystery. It makes me seem cooler than I am," Brex confided in me. Lowering his voice, he added, "And less like a loser."

Clearly, I had picked a sore subject. "Shot you down?"

"I'm in security. I do risk assessment," he explained. "I didn't even try to breach the walls she put up. Whatever she's protecting, I'm not getting past her defenses."

"You're not even going to try?" I wasn't certain why I cared so much about this. I wasn't Georgia's biggest fan, but I liked Brex and it was obvious to me he was hung up on her. There was no explaining attraction. Although I did wonder how much he knew about her. Brex, despite his self-assured attitude, didn't strike me as being into the same things she was. Maybe he knew more about her than I thought. If Alexander had opened up about other things to Brex, had he shared his past with Georgia? "Is there a reason?"

Brex shook his head. "It might not seem like a good one, but I think there are some people you can't reach. Some people can't change. Or maybe they just don't want to."

"I don't believe that's true," I said softly. There had been a time when Alexander couldn't use the word love—a time when I'd thought a future with him was a fantasy. No matter what trials we faced, I remembered that we had chosen each other. I had reached him when it had seemed impossible.

"Weren't you the one punishing your husband earlier by sending away your bodyguard?" he asked.

It wasn't like Brex to speak so freely around me, but I didn't mind. I had been the one to bring up his personal life. It was only fair that he be allowed to do the same.

"Marriage isn't easy." I knew it wasn't much of an explanation. "Neither is love."

"You're really selling me on breaking down her defenses," Brex teased.

But never trying? How could I explain to him that it was still worth it? I had to try. "Love stories never really end. There are no happily ever afters. Love is fighting and compromising and choosing one person over and over again. No matter what."

"I guess that means you're going to forgive him for whatever he did to piss you off," Brex said with a low chuckle.

"Maybe not immediately," I confessed, but my spirits felt lighter. Maybe I would forgive Alexander. Maybe I would forgive him across his desk this afternoon. Then again, sometimes Alexander needed to sweat a little longer. Someone had to keep him in check.

"Don't worry. I want to... I don't want to settle for..." His words faded away as a distant look came over his face. I recognized what was happening. Someone was speaking to him through the security earpiece he wore. I didn't have to wait long for him to update her. I'd expected it to be an update, a heads up that they were nearly ready for me. Instead, Brex grabbed my elbow and gently started pulling me toward the hallway. "We need to leave here now."

It was remarkable how calm he sounded given the implication in that statement. I had been trained on this by Norris. When a member of the security team—as long it was it was my personal security—informed me it was time to leave, I was to do so without question. The problem was that I wasn't very good at not questioning things. My head whipped around and I pulled against his hold, nearly crashing into Georgia.

"What about those people?" I asked. The auditorium was full. Any threat I faced was also a danger to them.

"Our job is to get you out of here," Brex explained, tugging at me. I refused to budge. "Look, the important thing is to get you out of here now and then to make sure everyone else gets out in an orderly fashion."

I didn't ask what the threat was, but if this whole building needed to be evacuated, it wasn't good. "I don't care what Alexander's orders are. My life is not more important than any of theirs."

Brex looked like he was seriously contemplating picking me up and throwing me over his shoulder. I silently dared him to try. I didn't care how much I liked him. A move like that would earn him a swift kick in the gentleman's sausage.

Georgia moved forward and took my other arm. "I'll get her out of here and you go help them."

He looked from me to her, a muscle twitching in his jaw before he jerked his head in agreement.

"Stay on comms," Brex barked, before disappearing back into the wings.

I stared at my newfound ally. Georgia had sided with me. I didn't know what to think about that. "Thank you."

"For what? You were being a stubborn ass and someone has to oversee the evacuation. He's better at leading people." She was less gentle than Brex as she dragged me out of the backstage area. "I'm less of a people person than Brex."

My arm hurt from her tight grip, reinforcing the truth of that statement. "You don't say,"

She guided me to the corridor, checking things out before allowing me to head toward the exit. Part of me—a very surprised part—found myself glad she was with me now.

There really was a first time for everything.

"Where are we going?" I asked when we didn't head the direction we'd entered through.

"I'm sure your husband would prefer as few photographers catch this as possible," Georgia said tightly.

I tried to ignore the pit opening in my stomach. Being taken out the back was never a good sign. I dared to glance over my shoulder and saw a line of people streaming out the front. It would be chaos to be with them there now. There was no way my security team could keep track of me in such a large crowd, which would only make Alexander panic more when he found out what was going on. But I couldn't shake the feeling of being singled out. I had meant what I'd said. I was no more important than these people. At least, to no one but Alexander. Didn't they all have their own families to go home to? Children or husbands or wives?

We had almost reached the exit when the entire structure shook. I'd been in a few earthquakes when my family lived in California and I stopped, trying to remember what I should do. Georgia handled it for me. Her arms shot around my shoulders and we raced toward the exit until another small blast shook the walls. Debris fell from the ceiling and smoke poured from the center of the building. There were screams. Chaos. I wanted to help—to turn back. I didn't have an option now, Georgia kept a tight hold on me, shielding my body. Two more small explosions rocked the building. I tried to ignore the first sharp spikes of panic and focus on the glass doors ahead. Only a few more steps...

We were out the doors before I'd begun to process any of what happened. The moment the sunlight hit my face, I whirled around, yanking out of Georgia's grasp and turning to stare. I was barely aware of the security forces swarming around me, pressing me back and away from the scene. On the outside, it didn't look like much had happened. Had it all been my imagination? The building answered with a final blast, bigger than the others. The deafening sound split the air and a small scream escaped me as part of the roof caved in.

"Brex!" I yelled, fighting against the guards trying to keep me back. Brex had stayed inside. He'd stayed because I'd asked him. Next to me Georgia stiffened as if she was thinking the same thing.

"He'll be okay," she said fiercely.

I wasn't certain if either of us believed that.

Before I could so much as say a prayer, Brex came out the back door, yelling, "All clear. Building is clear."

I relaxed immediately, and I noticed Georgia did as well. Brex ran toward us, his suit dirty, smoke smudges on his hands and face, but he didn't stop when he reached them. Instead, he skidded to a halt a few paces past me, his attention on something slightly beyond us. The crowd of security guards parted and I turned to see the one man who could command any situation. The one man I most wanted to see and the one man who definitely should not be here. Because Alexander's life did matter more. To the country. To the world.

To me.

He strode past Brex, giving him a cursory nod, but keeping his eyes on me. One step. Two steps. Ten more steps. And then his arms were around me, erasing, if only temporarily, the horror of what had just happened. He held me for a long moment, before the security teams began to move us towards the cars that had been brought around to get us out. He seemed reluctant to let me go, but when he did, I looked up to find his beautiful face as hard as stone. I knew that face all too well. His eyes were cold sapphires—set, determined, deadly. I also knew what came next. There was no escaping it.

CHAPTER FOUR

ALEXANDER

I kept checking her—touching her—as if she might vanish if I looked away. Since we'd married I had always preferred to drive her, but today I let Norris take the wheel. I didn't trust myself not to stare at her instead of keeping my eyes on the road. She'd faced enough danger today. I wouldn't risk her again.

Clara kept her face pressed against my shoulder. On another day, she might have done it to avoid the paparazzi. But the Range Rover's windows were tinted and I suspected the reason Clara kept her face turned away from the glass was to avoid seeing the destruction outside. I'd had an initial briefing and knew the situation wasn't as bad as it looked. Because it had looked bad—very, very bad. Somehow, now didn't feel like the time to update her, though. Not while she was still shaking. Not while the memory was still so fresh. She would ask soon enough and then I would. Not a moment before.

"Are we going home?" she asked in a soft voice. Her words were searching, her lost eyes looked into mine.

I shook my head, knowing how she was going to react to this bit of news. She had a stubborn streak that I loved, but right now I didn't want to deal with it. I wanted to be in control. Of something. Of anything. Later, everyone would tell me this wasn't my fault, but it wouldn't matter. I hadn't put my foot down when others had changed the plans. I should have sent Norris immediately rather than wait. I wasn't budging on what I wanted now. "I want you checked out by a doctor. Both of you."

She couldn't argue with me on that, even as she looked to Norris, who gave no hint of having heard our "secret." It might be poor form to bring up the baby, but I wouldn't be able to focus until I knew they were both unharmed. I wrapped an arm around her shoulder and pulled her closer to my body, wishing I had never let her out of my sight.

Most of the injuries from the explosion had been routed to a small hospital near the school. I wanted to avoid that, knowing the press would descend like vultures. It took us longer to get to St. Mary's, but we had family doctors there. Right now, I needed to be surrounded by people I trusted. Norris had sent a team ahead of us, enabling us to utilize the south door. Since most of the media had swarmed the other hospital, it was an extra cautious move—one I appreciated.

Doctor Ball met us at the entrance along with a nurse who had been present for the birth of Elizabeth. An ounce of weight was lifted from my shoulders at the familiar faces, not enough to make a difference—but felt all the same.

"Your Majesty," Dr. Ball said in a clipped tone, ushering us toward a private exam room. I appreciated him dispensing with the formalities in favor of getting down to business. "We'll need to do a full physical exam. The nurse will take your blood pressure and other vitals."

The nurse bustled around the room, laying out an exam gown for Clara and prepping a blood pressure cuff.

"We should do blood work as well and possibly have an ultrasound," I said, stepping in. Clara had an appointment coming up where all of this would have taken place. I was unwilling to wait that long given the circumstances.

There was a moment of hesitation. Then the nurse hurried to a cabinet and began prepping a needle. Dr. Ball smiled uneasily. No doubt he was remembering some of the complications Clara's last pregnancy had involved.

"I assume congratulations are in order then," he said. "We can do our best to check her out and see what we can find out about the baby. We'll do a blood draw and rush it to the labs."

"And the ultrasound?" I pressed, wondering if I was going to have to issue an actual command. I was teetering on a very fine edge. The wrong word was liable to push me over.

"Unfortunately, we've been having difficulty with our machine. It might take a while to get one from obstetrics. I will phone down, of course."

"That won't be necessary." Clara's trembling had subsided and although she still looked small and scared holding onto a folded hospital gown, her words were spoken like a queen's.

"We'll leave you to get undressed." The doctor stepped outside, holding the door open.

"I'm glad you're okay, your Majesty. We'll take good care of you," the nurse promised before disappearing behind the doctor.

I turned away as Clara undressed, not trusting myself to the sight of her body. I wanted to touch her. To claim her. The need to possess her ached through my blood and burned deep into the marrow of my bones. "Don't tell me you've developed a sense of shame?" she said to my back. It was meant as a joke, but her voice was hollow and lifeless. I couldn't find the heart to even laugh. "You can turn around now, X."

Even the few moments with her out of my sight had been excruciating. My eyes drank her in as I turned, studying her. She was so physically fragile. I'd once believed nothing could break her spirit. Then, I had wanted to protect her body. Now, I couldn't help but look for a sign she was cracking elsewhere.

"Stop looking at me like that," she demanded.

"Like what?" Had she seen the naked want in my eyes? Was she still angry about this morning? Could it be possible that after what she'd gone through, she wouldn't see why I hadn't liked the idea of her going to the symposium?

"Like I might shatter," she said, her gaze darting away to the window and the world outside. She'd seen through to the truth I tried to bury inside me. She'd seen that I was afraid. "I'm not so easy to break, remember?"

"I know." But I said it for her benefit, not because I believed it. How much could one woman endure before it was too much? I never wanted to find out.

"Do we know...?" The question trailed away. I couldn't tell if she wanted me to answer what I knew she was going to ask.

I did anyway. This I couldn't keep from her. "There have been no casualties reported so far. There have been some injuries and some people are being treated for smoke inhalation. All in all, it seems we were lucky," I said, unable to keep the wild edge from my voice. A rational man—an outsider—would be able to see it that way. But I was no ordinary man and this was my wife. I couldn't be rational about this. I couldn't separate myself from the who and the what and the why.

"Do we know why?" This question she seemed more sure of like she didn't want this answer, she needed it.

"We received some intelligence this morning—just in time. The assumption is that you were the target," I told her. I wanted this to sink in. There was a time I wouldn't have wanted to scare her, but I needed her to acknowledge that her life was different now. Clara craved control, but at what cost could I allow her to have it? Losing her was a price I was unwilling to pay, even if it meant a fight.

"No one knew I was coming, only a few council members and our security team. It's as likely this was a group of radicals."

It was a fair point, but I wasn't about to concede. If there was even a one percent chance that someone who knew she would be there was responsible—it was unacceptable.

"Why wasn't Brex with you?" I asked, ignoring her rationale.

"I sent him back. I wasn't about to let a bunch of people get hurt just so I could make a clean getaway."

"Christ, Clara, that wasn't your call. You could—"

A knock on the door stopped my lecture before it got started. When Dr. Ball walked into the room, we were glaring at one another. He looked between us, probably sensing something was off, but didn't say anything. The nurse bustled in and began taking vitals before drawing Clara's blood.

"She'll send those to the labs now. That shouldn't take long. But I did find this." He held up a small instrument that looked like the baby monitor we used for Elizabeth.

"Ultrasound machines have gotten much smaller," I said darkly.

"We weren't able to get the sonogram. This will help us find the baby's heartbeat. No need to worry if it's hard to find at first. There's a lot of factors at this early stage. How far along do you think you are, Clara?"

Clara bit her lip, daring a quick glance in my direction. "My period's been irregular since Elizabeth."

"That's quite normal," the doctor reassured her. "How many have you had?"

Clara filled him in on the details of her cycle. This wasn't news to me. It had become a bit of a running joke actually. Every month I would tease her that I hoped her period wouldn't come.

"The last one was probably two or three months ago," she told him.

"Then it's still quite early, but this should work."

The nurse covered Clara's hips with a blanket and helped her shimmy the hospital gown up to reveal her tiny bump.

"I kind of thought"–she gestured to the swell–"that I might be further along. I seem to be starting to show already. And there was the issue with the placenta last time."

"There's no greater chance of placenta previa in a second pregnancy. Obviously, it could account for bleeding if you thought you had experienced your period. However, most women show much more quickly in subsequent pregnancies." The look he leveled at her stomach was meaningful.

I translated it as we'd better tell everyone sooner rather than later. It was getting quite obvious.

After today, I would tell the world and then no one would blame me if I locked her up in the palace. I pressed my lips together to keep these thoughts to myself. Clara pretended to watch him but her gaze kept skipping in my direction. The doctor applied a sticky gel to her bump and then used what looked like a small microphone, moving it around as he adjusted knobs on the attached device. After a moment a soft swishing noise began.

"There we go," he said with a smile. "Hold on."

He moved a dial and there underneath the swishing of amniotic fluid was a rapid, perfect heartbeat.

He beamed at us. For a doctor, it must be nice to give good news for a change. "Everything sounds in order. I'd like to see you soon though. Can we make an appointment?"

"She has an appointment," I realized how stupid it was when I said it. If Clara had had an appointment the doctor would have known about it. The doctor would not have been surprised when I'd asked for an ultrasound. The Queen of England coming in to confirm her pregnancy wasn't likely to slip his mind. I turned to her. "You told me you had an appointment."

"I forgot," she said sheepishly. "I knew they'd get me in right away and I meant to do it. I'm sorry."

She sounded defeated, and my heart sank. I was punishing her. After what she'd been through, I was being a dick. Maybe I was angry with her for trying to make a statement this morning—angry that she'd pushed back—and feeling sickeningly self-righteous over the fact that something had happened. But it hadn't been her fault that something had actually happened. She must know that. Everyone must know that.

Everyone but me.

"We'll leave you two alone. Clara, you can get dressed. Everything looks fine. If you can wait a few moments, we will see to those lab results." The doctor gestured for the nurse to follow him, clearly aware that we needed privacy.

And I needed to apologize. Anyone could see that.

Clara began to strip the gown off, not bothering to wait for me to turn away. Perhaps, she sensed that this time I wouldn't—this time, I couldn't. But she didn't make a show of it. Her movements were deliberate but cautious as though I was the real threat. I hated myself for making her feel that way. I hated myself for knowing what I was willing to do to keep her safe.

I caught her in my arms before she could finish

slipping her second stocking on. By some miracle—
and her body was so perfect it was a miracle—I was
hardly aware of her bare flesh. I ignored the insistent
twitch in my groin. There was something more
important. Cradling her face in my hands, I looked
into her grey eyes and told her the two things she
needed to hear. "I love you, and I am so, so sorry."

I didn't clarify why I was sorry. The list was too
long. There were the obvious reasons. I'd been a first
class knob head since I'd reached her. Others I
couldn't bring myself to say out loud. Because I had
failed her. I had promised her a life—I promised her
protection—and I had failed to keep her safe. I might
have been able to forgive myself if it were the first
time. But danger seemed to follow me. I had known
that and I'd selfishly fallen in love with her. I had sold
her lies as promises, afraid that if I faced the truth
that she would have run.

"I love you, X." And then she did the last thing I
deserved. Her face tilted toward mine, offering her
mouth.

I couldn't resist. I could never resist her.

I swallowed a groan of relief as our lips met, her
soft body molding against the hardness of mine.
Clara's palms pressed to my chest, pausing over my
heart. Her touch sent a jolt of awareness through me
as if she'd reset its rhythm, freeing it from the racing
panic I'd felt since Norris had come to me this morning. But though it soothed me, the calm was momentary as her hands descended lower, tracing the scars

she knew lay hidden beneath my shirt. Finally, they found my belt and unlatched it with practiced ease. She slid past my slacks, her movements growing more urgent, and closed her fingers around my cock.

I still held her face, unwilling to let it go or to stop kissing her. Slipping one hand to hold her neck—to keep her where I needed her to be—the other fumbled with the button she hadn't bothered to undo. It popped open and I shoved my pants down, freeing my erection. I didn't bother to step out of my pants. "Thank God, you're naked," I murmured against her lips, finally relinquishing her mouth, so that my arms were free to scoop her up.

Pausing a fraction of a second, my eyes met hers, waiting for a signal. After what had happened, I needed to know she needed this as much as I did. Clara pressed her forehead to mine, our skin already damp and heated. Her legs wrapped around my waist.

"Yes, please." It was a sigh. It was permission. It was everything.

I slid into her slowly, savoring the slow union. But with each inch, I lost more control. Clara seemed to sense this and she locked her arms over my shoulders.

"I'm sorry," I repeated, somehow torn between the numb terror that had driven my day and the feverish want building inside me now. My thoughts drifted to the horrible moment when I'd heard the first explosion. My own life—a life without her—had flashed before my eyes. "I could have lost you."

"I'm here, X." She kissed me swiftly to prove it, drawing me from the shadows and back to her. "Take me. Take what you need."

With those words, she released me from the caution holding me back. I thrust into her, giving in to the raw emotions I'd held at bay. She turned her face to my shoulder, sinking her teeth into its flesh to stifle her cries. I couldn't tell if the muffled sounds were from pain or pleasure. Later, I would make sure she was okay. I would check that I hadn't hurt her. Now, I would take what she had given me. I would take everything.

"Say it," I groaned as the pressure built in my groin. I needed to hear those words. The words that had set me free once.

I came violently as she followed my command, her own pleasure tightening around my cock. The words spilled from her lips, soaked in a moan, and shackled me to her. They built a new prison which we'd never escape.

"I love you."

CHAPTER FIVE

ALEXANDER

The test results showed what we already knew: Clara was pregnant. They also confirmed she was further along than we thought. Once the baby was born, I was going to have to institute monthly pregnancy tests. This was the second surprise baby we'd been blessed with, and, in the future, I wanted to worship for every second of her pregnancy. I'd already lost out on three months. She had enough to worry about without keeping track of her cycle.

Clara looked near the point of collapse as I led her inside the palace an hour later. The day's events had caught up with us rapidly. As soon as we reached our private quarters, I lifted her into my arms. She curled into me, her eyes drooping even as she tried to stay awake. When we reached our bedroom, she jolted fully awake.

"Elizabeth." The one word explanation was

enough. I wanted my wife to rest, but we both needed to see our daughter.

Turning, I took the few steps to the nursery and placed Clara carefully on her feet. She swayed a little, but caught herself on the door. Elizabeth had only recently moved full-time to her own bedroom, a transition we'd found difficult. With a new baby coming and a tired mum-to-be, it had been a necessity. I wondered if that new arrangement would last.

We entered quietly, afraid to disturb a nap. The curtains were drawn, filtering the fading afternoon light. It fell across the room, not casting shadows, but rather making the delicate furniture and creamy fabrics glow. In the middle of the ethereal space, a tea party was taking place.

Penny, the part-time nanny, scrambled to her feet, abandoning the tea party she was having with Elizabeth. Her red hair was pulled back in a tight knot, revealing that her fair skin was red and splotchy.

"You're back! No one would tell me anything," Penny kept her voice low as she glanced over her shoulder repeatedly to check on her charge.

"Did she hear anything?" Clara had a frantic edge to her, even after our life-affirming interlude. She had soothed me, but I'd failed to give her the same comfort.

"No. I've kept her busy all day."

I didn't bother reminding my wife Elizabeth was too young to understand even if she did hear.

Elizabeth toddled over and Clara scooped her up, showering her with kisses. Then she paused to examine her fingers and toes like she had discovered a tiny miracle. Elizabeth clung to her mother. I guessed it would be a long time before our daughter went on any public outings. If only her mother could be so easily ruled.

Clara wasn't a child and I couldn't keep her here, but watching her with our daughter made me realize that, as much as I didn't want to hurt them, I would do anything to keep them safe—even if they hated me for it.

A call buzzed in my pocket. "Excuse me." I silenced it and took a step towards the hall. "When I come back, you're both taking a nap."

My mobile had been ringing for the last few hours. I hadn't bothered to answer it since I'd found Clara. She had been more important, but I couldn't ignore the outside world forever, especially since the outside world kept intruding in our private lives.

I was relieved to discover it was Edward. I hoped it was a coincidence that he was calling, but I had little hope that even honeymoon bliss could keep news of this magnitude quiet.

"I've been calling you for hours!"

So much for letting him have his honeymoon. I decided to bypass the whole update and give him the highlights. "Everything's fine. She's fine."

I nearly told him the baby was too before I remembered that he didn't know about that yet.

"She's fine?" His voice peaked on the final word like I'd lost my mind. In all fairness, I probably had.

I pinched the bridge of my nose. I supposed I deserved my own lecture after starting in on Clara. "Hang on, how did you find out?"

In my head, I said a hopeless prayer that Norris or a security team member had called him.

"It's all over the news." He was shouting now and I suspected it had nothing to do with trying to be heard from the Seychelles.

I'd dropped the ball once again. I should have called him before he'd heard it that way. It seemed my inability to protect my family was matched only by my miscommunication with them. "The news is probably exaggerating."

"I don't care if someone lit a match near her," Edward exploded. "I want to hear about it from you."

"You will. I wasn't thinking. Listen"—I glanced up and down the hall to make certain no one could overhear us—"can you come home? I need your help."

There was a pause, which lasted long enough for me to regret my request. He'd just gotten married. The last thing he wanted was to come home and help me run the country.

"We'll be there," he said at last. He hung up without saying goodbye.

It took a concerted effort to coax Clara

from the nursery. Finally, with Penny's help, Elizabeth was in her crib and I'd taken Clara to bed. She climbed in with her clothes on, mumbling sleepily as I began to undress her.

"Come on, Poppet." I tugged the dress over her head. Throwing it on the ground, I rolled off a stocking. Without thinking, my lips went to the creamy skin it revealed. Clara sighed as I slowly repeated the action with the other, trailing kisses down her leg.

When I finally tore myself away, she reached out, her languid eyes widening. "I don't want to fall asleep."

I understood what she meant. Dreams awaited her on the other side of closing her eyes. I also knew that she couldn't avoid nightmares forever. Once, I had suffered from night terrors, reliving the car accident that claimed my sister's life. The dreams had faded when I'd fallen for Clara and she had come to my bed. Tonight, I would protect her from the horrors she'd seen.

"Let me help you," I suggested. I stayed where she could see me, taking off my clothes quickly. Clara's gaze didn't stray, it saw through the mask of strength I'd worn all day. It laid me bare. Only she could see what I so carefully hid from everyone else. My scars. My fears. I could only face them—face myself—with the strength she gave me.

Now I needed to take that strength. Take her. But not tonight. Not after what she'd experienced. Still, we needed more than quick and raw. Taking her at the hospital had held me, but I realized now that what we both needed was skin on skin.

"Alexander," she began as my body lowered over hers, "I know that you think I need"—

"Not now," I said gently, stopping her mouth with a kiss. There would be fighting later. We both knew that. It was inevitable. Right now, though, we needed this. My hand slipped under her back and unhooked her bra. She shimmied in my embrace, until it was gone and there was nothing between us.

I began a slow descent, pausing to pay homage to my favorite spots: the freckles on her shoulders, the hollow of her collar bone. When my mouth closed over her nipple, I sucked it gently between my teeth, relishing the satin-soft skin and her breathy cry. My tongue traced a line down until I reached the apex of her thighs. My arms curved around her hips, my hands pressing her legs open. Clara flowered before me and I drank in her perfume before my tongue found a new, more delicate spot to tease.

Her hands fisted in the sheets as her body arched in greeting. I wanted to stay here and let the world fade away. Drive her wild with my mouth and make her come again and again. More than that, though, I needed to feel her body clench possessively on my cock once more. She was soft and wet and I needed to bury myself there and watch her fall apart.

There was a moan of protest when I pulled away, her hips writhing at the loss of contact. When I replaced my mouth with the crown of my cock, she opened in welcome. Entering her felt like coming home. I drew her body against mine and our lips met in deep, hungry kisses, our teeth and tongues nipping and sucking. I wanted to consume her, make her such a part of me that we were never separate. Her fingers found the scars I kept from everyone but her and lingered there.

We claimed each other with thrusts and moans, giving and taking, until there was no her. No me. Only us.

She met me at the first shattering pulse of my cock, her channel rippling over me as she melted in waves in my arms. We rolled in a sweaty heap onto our sides, not breaking contact.

Clara's eyes were heavier and if she minded that I'd fucked her to sleep, she didn't show it. I whispered that she was safe and loved and home until her breathing slowed to a soft, regular rhythm.

I didn't want to leave her. It felt like ripping my heart out to untangle my body from hers, but there were matters to attend to, especially if I was going to see that she was safe. I dressed quickly and quietly, planted a kiss on her forehead, and hoped I'd chased the nightmares away.

Leaving our bedroom, I blinked against the bright lights of the hallway. It was early evening, the world outside had fallen to the early night of winter, but the household and the offices were still running.

No one questioned where I had been when I strode into my office and found Norris, Brexton, and

a few others waiting there. Under normal circumstances, Brex might make a few insinuations about
what I'd been up to. He might wink. Today, he
couldn't muster so much as a smile. That made two
of us.

"Sir, I'm sorry," he began instead. "I went—"

"You left her," I cut him off. "I don't need an
explanation. Norris, I want to speak with you
privately."

The other men left the room without protest.
Brex followed without a word. I recognized the self-
loathing written across his face. I knew the feeling
well.

When they were gone, Norris spoke first. "It's not
his fault. Clara refused to leave. Georgia had the
Queen's safety in hand."

"It was not her responsibility," I roared. My fist
slammed into the oak desktop. I didn't even
remember taking my seat behind the desk. Norris
took the chair opposite, a well-worn expression of
patience taking over his features. There were times
when he looked so much like my father—or what my
father might have looked like if he'd had a soul. This
was one of those times.

"It was mine," Norris said after a moment. "The
blame lies with me."

"Brex was with her."

"Because I allowed him to take my place. If
you're going to blame someone for following Clara's

wishes, the blame belongs on me." Norris folded his hands in his lap as if awaiting his punishment.

"Or maybe Clara," I said darkly.

His eyebrows lifted. "That would be an ill-advised stance to take. Particularly if you want to touch her again. I assume you didn't insinuate that this evening."

We both knew that I couldn't keep my hands off her. Norris was the best at pretending not to notice rumpled clothes and mismatched buttons and freshly yanked hair, but he wasn't stupid. He also knew me well enough to know why I'd spent the afternoon in bed with my wife. It was something we'd never had to discuss. He just seemed to understand.

My anger ebbed into a dull frustration. He had a point, and we both knew it. It wasn't Brexton's fault. It wasn't Norris's. Or Clara's. "It's my fault."

"There was no way to know what would happen. You can't spend your life expecting the worst," he said. "And neither of you can spend your marriage making power plays."

He misunderstood me. I wasn't to blame for not being there or for fighting with her over her security. I was to blame for not overruling her when I knew what was best for her safety. "But I have to plan for it. She's not going to like it, Norris. But we have to increase security or..."

"You can't lock her away," he said, guessing what I was thinking. "Perhaps a dedicated team chosen by yourself and your wife would help to ease her into an increased security presence."

"I need you overseeing the entire family's security," I mulled aloud. "I'll want you to attend any events she has scheduled, but day to day, I need you."

"Even I can't be in two places at once," he said dryly.

"Georgia got her out of there. Perhaps—"

"She's not going to like that." There was warning in his voice.

I was well past caring. I would do anything to keep her safe. "I'd hire the devil himself to keep her safe. She'll get used to it."

He didn't argue with me. He would later. Clara would, too. We had all known this was coming. We'd never defeated the darkness that plagued this family. It had only retreated for a moment. Now it was sweeping towards us—all of us.

"And the rest of the family?" he asked.

"Edward is coming home. I'll brief him, but there's no need to wait. I want dedicated security on each of them. All hours. People we trust explicitly."

Norris's jaw clenched as if it was hard to hold back his opinion. "The usual family then?"

"No," I said with a shake of my head, choosing my words with a meaning only he could understand. "All of my family—seen and unseen."

CHAPTER SIX

CLARA

Alexander had become even more unbearably paranoid, a feat I wouldn't have thought were possible if I wasn't experiencing it firsthand. For the last week even my movements inside the palace had been tracked. There were more security guards than ever before. At one point, I thought I saw one of the cooks wearing a gun holster. I wouldn't put it past my husband to arm everyone down to the gardeners. Despite my unofficial house arrest, there was one bright spot: Edward had returned to London.

Part of me felt horrible that his honeymoon had been cut short. The other part of me—the selfish part—was glad to have the company. Not that I had seen much of him yet. He'd been laying low with David as he prepared to move into the new house Alexander had gifted him. If I felt like I was under scrutiny at the castle, it was nothing compared to what Edward was facing on the streets of London. Paparazzi were following him and David's every movement. It was one of the perks of being the most recent Royal to wed. They were also pestering him for details about last week's attack.

Not that Edward had any answers. None of us did. That was probably what was driving my husband so crazy. But regardless of what we did and didn't know, he couldn't keep me here forever. The first few days I'd been more than happy to stay home and process what I'd experienced. Now things were getting out of hand. If I didn't put a stop to it, there was no telling how far X would take this.

Alexander was leaving our bed earlier and earlier each morning and taking meetings and calls later and later each night. I'd had enough. As I stepped out of our private quarters on my way to tell him that, Norris met me in the hall.

"Your Highness," he began, but I held up a hand to stop him.

"If you're going to tell me to go back to my rooms, I'm afraid you aren't going to like my response."

Norris had always been an ally, which was why I wasn't telling him the response rattling around in my brain at the moment. It included a few choice American words coupled with a few choice British words. None of them were ladylike. None of them were suited to the vocabulary of a queen. I didn't give a fuck.

He mustered a slight smile, shaking his head. He knew better than to try to convince me that

Alexander was right. Probably because Norris often thought he was wrong, too. "I'm here to tell you Prince Edward is here to see you."

"Finally! Where is he?" My eyes darted around Norris as though he might be hiding Edward behind his back.

"I'll take you to him," Norris offered.

My excitement grew as he led me through the castle's long corridors. It wasn't going to solve my problems. I still needed to talk to Alexander. But if I couldn't go out into the world, at least the world was coming to me. It also meant there would be a friendly face around. Edward always sided with me over his brother. I could use the back-up.

He had been shown to one of the formal sitting rooms. One of the parlors we reserved for entertaining important dignitaries and diplomats. Occasionally, we used it for larger family gatherings. It seemed a bit grandiose for a meeting between best friends. Was X keeping everyone but top level security out of our private rooms now? We seriously needed to talk. Edward looked ridiculous sitting alone in the giant room, but the smile that lit up his face when I rushed into the room filled the whole space. We collided in a fit of giggles, hugging one another. I couldn't tell if I was just really happy and therefore prone to laughing or if I was going quietly mad and likewise prone to laughing. I trusted him to tell me.

Edward backed up a step, grabbing my hands and turning them over in his own.

"What are you doing?" I asked.

"Checking to make sure you're all here. Thank God, you still have ten fingers." He pulled me into another hug. "I'm so glad you're okay."

"Don't start," I warned him. "Your brother is bad enough. I can't take one more overprotective prince in my life."

"Too bad for you. If you'd wanted to stay a common tart"—he winked at me—"then you shouldn't have married him."

"I probably would be having more fun, if I hadn't," I grumbled. It had been our joke when Alexander and I were only dating—a nod to the trashy tabloid headlines that had followed my every movement during that time. I'd been called a gold digger, a commoner, and worse. It still raised my blood pressure to think about it.

"Earth to Clara," Edward said, taking my hand and leading me over to a stodgy divan upholstered in silk damask.

I gave him a sheepish grin. There was so much to tell him. We needed a catch up, and I wasn't certain where to begin. Some of my news was big—Edward still didn't know I was expecting—and some was garden variety gossip. "Sorry, I'm not used to getting to talk to people."

We took a seat and Edward turned, casually

throwing his leg over the antique furniture as he gave me a sympathetic nod. "Is he that bad?"

"Remember my honeymoon?" I said flatly. "Or lack thereof." We hadn't had a honeymoon. We'd been dealing with the aftermath of his father's death. Alexander had shut me up inside these very same walls. It had nearly ended our marriage before it began.

"That bad, huh?" Edward whipped his horn-rimmed glasses off his face and wiped the lenses with a cloth from his pocket. "Speaking of honeymoons—"

"I'm so sorry!" My hand flew to my mouth. Here I was complaining about my husband's behavior, and my best friend was listening after being forced to abandon his own honeymoon.

"No one needs a month-long honeymoon," Edward said seriously. "David wanted to come home. We wanted to be here for you."

"If I were you, I would have stayed. It's a circus here," I warned him.

Edward didn't need the warning. He was used to the sideshow that was his birth family. He'd grown up with it. He, unlike me, had a much better grip on this kind of thing. I was glad he was here now to help me through it. When Alexander shut me out, it helped to have a sympathetic ear.

"Alexander asked me to come home," Edward confessed.

I sucked in a breath and tried to digest this infor-mation. Alexander had barely spoken to me since that day. It wasn't that he was angry with me—he was obsessing. He'd stumble into the bedroom exhausted. We'd make love and he would fall asleep. I could set my watch to this new schedule, and I didn't like it. I'd gotten updates from Norris and Brexton, but hardly any from Alexander himself. Probably because there wasn't much to know. The intel that had warned our security teams about the attack had led to a dead end. Now Alexander seemed to be checking under every rock in London, knocking on every closed door, and reading every security file held by SIS and MI5. "He needs to learn to let other people do their jobs."

"He sees his job as protecting you," Edward said sagely. He squeezed my hand, which was still in his. "So he's keeping you locked away?"

"You know how he is. Especially with the baby," I whispered. Edward had guessed our secret over the holidays, even Alexander didn't know that he knew.

Edward leaned back, shaking his head as he let out a low whistle. "Can you blame him for acting crazy? You're pregnant. I lost my mind when I heard the rumors you'd been there."

"I keep telling him that it was all a bizarre coincidence. Hardly anyone knew I would be there, but..."

"He's not letting you out of his sight, is he?"

"He seems to content to know that I'm in the house. That's why I'm so glad to see you." I turned a pout on him. This was where he came in.

Edward held up his hands in surrender. "I'll do

what I can, but I'm not promising you anything. You're the one he listens to."

If that was true, then this was hopeless. Edward seemed to sense what I was thinking. He looked around the room and my gaze followed his, taking in the outdated fashions. "I don't think this room has been redecorated since before I was born. You know..."

"Are you suggesting I spend my time redecorating?" I asked, unable to keep a note of distaste from my voice.

"There are worse ways to spend your time." Edward continued to study the room as though plotting exactly what he would do with it. He was welcome to focus on interior design. It was one of his strengths. My strengths lay elsewhere. It was time to make a plan of my own.

I HAD A PLAN BY AFTERNOON TEA, WHICH WAS when I remembered we had guests coming for dinner. Guests who were the perfect, if unwitting, accomplices to my new scheme. I had purposely forgotten to remind Alexander that his grandmother and uncle were coming for dinner, knowing he'd purposefully forget and stick me with entertaining them. I might have also told his secretary to leave it off his official schedule. I did, however, take the opportunity to send him a note reminding him his brother was home and that I expected to see him at seven sharp.

Edward and I spent the afternoon in my closet, plotting what I should wear into battle. I'd let him in on the bare bones of my plan. Then we called Belle and put her on speaker phone. Smith had swept her away to the Scottish countryside, so she couldn't join us. It would have been nice to have more backup, but I understood. If I had the option for a normal life and babymoons to the country, I would have seized it.

By 6:30, Edward was helping me put the finishing touches on my makeup. He passed me a tube of red lipstick, but I shook my head, a wave of nausea rolling through my stomach. I had worn that shade that day. It was the one Georgia had commented on. Edward didn't notice I was upset. Instead, he began rummaging through my lipstick drawer until he found a more muted option. The nudish-pink worked well with what I had chosen to wear. Somehow, despite only a week passing, my baby bump had grown even more pronounced. Most of my clothing did little to hide it. I'd warned Edward not to mention this while we were on the phone discussing options with Belle. I still wanted to tell her in person. It was the only perk of being locked away at home. No one here was taking photos of me and disseminating them on the Internet. No bump watch sites were poring over my wardrobe. It was a small victory. I stepped away from the mirror and studied the wrap dress we had decided on. The cobalt blue was shockingly bright and hard to ignore. More importantly, I felt powerful in it, and that was what I needed now: to feel powerful. I was going into the lion's den, but I wasn't a piece of meat. Their grandmother, Mary, was vicious and manipulative— a cruel lioness. So, I was walking in with my proverbial whip in hand, ready to take control of the entire room.

I swiped a coat of lipstick on and nodded with satisfaction to Edward. He pulled out his phone and took a quick picture. I glared at him. "That better not wind up on the Internet."

"I'm sending it to Belle. Don't worry," he said quickly, "I'll crop it! Although, do you know what this photo would sell for? The first picture of the Royal baby bump?"

"Don't remind me," I groaned. Soon there would be betting pools across the world regarding everything from the sex of the child I carried to what we would name him or her. I was going to need a brave face over the next few months. I knew I could handle whatever they threw at me, but Alexander needed to know the same.

"At least it's only grandmother and Henry tonight. Good practice," Edward said sympathetically. "On second thought, she might be worse than the press."

We exchanged a worried look. The truth was that if there was one person in the world more set on destroying me than the tabloids or our enemies, it was a member of my own family—and she was coming to dinner tonight.

I'd asked the kitchen to prepare something that would be easy on my stomach and meet his grandmother's dietary requirements. I was still struggling with keeping food down. The morning sickness never seemed to end. It was different than my first pregnancy when all I did was cry. The chef, who was in my on my secret, had chosen a salad and mild chicken soup to start and even more bland roast chicken for the main course. It probably wasn't the fancy, extravagant meal the Queen Mother was expecting, but it was one I expected I could keep down. It would seriously undermine my plans to lose my supper in front of her.

Edward and I arrived early, wanting to make certain that all of the arrangements had been made. We had obsessed over every detail: who was sitting where, what wine was being offered, and how sharp the butter knives were. The family had never resorted to using cutlery as weaponry before, but there was a first time for everything. Between Mary's constant criticism and my hormones, it was best to be on the safe side.

"This was the right choice," Edward said with approval as he looked over the place settings.

"Do you think?" I needed every detail to be perfect.

"I believe this was created for my father's coronation." He picked up a plate and looked it over before carefully replacing it. "My mother picked it out."

The table was set with a china pattern that had been a favorite of Alexander's mother. We used it often for private family meals. Right now, I wanted to remind my husband of the strength of family. I also wanted to send a clear message to Mary, who had been the one to pick out the last 25 years' worth of China. This family could both respect tradition and stand on its own. My fingers skimmed over the elegant silver design of the plates, lingering at the monogram centered on the rim. The A and C had represented Albert of Cambridge. I could imagine how Elizabeta had felt as she picked out these plates. I'd never met her—she had died when Alexander was very young—but there were touches like this all over Buckingham Palace—small nods to the love she must have felt for that man. Alexander's father had changed after her death, so I had never known the version of him that had inspired such obvious affection. Now, the A and C represented something else to me entirely.

Alexander and Clara.

It was a merging of the old with the new. It was also a reminder that we were in charge of the monarchy now, and I wasn't about to let anyone, even Alexander's grandmother, forget that.

As seven o'clock approached, Mary and her younger son, who I'd only met in passing at my engagement party and a few other family gatherings, appeared. It was always a shock to see Henry. He looked so much like Albert that sometimes, when we were in the same room, I caught myself doing a double take. The looks they shared were the Cambridge family genetics before Elizabeta had introduced her Greek lineage. My own child had dark hair and electric blue eyes. It was hard to say whether Elizabeth's skin would take after her father's golden hue or my own pale porcelain, but I wondered what Mary thought when she looked at her. Perhaps, it was the striking difference between Alexander and her own sons that made her wary of him. It has been clear since the moment we'd been introduced that she despised her grandchildren. I'd never bothered to find out why. The mere fact that she hated them was enough for me to return that feeling towards her. Alexander and Edward were the best men I knew, and if she couldn't see that, I wanted nothing to do with her. Now, I was about to do the unthinkable. I swallowed as I considered the olive branch I was planning to offer to her tonight.

Mary's lips pursed, her expression sour, as she swept a scathing look over me. Her eyes landed on the small bump I had chosen not to hide. That was one secret out of the way. I could only hope she wouldn't go blabbing it to the press herself. Next to her, Henry's face was serenely unaware of the tension. My limited experience with him had been friendly. He had been the spare to the heir. Maybe that was why he had always been kinder to me. Like

Edward, he'd known that the moment his brother had his first child, his chances of landing on the throne were limited. He also didn't seem to mind passing on that responsibility.

"I see you're pregnant again." Mary didn't bother to hide her disapproval.

I'd been expecting it, but it still stung. Part of me hated my hormones for making me more susceptible to her barbs. I shrugged, willing the comment to roll off my shoulders.

Edward, however, had gone rigid. "I think what you meant to say was congratulations."

"And where is your husband?" Mary asked him, turning on him. "Or are you hiding him away, too?"

"I'm not hiding anything," Edward said coolly. He went to the seat next to the head of the table and pulled out my chair. It was a cue we'd discussed. It was time to take our places and remind her who was in charge of this palace now.

"Not hiding anything?" She guffawed, adding a dramatic huff for good measure. "I don't remember a wedding invitation. In fact, I had to read about it in The Daily Mail."

"Mother," Henry said in a quiet voice. Was this why he had come? Was it his job to keep her in check? And who had put him in charge of that position? Or had the duty fallen to him with the death of his brother? I couldn't imagine that Mary suddenly cared what she said or who she hurt. She never had before.

I took the seat just as Alexander arrived, buttoning his jacket and straightening his tie. He had obviously come straight from a meeting and he wore the weary look he usually had after a long discussion with Parliament. His eyes, which had been slightly glazed over as he entered the room, as though his mind were on something else, zeroed in on his grandmother and uncle and flamed to life. Instantly, his whole demeanor changed. This wasn't a simple family dinner with his wife and brother. I saw the recognition of that dawn on his face. Anger flashed so quickly over his gorgeous features that I was certain I was the only one who caught it. I suspected I'd be seeing more of that look later.

"We have guests?" he asked through gritted teeth. His eyes looked down to where I sat next to the seat he was supposed to take. I had expected to see anger or rebuke reflected there, instead, I found only frustration. A pang of regret bounced in my chest. This was worse than him being mad at me.

"Yes, I thought you knew," I lied, hating myself a little for it. Later, I would admit the truth to him privately. I had no intention of being dishonest with my husband, but there was no way I was going to show all of my cards now. It was better to let them think he had forgotten after a harried day of meetings than that I had purposefully manipulated the situation.

"We were just discussing your wife's condition," Mary said, as she took a step toward the seat across from mine. She waited, but Alexander didn't move. After a tense minute, Henry stepped forward and pulled the chair out for her. Alexander was still standing, still taking his measure of the situation.

"Her condition?" he asked.

That I hadn't planned on. Immediately, my hand went to my stomach, rubbing it absentmindedly as I tried to think of a way to smooth this over. He hadn't seen what I was wearing. He also hadn't been told that Edward was now in on the news. We hadn't discussed whether or not anyone outside of the security team should know that I was expecting yet. I'd wanted to keep this a secret. Now I'd spilled the news without consulting him.

"I'm running out of things to wear," I said in a soft voice. It was the truth. It would have been hard to find anything appropriate that didn't scream maternity dress.

"Is she trying to hide it? I don't see how that's possible." Mary picked up her water glass and took a sip. She hadn't said it to be supportive. In fact, it was the opposite. But it did the trick.

Alexander glanced down, his eyes landing on the unmistakable bump, and a slight smile twitched across his lips.

"I think you're bigger than this morning," he said. There was no mistaking the love in those words. It soaked through me like a warm ray of sunshine. We were in this together. He finally took a seat, his hand stretching across the table in invitation. I took it without a thought.

Henry rounded the table and sat next to me. Edward sat next to his grandmother as planned. I felt safer having her surrounded by my husband and his brother. At least, it was safer for her.

"You two are very affectionate," Mary noted, glaring at our entwined hands. "It isn't dignified. No king holds his wife's hand."

Henry laughed, which earned him a sharp look from his mother. "You seem to forget how Albert and Elizabeta were when they were together."

"How were they?" I asked before I could stop myself. I knew so little about Alexander's parents and this was a surprise. Albert hadn't been the affectionate type.

Henry leaned closer to me and lowered his voice. "I swear that I caught them shagging in the hallway."

"That is quite enough!" Mary said. Her hand flew to her chest as though she was in danger of a heart attack.

One could hope.

I made a note to ask him about it another time. The conversation at dinner faded into small talk and safe conversations about a variety of parliamentary measures that Alexander had been briefed on today. We avoided anything that might inadvertently cause someone to lose their temper. It felt like walking on eggshells, and it was the most uncomfortable dinner we'd had in a long time, even worse than the time my parents had practically gotten divorced before the salad had been served.

It all changed over the dessert course.

"How long will you be staying in London?" Edward asked his grandmother.

It was a simple question. I'd asked Edward to wait until everyone had finished eating before he brought it up. There was a reason I had planted it amidst the conversation so carefully. I needed them to have this discussion now, even knowing it might devolve into a fight.

"We will be here through the end of the games." Mary moved so the server could place a small plate of fruit in front of her. She looked at it and sighed with disappointment. "Fruit?"

"I sent along your dietary restrictions," Henry told her reproachfully. He glanced over me and rolled his eyes. "Thank you for seeing to them. We appreciate it."

I nodded. I wasn't going to win over Mary with a plate of strawberries, but seeing to her health seemed to be a priority of Henry's. He was the one I had a chance to impress, and I seized my opportunity.

"Who have we appointed to work on the games?" I asked my husband.

He abandoned his fork, his eyes narrowing and his mind translating my simple question. "That's not our concern."

"It was your father's pride and joy," Mary said coldly. She speared a strawberry violently and waved it on the end of her fork. "I would think you could muster a shred of respect for him after what he did for you."

"If you mean dying for me, I haven't forgotten." The temperature in the room dropped another ten degrees at his words. This was spinning out of control, and I needed to take the reins.

"Of course we want to support Albert's legacy," I broke in, ignoring how every head at the table swiveled in surprise. Well, except for Edward's. He was trying to hide a smirk. "That's why I'm going to do it."

"Do what?" Alexander and Mary asked at the same time. They were both staring at me as though I had grown a second head.

"Host the games," I told them. This time, all of them went completely still. I hadn't discussed this part of the plan with anyone, not even Edward.

It was time I stopped allowing all of them to criticize and control me, which meant taking charge. I waited a second to make certain they were paying attention. No one could leave here with any doubt of my intentions. "I will be the host. After all, it is the Sovereign Games, and *I'm the queen*."

CHAPTER SEVEN

CLARA

We made it back to the bedroom before the argument began. I kicked off my heels as soon as I was through the door. Taking off my earrings, I flinched as Alexander slammed the door closed behind us. I'd expected this. I'd mentally prepared as best I could. Now I had to face him, it was hard not to have second thoughts. Alexander's hands grabbed my shoulders and spun me around. His lips crashed into mine, his strong body backing me toward the wall. His kiss was rough and hungry, but, more than that, punishing. I gasped as his teeth nipped at my lower lip. His hands were everywhere, shoving up my skirt, gripping my ass, tangling in my hair.

"I thought you were mad at me," I said, barely containing a whimper as his hand delved past the neckline of my wrap dress. He caught my nipple with his thumb and forefinger and began kneading it roughly.

"I'm not mad, Poppet, I'm *furious*."

"Then why—"

But his mouth smothered mine once more. He didn't want to talk. Maybe he knew that we were about to have the fight of our lives. Maybe we needed to get this out of the way. Sex drove Alexander. I had always known that. I had always responded to it, as well. Even now, knowing this was the storm before the hurricane, I didn't want him to stop.

Alexander dropped to his knees, his hands bunching the fabric of my skirt at my hips. "Christ, Poppet. No knickers?"

I dared to look down at him. His eyes blazed into me, white hot and furious, his face hovering over my bare sex.

Oh, was he pissed.

I did my best to sound nonchalant. "I don't go into battle unprepared."

"You knew how I would react?" The words grated out, his breath hot on my skin. "You knew I would need to claim you—take you—and you came *prepared*? We are not through discussing this."

Before I could think of how to response, his mouth closed over me. There was no love in the act, only blind, driving need. He was wild. He was out of control. I had pushed him past a breaking point I didn't know he had. His tongue parted me, accessing every part of me. He devoured me, driving my body toward climax, taking my pleasure. It was primal—somehow terrifying and thrilling at the same time. My fingernails scratched across the papered walls, seeking purchase and finding none.

Usually, Alexander was my anchor, the center that kept me tethered, no matter what his body asked of mine. Something had shifted now. The hold he had on me was no longer a tether but a leash. He was binding me, asserting his ownership. I felt my muscles tighten, my body responding to his attack even as my mind warred against it. I cracked apart, his name on my lips, and my thighs closing around his head. It was too much. Too fast. He kept going, and I pushed against him until he vanished.

I clung to the wall, and his strong arms bracketed me, his still-clothed body pressing against mine. I felt his cock, hard against my belly, as his lips danced across my jaw and paused to whisper in my ear, "You know what to say to make me stop."

My safe word would end this. All I had to say was *brimstone*. It was a reminder I didn't need. Instead, my hand flew, slapping him hard across the face.

His face snapped to the side, and his eyes stayed on the ground a moment before he shook his head slightly. He turned back to me with a wicked smile. "Wrong answer, Poppet."

I surged forward, my lips finding his. He met me, his arms lifting me off my feet and carrying me to our bed. My dress came off entirely, followed by my bra. I bucked against him, wanting him and hating him for it at the same time. He dropped me on to the mattress, and my fingers fumbled with his buttons and his tie as Alexander shucked off his jacket. It fell to the floor in a heap.

I couldn't get him undressed fast enough. He reached down, pulling off his belt and unfastening his pants. My feet found his hips, pushing down the last barrier between us. I didn't even see his cock before it was inside me. My body arched at the sudden intrusion.

There was no gentle pause to prepare me. He was there, pounding into me with strong, fast strokes. He clutched my hips, rocking them in a desperate rhythm. His eyes darkened as he watched where our bodies collided. I seized my chance before he could release. Hooking an arm around his neck, I threw my weight against him, knocking him off his feet. He fell to the bed and we rolled over one another until I found myself on top. Without waiting, I slammed over him, yelping as his length speared me to the core. Alexander paused, concern flitting over his face, but I didn't stop. My hips circled and ground, pushing him towards his orgasm. His hand reached to brush my breast, but I forced him down, holding his chest with my hands. I was the one in charge now and he needed to see that. Two of us could play this game. He could drive me crazy, too. I needed him to see that no matter how much I gave him, I could take it back.

"Tell me, X. Tell me what you want me to do." I bit out, my demand coming in quick, frantic bursts.

His hands caught the bedsheets as he grunted and thrusted, trying to match my movements. "Fuck me, Clara. Fuck me."

"Who do you belong to?" I asked him, lifting myself to the tip of his cock and hovering there. He strained, trying to slide inside me once more, but I held firm.

"You," he said darkly. "I belong to you." I plunged over him, lost to his words.

The first hot spurt of his climax undid me and he threw himself free of my imprisonment, rising to catch my waist so that, in the end, we fell together. He pressed a kiss to my lips, our breathing still shallow and rushed.

"That was very wicked of you, Poppet." His words were low and dangerous, but the rage in his eyes had cooled. He brushed a strand of hair from my forehead and took a deep breath. "*You're* wicked."

"I'm yours," I breathed.

"Yes, you're my wicked queen." He brushed his mouth over mine. "I get the feeling you're trying to prove something to me."

"I could say the same thing," I said dryly. Had he forgotten where this had started? With me pressed against a wall as he forced me to come on his mouth? "I belong to you, X. You seem to keep forgetting that."

"Maybe I just wanted a reminder," he suggested.

I trailed my hand down his face, lingering where

I had slapped him. He turned into my hand, kissing my palm. I guess that meant I was forgiven for that indiscretion.

"Sometimes I need you to remind me when I'm being an ass," he muttered.

"Does that mean you're not mad at me?" I asked. Not that I cared if he was. He might be mad, but he was also in trouble. We'd gotten sex out of the way. Now it was time for the fight. I braced myself.

Alexander bit his lower lip, his eyes darting up and then away. "I'm still mad, but I think that makes two of us."

"Are we going to talk about it or are we going to fuck it out?"

"Is that an option?" He dropped a playful kiss to my shoulder.

The time for fun and games was over. I leveled a glare at him. "No, it isn't, X."

"I didn't think so," he sighed.

I pushed off him, my body instantly missing his warmth, but I did my best to ignore the pang of longing I felt. I stood on shaky feet, bent down, grabbed his pants, and threw them at him. "Put these on."

"I thought you liked me better naked." A smirk twisted over his face, and I fought the urge to kiss it off.

"I can't think with that thing"—I waved a hand in the general direction of his crotch—"staring at me."

"It is my secret weapon." He stroked it sugges-tively while pulling on his pants.

"Stop," I demanded.

He paused, one foot into his slacks, and a look of genuine apprehension crossing his face. "Stop what?"

"Being charming."

"Isn't that my job? Prince Charming?"

I laughed at this. "You're no Prince Charming."

"I'm not?"

Alexander was many things. That wasn't one of them. He was cocky and broken and sexy as hell, but he wasn't some white knight. "No, you're the King. I'm the Queen."

"As you so aptly reminded me earlier this evening," he grumbled.

"You are the only one I bow to," I reminded him, "but you seem to have forgotten where your place is."

Alexander stood, his fingers fastening his pants. He stopped and took a hard look at me.

"Is that what this is about?" he asked in a soft voice.

"You tell me." I wasn't certain what any of it was about anymore. I'd known what I was signing up for when I agreed to marry him, or so I thought. Alexander had known what he was asking of me. "You seem to forget that we're equals."

"I've never thought we were equals," he said quietly.

I sucked in a breath as his words shattered my heart. At least he was being honest. I wished I had known before now that he felt that way. Was this his plan all along? To trick me into believing I had as much power as him—as much say is him? As much control as him? I couldn't find the strength to argue with him. Suddenly, I was tired and my heart hurt.

He took a step forward and I backed away.

"Clara," he said my name gently, "I think you've misunderstood me."

"I think I understood you fine." Anger, hurt, and resentment simmered in my voice, and I hoped he heard it. I hoped it hurt him the way his words had hurt me.

"No, you didn't. We aren't equals," he repeated.

I closed my eyes, shaking my head. I didn't want to hear this.

"I could never be your equal," he confessed softly.

My eyes flew open and I stared at him. Anguish lined his handsome features. He stood before me, the scars of his past no longer hidden, the fears for his future written in his eyes. This was us—messy, complicated, damaged. He had never believed he was worthy of love. Why had I lost sight of that? Why had I forgotten that under the face he showed to the world, he was lost. I'd believed that I could fix him— that I had fixed him. But maybe some people could never be fixed, maybe some people were held together by love alone.

"Alexander, you are a good man," I said, because

he needed to hear it. He needed to face the demon that frightened him the most: himself.

He crossed to me with tired eyes, and I didn't resist as he took me in his arms. No matter what happened this was where I belonged. It was what I had promised him. My heart. My life. My faith.

"No matter how hard I push back, nothing changes between us. I love you. I chose you. You are a good man," I repeated.

He looked down at me, sorrow tinging his blue eyes, and smiled sadly. "I'm not, but you make me think I could be."

CHAPTER EIGHT

ALEXANDER

Clara had not budged on her position by morning. I'd pulled out every argument I could think of and she still wouldn't acquiesce. It was a dangerous play on my part. The last time I tried to talk her out of doing something had nearly gotten her killed. That was probably the only reason she was still at Buckingham the next morning. Even she couldn't deny my concern was warranted. Not that she would admit that to me. She'd made that clear last night. When I brought it up, she'd laughed, albeit nervously, and reminded me that we still have no proof she had been a target at all. To her, it was simply a matter of being in the wrong place at the wrong time.

That was bullshit. Members of the Royal Family didn't coincidentally walk into a place where a bomb was about to go off. I wouldn't admit this to her—but we didn't have any proof the attack had had anything to do with her yet. It was frustrating. It was exhausting. I was at the end of my patience trying to understand what had happened. We almost got the intel too late that day. There had been a breakdown somewhere in our communications and in our security precautions. I was determined that wouldn't happen again.

However, maintaining my family's safety was going to be infinitely harder if Clara continued to insist on putting herself in the spotlight with these stupid games.

I reached my office before sunrise and found Norris already there. I took a long look at my old friend, noting the dark circles under his eyes and how much deeper the creases in his face ran these days. He carried the responsibility of protecting my family on his shoulders as much as I did. I shouldn't have been surprised to find him here, waiting to consider our options.

He didn't move from the sofa as I came in. There was no point. Norris and I didn't rely on ceremony and protocol. I liked to pretend that he felt he was my equal. Still, I couldn't deny that on more than one occasion I had played my trump card by issuing a command. He had always followed them. It was the one lingering sign our relationship was not built entirely on love and accountability, but rather respect and duty. Sometimes I wished my wife shared his amenability.

"I took the liberty of ordering coffees," he told me as I shut the door behind me.

What I had to say to him needed to remain between the two of us, and the staff would be arriving within the hour. I only wished we could sort out this mess in that short an amount of time.

"Did you sleep at all?" I asked him, taking the sofa opposite his. Someone had lit a fire, perhaps Norris, and I was grateful. Even inside the palace's thick walls, I felt January's chill.

He studied me for a moment, no doubt taking in my haggard features, and shook his head. "Did you?"

"I had to reason with her," I said. I didn't bother to tell him what methods of persuasion I'd resorted to. He could probably guess.

"Maybe *reasoning* with her isn't the right method," he suggested.

I arched an eyebrow in surprise. It wasn't like Norris to take my side so easily. If he could see that Clara was being irrational, then maybe I'd been right to try to stop her. "What would you suggest? I could demand she not host the games. I could—"

"I don't think that will work out the way you hope." Norris snorted as if in on his own private joke.

He was probably right about that, which left me fewer options, but much more decisive ones. "I could call off the games. If I announce it publicly, no one will dare to undermine me, not even Clara."

"You should consider how the people will feel about it, though," Norris said. "It won't be a popular decision. I don't need to remind you that when certain other matters come to light, there might be a public reaction. I wouldn't court more controversy if I were you."

"And what would you have me do?" I exploded, all of the frustration I felt for the last twelve hours coming to a head.

"Have you spoken to your grandmother?"

"What do you think?" He knew enough about our relationship to know better. She hadn't come here on my invitation, but rather left a message telling me to expect her. She still believed that this palace—that this monarchy—belonged to her. Now, she wanted to come stir an already simmering pot. No, I hadn't invited her. In fact, I should have told her she wasn't welcome at all.

"I suspected." Norris, who'd been fiddling with his cufflinks, abandoned them and turned his attention to me. "Perhaps, that's where you start. Speak with your grandmother. Speak with your uncle. Explain to them the security issues that we're facing and how the games would exacerbate the situation. You always presume one will respond unreasonably, but you might be surprised how they will react when given the facts."

"I doubt that. Besides, what good will it do me?" It wouldn't convince Clara to let this go. Even if my grandmother agreed to cancel the games, would my wife?

"Who cancels the games will make a difference,"

he advised me. "Most of the countries still perceive your grandmother as a grieving mother. If she were to announce a stay in the plans out of respect for your father's memory, no one would question that."

"And you really believe she'd go along with that?"

There was a knock on the door and we exchanged a glance. It appeared our time was up, and we were no closer to finding a solution to our problems. Norris stood, straightening his suit jacket and offered me a sympathetic smile. "We won't know until we ask."

I wished I had his optimism.

Norris told me my grandmother had agreed to speak later in the morning, which was a promising sign. She'd agreed to come with Henry. Even though the meeting would be in my office and on my terms, I still wondered how a man like Norris—who'd seen so much—could hope for a good outcome.

She arrived wearing one of the stiff, formal dress suits that had been her signature when she'd held the role my wife now did. That was the difference between her and Clara. Mary had made every decision, even when choosing how to dress each day, out of a sense of duty. Even now, when she was free from the restrictions of her previous title, she continued to uphold an outdated persona. That was probably why she despised my wife so much. Not only had Clara been an outsider, but she'd fought me and my family's rules nearly every step of the way. I loved her for it, even when it drove me insane. I could only imagine how Clara would punish me when she found out this meeting had been held without her.

My cock twitched at the thought of my wife's face flushed with anger. It always did when I pictured her rising to challenge me. It was a bad habit —getting turned on by angering my wife—and one I needed to break.

Norris coughed politely, and I shook myself from my thoughts. Now definitely wasn't the time to be thinking about Clara in that way. One look at my grandmother erased the thought from my mind entirely.

I left my desk and joined them in the sitting area. "I've ordered some tea."

"It's a bit early for that," Mary sniffed as though somehow the thought of tea before noon was offensive.

"Thank you," Henry added hastily, shooting a barbed look at her. She huffed but didn't say another word.

In some ways the dynamic of their relationship reminded me of what she'd been like when my father was alive. My grandmother had always been prone to insulting everyone around her. The only person she'd respected had been my father, probably because he was also cruel. Now, it seemed that Henry had taken his place in her eyes without being the cold, domineering man my father had been. It was strange to think that a woman as opinionated and outspoken as her needed a man to oversee her affairs, but that was clearly the case. She'd left to live with him before my coronation. I'd nearly sent my apologies to my uncle ahead of time. Judging by the interactions we'd had so far, my concern had been unwarranted. The two of them seemed to work. My uncle actually held her in check, something she desperately needed if she was going to have any relationship with me or my family going forward. It seemed Henry understood their place in the family. Perhaps that meant he would see reason today.

"You're probably wondering why you're here," I began.

"Of course, we aren't. Your wife made it quite clear that you two were taking over the games." There was another sniffle of resentment from her at these words. Despite her earlier objections, she'd taken a cup of tea. Hypocrite.

I hadn't expected her to interpret last night that way. Surely, she had seen my reaction. How could she think I wanted anything to do with the bloody games? Then again, after Clara had made her announcement at dinner, I'd waited until we were in private quarters before I'd disagreed with it. Allowing my grandmother to see even a hint of division between us wasn't an option. She would take advantage of that, which would only make matters worse. This now left me on dangerous ground. If I admitted to her this was Clara's idea and appealed to her for the cancellation of the games, she would know that division existed. On the one hand, she would have no reason to stay in London once the games were canceled. On the other, I wouldn't put it past her to make breaking up my marriage her new hobby. I needed to tread carefully. I couldn't admit to her that I wanted the games discontinued any more than I could do nothing. I had to spin this.

Next to me, Norris spoke before I'd landed on an answer. "This morning, I had the unpleasant duty to inform his Majesty that early security assessments for the games have revealed a number of concerns."

"What's that supposed to mean?" she hissed, abandoning her teacup to its saucer and glaring at us.

"We're still conducting an investigation into last week's attack," he explained.

"We are aware of that," Henry said in a clipped tone that chipped away my confidence that he would see our side. "Our own advisers informed us there's no reason to think the attack had anything to do with the Royal Family."

It took every ounce of restraint I had to stay silent. I'd heard this before—from my own team. Even Clara had thrown it in my face. I didn't believe it and I refused to write it off as paranoia.

"Yes," Norris confirmed, and I shot a scathing look in his direction. He was supposed to be on my side. He continued without acknowledging me. "Our teams seem to be reaching the same conclusion. We will, of course, continue to look into the matter. It's important to consider, though, that the general state of security in the country—and indeed, the world—is unstable. We're seeing more and more attacks of this nature at public events, targeting ordinary citizens and charity organizations, as well as the usual targets. In a way, these attacks are aimed at our very way of life."

"I don't see what this has to do with the games," Mary said, but her attention had turned to the floor. My grandmother had always had a knack for ignoring what she didn't want to hear.

"What Norris is saying," I interjected, "is that hosting a large, public charity event will be a risk to everyone involved, even ordinary citizens. This isn't a matter of *our* personal security. This is a matter of protecting our people."

I had to hand it to Norris. It was brilliant. More than that, it was the truth. I'd been so focused on Clara and my family's personal safety that I'd failed in my other responsibilities as King. Hosting the games would put more than the people closest to me at risk. It endangered the lives of attendees.

"I understand where you're coming from," Henry began slowly, taking the measure of the room as he spoke, "but to cancel the games would be a clear show of cowardice."

"I'm not interested in what people think of me," I said roughly.

"Well, that's obvious." Mary shook her head as if she was recalling every moment in which I'd disappointed her. If she was going to try to get through them all, she would probably be on the couch next week.

"It isn't about perception, Alexander. It's about how you choose to reign over this country. I hadn't expected you to allow fear to control you. It wouldn't have influenced your father, at least." Henry leaned against the arm of the sofa. He'd never bothered to take a cup of tea, and I realized that of everyone here, he'd been most aware of the path this meeting would take. He'd foreseen it. I'd never had a shot at making him my ally. He'd come here to call me out.

I'd always thought of my uncle as a friendly type that showed up on occasion with a birthday present or in his funeral suit. He seemed so unlike my father, but maybe that had changed with Albert's death. He'd stepped into the role of dutiful son, but I hadn't expected him to take up the mantle of disappointed father as well. That was what he was doing now, trying to get me to do something by accusing me of being afraid. But this wasn't a matter of refusing to eat my vegetables. Lives were at stake.

"I don't expect you to understand." I met his eyes as I spoke and he didn't look away. I'd drawn a line in the sand. Would he cross it?

"Could Clara not join us?" he asked.

There was my answer. He'd taken a look at my boundary and stepped right over it.

"She's quite tired these days." I gave him a tight smile. This battle would be fought with civility—

handshakes and apologies and outsmarting one another.

"Given her interest in being the one to host the games—and given your obvious responsibilities in addressing current security measures—perhaps we should continue our plans with her," he suggested.

"Henry," Mary said sharply.

"Mother, we discussed this," he said to her in a low voice. "Clara is Alexander's wife now. We should respect her contributions to the family."

He had me by the balls, and he knew it. I couldn't help but see him in a whole new light. Perhaps Henry was more like my father than I had ever realized. He wouldn't be my ally, but he would be Clara's. How hadn't I seen this outcome? Siding with her got everyone what they wanted. The games would go on, my wife would be happy, and Mary and her son would be in a new position of power. Everyone got their way, but me.

I only had one way to play out the lie we'd told. Had Norris foreseen this? Was that why he'd broached security concerns? Either way, it was my only way to save face and avoid all out civil war.

"I'm certain she'll want to talk to you further," I said. "I had a duty to inform you of what we knew."

Norris stiffened, the movement was imperceptible to the others, but I caught it. He knew, as did I, that I'd just given my unofficial approval to the games and thrown him under the bus at the same time.

"You understand," I added, more for his benefit than theirs.

"Of course, a king must consider all his movements carefully." Henry's genial smile stopped at his watery, blue eyes.

My family left after exacting more promises they would hear from Clara soon. Mary stopped on her way out and turned her shrewd gaze on me. "We've already delayed enough. Don't try to drag this out any further, Alexander."

I'd fooled neither of them.

She left her warning hanging in the air between us. I didn't bother to shut the door. Soon we'd move onto the next appointment on the agenda, leaving me no time to consider my next move.

"That went well," I said flatly.

"No matter what you might've said, we still have options."

I shook my head, laughing a little at the idea. "I think our options just walked out the door."

"Talk to Clara further. Maybe try a different form of persuasion," Norris said.

"What did you have in mind?" I'd tried every persuasion I could think of with her. Some twice.

"Perhaps, actually *talking*."

"She doesn't listen to me," I said, leaning against the wall, frustration overtaking me. "I'm supposed to be the King, but I can't control my wife."

"Maybe you should stop trying to control her," Edward's voice broke into our conversation. He stood in the doorway, eyeing me reproachfully. He was dressed down for the day in a sweater and jeans. There were no meetings or debates on his agenda, which left him all the time in the world to harass me. My brother had always sided with Clara. They were best friends, and I wouldn't take that away from either of them. Even having him here, discussing this now, seemed to undermine the trust between them.

When I didn't respond, Edward walked to my desk and picked up the framed picture of Clara and Elizabeth. "Have you ever asked yourself why you believe Clara needs to be controlled?"

"She needs to be protected," I corrected him.

"You said controlled. You said 'I can't control my wife,'" he repeated my words back to me.

I hated the way they sounded, but it didn't change facts. Why couldn't he see that? He'd panicked after the attack. I'd spoken with him. Now he was acting like there was nothing to fear.

"Why do you want to control her?" he asked again.

"She's in danger." That was the most obvious thing in the world.

Edward replaced the photo and turned a penetrating stare on me. "So are you."

"That's different." He was baiting me and I was biting.

"How?" He stuffed his hands in his pockets, daring me to come up with a good answer.

I couldn't.

"That's what I thought," Edward said. "I'm in danger. David is in danger. Elizabeth is in danger. It's a fact of our lives and one you must come to grips with."

"It's not the same thing. There've been no attacks on you or David. Elizabeth is home safe."

"She won't always be. Someday, she'll fight you on this, too. And you better have found a better way to handle it by then or you'll wind up becoming our father."

He might as well have crossed the room and thrown a punch. His words sliced through me but even as blood heated, I couldn't deny the truth in his words. Was that were I was headed? Was I doomed to become a man I despised?

"Edward," Norris began gently, sensing I was on edge.

I held up a hand. It was time to show that I could be reasonable. "It's okay. He's right."

"Now we're getting somewhere." Edward dropped onto the sofa and folded his hands into his lap. "It's okay to worry about her, Alexander. I do, too. But you can't lock her away—or you're going to lose her."

That was the heart of the issue. Allowing her away from here, away from me, away from safety, felt like a terrifying risk. Why couldn't he see that?

"But if I don't protect her, I lose her forever. How many times has someone tried to take her away from me?"

"That could happen. No one can control the whole world—not even you. But if you keep levelling demands at her, keep blocking her way, keep presuming to know what's right for her, you will lose her without question."

"But she'd be safe," I said in a small voice I rarely allowed to speak. This was the voice of my fears, the one I tried to force deep inside until it was so distant, so hidden, even from myself, that I could barely hear it.

"Either way, it would be a life without her." He paused and gave me my answer. "There's only one chance at keeping her."

I knew I could no longer win. Not the way I had wanted. In the end, there was no decision to be made. Everyone seemed to have conspired to make it for me. I turned to Norris and sucked in a deep breath. "Cancel my meetings. Call Brexton and Georgia."

CHAPTER NINE

CLARA

A half dozen cars flew past, and I clapped my hands over my ears as the deafening roar of the engines pounded in my head. Next to me, Belle bounced up and down on her heels. I stole a glance at her, wondering if this was some weird pregnancy thing. I never realized that she was into cars before. Maybe she could explain what was happening later, because I wasn't getting anything except that cars were going around the track very, very fast. It was making me nauseated to watch them.

I hadn't known what to expect at Silverstone, except the obvious: fast cars and a hovering security team. I still couldn't believe I was here. My new role as official host of the Sovereign Games came with a few unwanted perks, though. Alexander had been perfectly clear on that.

At one end of the stands, Georgia's attention was on everything but the track. On the other side, Brex was doing the same thing. I couldn't help but notice they'd been keeping their distance from each other the whole time. Splitting up meant they could cover more ground, but it wasn't as if they were the only two members of my security team. Alexander had sent an embarrassing number of people to the track with me today. I felt like I was heading off to war, not to deliver an official invitation to participate in this year's Sovereign Games.

For the most part, my husband had stayed out of things. Ever since he gave in and told me the games would proceed—and that he supported my decision to be part of them—he'd holed up in his office. I suspected his focus was on matters of national and personal security, like studying every entrance and exit at the Silverstone track. As far as I could tell, he'd covered them all. It would take another nation's entire Armed Forces to reach me.

I didn't argue with him. After all, this was the most flexible he'd been since we were married. It might have seemed like a small step, but I knew it was huge. I hoped it was a sign of things to come.

The screech of rubber yanked me back to the present moment and I leaned against the guardrail to see a driver's backend slide off the track. It was particularly icy this morning and my breath caught as the car spun in a wild circle before narrowly clipping its rear bumper on a cement barricade.

I turned to Belle, who seemed to know what was going on, and yelled over the noise, "Is he okay?"

"He's fine," she called back. Then she yelled something about *opposite lock at the chicane.*

I suspected I'd heard her wrong or she was speaking another language.

The other racers finished their race and pulled into the pit, instantly dropping the decibels in the stadium to normal levels. I made a mental note to bring earplugs to drown out the sounds of the race next time.

"That was impressive. Your guy managed to keep from flipping when he spun out. Icy track and slick tires don't mix." She whistled as she watched the crew inspecting the vehicle. "Of course, he was out ahead of the others. That's why he lost control. He kept hitting that corner faster and faster. He stopped accounting for the conditions. He's good, but reckless. Of course, he *is* young."

My mouth fell open and I closed it quickly. "When did you learn so much about cars and racing and racecar drivers?"

I didn't even think she had a driving license. I couldn't remember her driving during the entirety of our university careers. It was like she'd just revealed she had an entire secret life. I wasn't sure how to feel about it.

"I've always loved cars," she said, a mischievous smile playing at her lips. It vanished, replaced by a sad one. "My dad loved them."

I reached out and rubbed her shoulder. She didn't talk about her father often. Belle had been the one to discover his body after he'd committed suicide. She'd been young, robbed of the chance to really know him. Instead, her memories of him were colored by the unimaginable. "I didn't know that."

"Most people don't." She shrugged, her grin looking a little forced now. "When I met Smith, I discovered he loved them, too. He gave me a chance to enjoy them again, outside memories of my father."

I understood that. Love gave us the courage to be the person we were afraid to be.

"Smith drives some fancy car, doesn't he?" I'd seen it on occasion when we'd gone out. Unlike Belle, though, I knew very little about cars. I could drive, of course. Part of me *was* still American, so it was practically ingrained in my DNA. But apart from knowing where the ignition was and what to do when the oil light came on, my knowledge was limited. I'd driven very little in the last year. Alexander wasn't a fan of me being behind the wheel. In all fairness to him, I'd nearly killed myself in an accident on our ill-fated trip to Scotland. He didn't need to worry, though, I wasn't about to take up racing.

"It's a Bugatti," she told me as if I should know what that meant. When I didn't respond, she rolled her eyes. "It's a *really* fancy car."

"Like a Ferrari?"

"Not quite, because a Ferrari probably has a poster of a Bugatti on its wall. And you can't just buy one. You have to know a guy, be worthy, that sort of thing."

"Oh, like a Birkin Bag?"

"Exactly."

I appreciated the translation. My eyes strayed to her midsection, which even under her coat was still deceptively flat. Now that she was pregnant, I wondered what Smith would drive. "Isn't it a two-seater?"

"Don't remind me," she groaned. "He wants to get rid of it."

"That's true love—coming between a man and his car." Alexander had never been one for cars himself, but I had been raised in the States. There, a man's car was almost as important an extension of his masculinity as his dick.

"What I mean is, he wanted to get rid of it, but I wouldn't let him," she added fiercely. "He wants to put it in the garage. He keeps talking about a family car."

I laughed at the obvious distress in her voice. Sometimes, it was hard to imagine Belle or Smith as parents, even though I knew they both wanted this baby more than anything in the world. "I can't imagine you in an estate car."

I'd learned to use the proper British slang when talking to Belle, who had a habit of screwing up her face when I sounded *too American*. Somehow, though, an *estate car* sounded even worse than the American term: station wagon. Maybe it was a toss-up.

"The next thing you know I'll be a footballer mom.

Taking the kids to practice and popping the recycling up to the tip on weekends." She shook her head, sending her blonde locks swinging over her shoulders. "Things really do change." She bumped against me, her eyes darting to my security team, who were watching us closely. "Oops! I touched you. Are they going to tackle me?"

"Don't remind me," I said. We both knew all too well that our lives had changed. My security team was a pretty stark reminder. Despite that, I knew neither of us would change any of it.

"Mind if I join you?" Henry asked as he sidled through the bench seats and came up to us.

"Is everything okay?" I tipped my head in the direction of the racing team who were looking over the car.

"They expected it with the ice." Henry's voice was muffled by the scarf he had wrapped tightly around his neck, but there was no denying the excitement in his eyes. It seemed I was the only one out of my element here. I was determined not to show it. This week I'd read up on racing stats, so I had some idea what was going on.

"So who is this guy?" I asked. Given Mary's demand that the games move forward on schedule, there had been very little time to go over initial invitations if we planned to start in March. A stack of candidates had landed on the desk of my private office yesterday. I hadn't reached the S files yet. All I knew was that the driver's name was Anderson

Stone. I'd planned to dig into his file before we left when morning sickness had sidetracked me. "I'm afraid I haven't made it through his file yet."

Henry waved off my apology with a gloved hand. He tugged down the top of his scarf. "He's young. Very popular and he's made his way into the world's top three. They're predicting he'll be number one by year's end."

"And he's hot," Belle added.

I didn't bother to hide my surprise. In fact, I did my best to look scandalized.

She shook her head with an impish grin. "I'm married, not dead."

"He is considered quite attractive," Henry confirmed. I wondered for a moment if Henry had more in common with Edward than I thought. He was unmarried and of a certain age. I didn't know him well enough to ask. "It's one of the reasons why we landed on him, actually."

"Is that why you're inviting him first?" Belle switched into business mode. "He would be the perfect face for the new Sovereign Games."

"That's exactly what we were thinking. The monarchy is younger now, social media is more important than ever, and if we're going to get national support for continuing this program, we need to have everyone's attention," he said.

I nodded. That made sense. I had worked on a number of similar, but smaller, campaigns. It always worked best when I had a celebrity backing up our efforts. "I'm excited to meet him."

Henry scanned me for a moment as if trying to ascertain if I was serious. After a moment, he relaxed. "Sorry," he explained. "My family rarely says what they mean. I can't tell you how thrilled my mother and I are to have your support on this."

I didn't bother to hide my incredulity, it was probably written all over my face. I sincerely doubted that Mary cared how the games continued, so long as they did. But I didn't kid myself that if she had her way, I would have nothing to do with them.

Henry seemed to sense what I was thinking, and added, "My mother will come around."

"Miracles do happen," I allowed.

The car's engine roared to life again, but this time, Anderson didn't peel out at speed. Instead he drove it off the track into the pit.

Next to me, Belle released a frustrated sigh. She was probably hoping for more action. I, on the other hand, was happy for the reprieve.

"I think this might be a good time to catch him. Hold on a moment, the team will bring you over when we are ready." Henry darted off to talk to Brexton.

I nodded, my stomach bottoming out. It wasn't like me to be nervous. Then again, this wasn't something I was used to doing. The last time I'd been asked to deliver good news, something terrible had happened. I shook off the memory. I couldn't live the rest of my life expecting a bomb to go off.

"You okay?" Belle asked, seeming to sense the shift in my mood.

I didn't want to spoil her mood, but I also knew I'd feel better if I talked about it. "I can't help but think about what happened the last time I was asked to do something like this."

"You can't live your life in fear," Belle said.

"I know that." It was easier said than done, though. Plus, it didn't help that my husband had the exact opposite opinion. I kept that to myself. "Was it hard to convince Smith to let you come?"

"Not really." She paused as if considering it. "Of course, he knows how much security Alexander keeps around you, so that probably made him feel better. He wanted to come himself, but something is holding him up in Scotland."

My stomach dropped another level. They had just gotten back from that trip. Now Smith was back there again? I didn't like the sound of it. Smith was Scottish and he'd made no secret of his desire to get the hell out of London. Given what the city had put him through, I couldn't blame him. But I couldn't handle the idea that Belle might be leaving.

"I almost had to cancel on you," she confessed, rubbing her flat belly. "My morning sickness has been a little bit more active. I'm hoping that's a good sign."

"It is," I promised her. Even after her ultrasound had come back with good news—the baby had a heartbeat—she still seemed worried. I wanted to wait to share my own news until she felt more confident, but I was running out of time. I hesitated and then decided to dive in. I couldn't keep this from her forever. "At least you don't have it all day."

She nodded vigorously. "I don't know how I would deal with that. As it is, I'm constantly sucking on ginger lollies. It's the only thing that settles my stomach."

"Try mint," I suggested. "It works for me."

"I don't remember you having much morning sickness with Elizabeth," she said slowly.

"I didn't have much with her," I said, taking a deep breath.

In the time it took me to steel myself for the final reveal, Belle's eyes widened. "You have one in the oven?" It was more accusation than question.

I bit my lip, to stop the sheepish smile creeping onto my face. "Yes. I wasn't sure how to tell you."

"Clara Bishop, how could you keep this a secret from me?" She cried as she grabbed me and pulled me into a hug. The sudden movement attracted more than the usual amount of attention from the security guards around me. I pulled back and waved them off before they could interrupt the moment. Then I hugged her again.

"I was worried you would be upset," I confessed.

"Why would I be..."

"I wanted to wait until after your doctor appointment," I explained. "Then everything happened."

"And I went to Scotland," she said. Her eyes narrowed and for a second, I thought she really might be angry. It was never a good sign when she called me by my maiden name. Finally, she snorted. "Look, I know you were looking out for me, but don't feel like you have to keep secrets from me. I love you and I will always be happy for you."

"I love you, too," I said, giving her another hug. My stomach flipped over, even relief made me queasy. Of course, the noxious combination of burnt rubber and motor oil hanging in the air probably didn't help. This was going to be a long pregnancy.

"Are you okay? You look green," she said when she released me.

"I think I need to find the loo," I admitted.

"Okay," she said, waving for someone to come over to us, "but then I want to know everything." She eyed my stomach suspiciously, but it was well hidden under a sweater, a coat, and scarves. I'd made it purposely hard to spot my bump.

I was grateful Brexton was the one who caught Belle's wave. He rushed over, and I told him in a whisper what I needed. Belle listened without speaking, but I had no doubt she was putting two and two together. She would figure out that others had found out about my pregnancy before her. I would have to remind her she had been the first one to know about Elizabeth and then beg her for forgiveness.

Brex led me beneath the grandstand and into a maze of corridors, some of which ran out towards pit lane. "There's a few down here," he explained. "You'll have more privacy than you will out there."

I was grateful he was thinking clearly. The press was out in droves. While none of them had been allowed inside to watch the practice laps, I knew how far a camera lens could reach. It was better to play it safe than to have someone catch me tossing my cookies in the bleachers. But the time it took to reach the pit was another problem altogether.

"Here," he said. "I'll be close."

That was the benefit of a male security guard. I tried the handle and found it locked. My eyes darted around, looking for another one. We were in what looked like a makeshift garage, and the fumes were even worse. My stomach heaved as the door opened and I took a few stumbling steps. But it was too late. I grabbed the rubbish bin the unlucky stranger held out and lost the little bit of breakfast I'd hoped would stay down.

"Whoa!" a surprised voice said.

I looked up, eyes watering, into a familiar set of blue ones. I relaxed for a moment, almost instinctively, before my embarrassment overtook me. I stood up shakily, apologies pouring out of me. He was about my age and far too good looking. A horrible thought occurred to me.

"I am so sorry," I continued before needing to vomit again. This time, I realized I was clutching a helmet, not a garbage can. Oh God. Tracksuit. Handsome. My age. I forced myself to look up. "You're

Anderson." I tried to think of a way to smooth over this situation, but there was no helping it. I decided I could at least be polite. "It's nice to meet you. I'm—"

"I know who you are," he said with a laugh, even as his face crinkled with concern. "Are you okay?"

"I'm fine. It's just..." I held a finger to my lips and placed my other hand on my stomach. "Please don't tell."

I couldn't understand it, but for some reason it felt like I could trust him.

"Your secret is safe with me," he whispered as Brex and a few other people surrounded us. It was made more awkward by the fact that we were still half inside the loo.

"I'll take that for you," one of my men said, gesturing to the helmet. I hoped it was replaceable.

"Are you sure you're not going to need it?" Anderson asked me.

"I hope not."

After today, I definitely wasn't going to be able to keep this under wraps. All of our security team members were carefully screened, but they were also human. Plus, I imagined a few members of the Silverstone staff had caught what happened. But when I looked up, I was surprised to see that Anderson's was the only new face in the crowd.

"If you want to..." He gestured to the bathroom.

I probably looked like a mess. I nodded gratefully.

"This probably wasn't how you imagined today

would go," I guessed as he stepped out and held the door open for me.

"I definitely won't forget it," he admitted as he closed the door behind me.

I did my best to freshen up, thankful that I'd thought to throw a pack of gum into my purse. There was no disguising the sickly hue of my skin or the slight sheen of sweat on my forehead. So much for a pregnancy glow. Finally, when I accepted there was nothing more I could do, I went back outside. The sooner we got the official invitation and the press conference over with, the better.

Belle was waiting outside the door when I exited, her arms crossed, a smug look on her face. She rounded on me the second I was out. Brex and the security team had created a perimeter around the area, giving me more than the usual amount of room. They were probably afraid I would splatter them in the next round of morning sickness.

"Did you really vomit in Anderson Stone's helmet?" she asked, a hysterical edge to her voice.

"Don't be a gossip," I told her, cheeks flaming.

"Oh my God, you did!"

"I'm not speaking to you."

"Is he hot?" she whispered as we moved away from the restroom.

"Belle, I had my face inside his helmet, I didn't really pay attention to him." That wasn't exactly true. I had gotten a look at Anderson. He wasn't *my* type exactly—tall and blond with a lean figure and broad shoulders—but he was charming. He'd barely flinched when I'd ruined his racing helmet. Who said chivalry was dead?

"I know, I know. You only have eyes for Alexander."

"Are you telling me you have eyes for someone other than Smith?" I hissed under my breath as we reached the group.

"Of course not," she said, sounding offended. Her eyes lit up when they landed on Anderson, who was busy talking with Georgia. I wondered if Smith's friend would inform him that Belle was checking someone out.

"I hear my best friend puked in your helmet," she called to him. He turned to us both in surprise. A smirk as slow and sweet as honey split his lips when he saw me.

"Anderson, allow me to introduce you to my former best friend, Belle *Price*." I emphasized the last name for Belle's benefit. She seemed to be a tad starstruck. Maybe Smith was a big enough racing fan not to care, but I could imagine what Alexander would say if he saw the look Anderson was giving us.

Anderson, held out his hand to Belle. She took it and he kissed it with a panty-dropping wink. "It's nice to meet you. I'm Anders."

"And she's married," I informed him.

His gaze swiveled to me and he shrugged, his eyes lingering a bit too long on me. "All the good ones are."

I wasn't certain whose marital status we were referring to anymore. There was something about him—something I couldn't place—that left me slightly dazed. Maybe it was his celebrity status or his shameless flirtation. Maybe I just needed to get out of the palace more.

"So, this is a secret?" he asked, tipping his head to my midsection, which was still hidden beneath my coat.

"I'd really appreciate it if you wouldn't tell anyone," I said. Somehow I already knew he wouldn't.

"I won't," he promised. "But when it does come out, when can I expect the blessed event?"

"Want a leg up in the betting pools?" I guessed.

"You can't blame a guy for trying. Easy payday." He waved it off, shaking his head with a laugh at my disapproving glare. "I'm only kidding. Never bet on anything in my life."

"Not even a race?" Belle asked, a note of disbelief in her voice.

"Why bet on a sure thing? What's the fun in that?"

"I assume you're referring to yourself," I said.

"Of course I am."

I couldn't help myself. "Oh, I was just wondering, because I've only seen you crash."

"Come back to the track when you're feeling better, I'll show you what I mean." Anders stretched out his hand and I took it, expecting him to shake it like we were placing a bet. Instead he held it for a moment, then squeezed. I pulled away, feeling oddly guilty. "I hope you're looking forward to the games."

Henry, who'd been talking with a group of officials, called over to us, "They're ready. The press is assembled."

"Guess we better do this," Anders said. "See you out there."

Belle spun toward me as soon as his back was turned and mouthed one word: *wow.*

"I'm glad we're both married," she whispered to me when we were out of earshot. "I think that boy could be trouble."

I couldn't have agreed more.

CHAPTER TEN

ALEXANDER

"Alexander," Norris's tone stopped me in my tracks. "You're being paranoid."

I stared at him, then considered his position. I'd damn near worn a hole through the carpet in my sitting room. Clara was scheduled to be home an hour ago, but she hadn't arrived yet. That wasn't what worried me, though. She'd left early this morning, as it was a long drive with the team to Silverstone. It said something about the current demands on my attention that I'd only realized an hour after she left *where* she was going and what that might mean. A call to Brex confirmed my suspicions. I'd reassigned him to watch over her, but somewhere along the lines the communications had failed. The left hand didn't know what the right was doing.

"You're telling me it's a coincidence she went to see him?" I glanced at the clock, twisting my wedding band around my finger. How could he believe that?

"There is such a thing," Norris said dryly. "You can stop checking the time. Brex told you they were held up."

"The press conference ran late, I can accept that. What I can't accept is that no one told me she was going to meet Anderson Stone." My fist shot out, seeking relief for the energy building inside me. Norris caught it before it hit the wall.

"Do you want to explain to your wife why there's a hole in the wall?" He released my fist and crossed his arms behind his back like he was now on official alert. That was probably best for me and my walls.

I pulled back, rubbing my fist in my palm. He had a point. Clara wouldn't be happy to come home and discover I'd been punching things. What would I tell her when she asked why? I didn't know what to say to her now.

"I can assure you that no one, outside of Brexton, knows there's any relationship between you and Anderson Stone. I've seen to it." There was no room to doubt him. Norris's word was his vow, and he took his responsibility to me as seriously as anyone could.

I trusted Norris with my life and, more importantly, my family, but the last few years had taught me not to make assumptions. It had taken considerable effort to trace my father's payments to Anderson's mother. Was that why he believed no one would bother?

"So the first invitation to the Sovereign Games

just happens to go to my father's bastard son?" I asked.

Norris flinched slightly at the barb. I understood what he was on about. It wasn't Anderson's fault my father had kept this dirty secret for years. Anderson himself didn't even know.

"If someone knew, the press would," Norris said. He hadn't budged from his spot by the door even as I continued to track across the room and back again.

"That's comforting," I muttered, rubbing my neck. I'd probably strained it checking the clock every other second.

"We were always going to have to contend with the fact that your brother is growing quite famous," Norris began.

"Yes, we were," I allowed. "I didn't expect to send my wife to contend with it though."

"May I ask..." he trailed off significantly.

I told Norris everything—eventually. It hadn't seemed important until today that Clara wasn't in on the particulars of this situation. "No, she doesn't know. I mean, she knows I found out I have a brother. I didn't think I needed to tell her who it was."

Norris's eyebrows shot up, but he did a good job rearranging his face back to a normal state as quickly as possible. "And why is that?"

"Are you my bodyguard or my therapist?" I snapped.

"Sometimes, it feels like I'm a bit of both," he said evenly, and a wave of guilt swept over me. Norris didn't dwell on the slight. "I think we're dealing with an unusual set of circumstances and nothing more. There's no intelligence to suggest that this is anything more than Anderson Stone, a rising star in the racing world, receiving an invitation from the crown to participate in an international charity event. You need to accept that."

"And if I don't?"

"Then I suggest you tell your wife the truth—the whole truth," he amended quickly.

I sighed and crossed to the mantle, where a number of framed family portraits smiled back at me. Clara was in each one: holding Elizabeth, carrying a rose outside the London Eye, smiling next to a Christmas tree. She was the common denominator of not only the photos, but every memory I cherished. Hell, of every breath I took. But it wasn't just Clara. It was a radiant, full-of-life Clara. I'd seen less and less of her over the last few weeks. It might even have been months. I tried to fool myself, writing off the change in her mood as early pregnancy. But that was a lie.

Edward said I was crushing her. Was that all I could offer her—a love that broke her? Every time I tried to trust that everything would be okay, life seemed to send me a warning sign.

I needed to know more about Anderson. I needed to know why he had been chosen. I'd heard he was a gifted racer. I'd been following his career since Brexton had uncovered who he was. Part of me had cheered him on, but I'd kept my distance. It was safer —for both of us. All of that cautious interest had vanished, replaced now by a creeping sense of dread. Nothing in my life was a coincidence; I had learned that the hard way.

"Maybe I should tell her," I admitted, "but I need to know more first. I want you to look into this. Find out who's in charge of the invitation list."

Norris opened his mouth as if he was going to respond when Clara flew into the room, dropping her bag at the door.

Her cheeks were rosy, her neck still wrapped tightly in a scarf, and her perfect body hidden under too many layers for my taste. She rushed to me, throwing herself in my arms and kissing me hungrily. Pulling back, she let out a giggle when she saw that Norris was here.

"Oops! Sorry, Norris." But she didn't move away from my arms.

The tightness in my chest relaxed as I held her. I plucked her scarf, drawing it away from her face to discover it wasn't just her cheeks that were glowing. She was luminous, lit from within with the happiness that I hadn't seen for a long time.

"Today went well?" I couldn't stop myself from checking my watch.

"I'm sorry. I know I'm later than I thought I would be. Belle and I were talking in the car. I should've called you." Her explanations came out in a rush, and I realized this was what I had brought her to. She lived in a constant state of apology. I had known where she was. I was in contact with her security team. She had been having fun and that had changed the moment she came home to me.

"I knew when to expect you," I told her. "Brex let me know."

She peeked at that me through her full, black lashes hopefully. "Then you aren't mad?"

"What would I have to be mad about?" I pulled her to me, wrapped an arm around her shoulders, and pressed a kiss to her forehead. Behind her, Norris didn't say a word. He considered us a moment, an expectant look on his face. I shook my head slightly. Now wasn't the time to tell her. I would. Later. I willed him to understand.

He tipped his head to indicate he'd gotten the message, but he didn't look at me as he excused himself. "I'll take my leave."

Clara glanced over her shoulder as the door closed.

"I think I scared him off," she whispered.

"He knows we need some alone time," I said.

"You have been working awfully late," she accused.

I couldn't deny that any more than I could deny the possessive urge filtering into my blood now. I began unbuttoning her coat. She cooperated, her teeth sinking into her lower lip in expectation.

"Tell me about your day," I said softly.

She understood the invitation, or she thought she

did. There was no way she could know what I was really asking. "It was crazy. Belle is into cars and racing. I can't even wrap my head around that," she told me, "and it's very loud. Oh, and I threw up in Anderson Stone's helmet."

"You did what?" It was the last thing I had expected her to say. The rosiness which had begun to fade from her cheeks flamed again reaching all the way to the tips of her ears.

She buried her face against my shoulder. "It was terrible. I didn't want anyone to see me having morning sickness, but the bathroom was locked and he opened the door and...the next thing I know I'm throwing up in his helmet. It was very regal."

I bit back a laugh. Clara worried so much about what people thought of her as Queen. I didn't want her to think I was laughing at her.

"How did he react to that?"

"He was kind—a knight in shining armor. He offered to let me keep it in case I needed it again." She sighed, burrowing deeper into me.

"He sounds thoughtful." I tried to keep my voice even, but it lifted, betraying my apprehension. Was he really just a nice guy or did he know? I couldn't imagine he appreciated his helmet being used as a toilet.

"I don't think he's going to be asking me for dinner." She poked me in the side. "There's no need to be jealous of the guy. I'm sure I made quite the impression on him."

There was another matter to consider. "Does he know why you were sick?"

She nodded. "I know I shouldn't have told him. I was kicking myself the whole way home for doing it. There was just something about him—it was like I could trust him."

My heart stopped and I stared down at her for a moment. Confusion crept into her grey eyes and I pulled away, moving behind her to draw off her coat. I didn't want her to see my reaction.

"X?" Too late.

This was my chance. It was time to come clean. My hands took her shoulders gently and spun her around, but the words didn't come. I saw my chance slipping away. I watched it go.

I forced myself to say something to end the awkward pause. "Any man would be lucky to have you vomit in his helmet, Poppet."

"Belle thinks he's handsome," she told me. She searched my face as if looking for a sign that she shouldn't have told me this.

"And you?" I asked in a strangled voice.

"He's cute. I think they were right to choose him as the face of the games," she said.

"The face?" I repeated. I had no idea what that meant.

"They want someone young. Hot. Henry's words, not mine," she quickly added. "Speaking of which, is he..."

"I have no idea," I said honestly. That was the

least of my concerns. My wife had just described my secret, younger brother as hot. She had just told me that she trusted him with a secret we'd shared with very few people. Things were spinning out of control. It didn't matter what Norris had said. Coincidence or not, I needed to take things in hand. "And you thought he was hot?"

"I can't find another man attractive?" she asked testily.

An alarm went off in my head, but I ignored it. Maybe another man, but not *that* man. "I'd prefer you didn't."

"Oh, X." She shook her head.

"I don't find other women attractive."

"Really?" Clara pressed, lifting an eyebrow.

"I don't even notice them."

"I think you're jealous," she said, her voice soft with amazement.

"Of some race car driver?" I swallowed on the truth of her accusation, turning away so she wouldn't see it.

"That's what I thought," she said with a sigh. Her fingers tilted my chin, leveling my gaze back to hers. "How many times do I have to tell you that I belong to you, X?"

"I know."

"Then act like it," she said. There was a desperate edge to her voice.

I needed to fix this. Back us up a step. Change the subject.

Before I could do any of those things, she grabbed my tie. "Maybe I should show you," she suggested.

I reached up, loosening the knot, and helped her slide it free. "I've heard actions speak louder than words, Poppet."

"Then I'll show you," she promised.

I couldn't tear my eyes from her as she lifted her shirt over her head. Her swollen breasts and pert nipples strained against the thin lace of her bra. She unhooked it and they fell free heavily. She took her time with her jeans, making certain she had my full attention before she pushed them to the ground along with her panties. I savored the sight of her body, the full curve of her hips, the subtle swell where my child grew.

She took a step toward me, holding out her arms and crossing them at the wrists. "Let's play."

My tongue darted over my lips, imagining it was her I was tasting. She always understood exactly what I needed. She hadn't offered her submission to me for weeks. In fact, she'd turned the tables on me. I craved it now more than ever. "Not planning to top me tonight?"

"Sometimes I need to remind you of your place," she said simply. She held her breath as I wrapped my tie around her wrists, drawing in a sharp breath when I knotted it tightly. "Sometimes I need to show you mine."

She lowered herself on to her knees turning her

face up expectantly. "You are my King. You are my master. Everything I am belongs to you."

I knew what it cost her to say this to me now, after she had fought so hard to prove she could be independent. But that was the point. She could be independent. She chose when and where and how to give me control.

Fuck, she was beautiful.

"What do you want?" My hand fisted in her hair, pulling it back to raise her face. I stepped closer to her, removing the distance between my body and hers. Clara tugged slightly against my hold and pressed soft lips to the bulge growing in my pants. My cock, which had been keeping track of our conversation with interest, hardened painfully. Clara continued to press soft kisses through the fabric. "Is that what you want, Poppet?"

She nodded, not abandoning her devotion.

I let go of her hair and reached down to undo my buckle. I drew my belt off slowly and allowed it to fall to the floor. There was a time when she would have tensed at the movement. A time when she remembered what that strap of leather felt like on her bare ass. Now, she didn't so much as blink. She trusted me, but I couldn't help wondering if I had earned that trust.

"Is this what you want?" I slid a hand past the waistband of my pants, adjusting my shaft against the restrictive clothing.

"Yes, please." She licked her lips invitingly. Her

hands were tied, but she tried to reach up and tug my pants away.

"Patience," I told her as I shoved them past my hips. My cock sprang free and I caught it in my fist, running my hand down the length of it. I stepped back just far enough she couldn't reach me.

"Who do you belong to?" I asked in a low voice.

"You." She stopped trying to move closer. She seemed to understand the silent instruction I was giving her. If she belonged to me, then she had to trust me. I continued to jack myself off—just the thought of her watching and wanting— getting me off.

"X," she whispered. "Together."

And there it was, her plea to me. It called me back to her.

I moved toward her, but I was no longer interested in watching her kneel before me. Instead, I kicked off my shoes and shucked off my pants in the process. Leaning down, I lifted her onto her feet.

"Together," I repeated, catching the shell of her ear in my teeth and nipping it. I captured her mouth, kissing her languidly, exploring with my tongue while our bodies pressed urgently toward one another. Her tied hands found my cock and gripped it possessively.

"Together or nothing at all," I told her, pulling free from her. Hooking one finger around the tie that bound her wrists I led her to the sofa, urging her toward its rolled arm. She sat gracefully on its edge, her legs spreading in invitation.

"Christ, you're perfect," I growled at the sight of her naked cunt.

"X, please. I need to feel you."

I grabbed her hips, kneading them roughly before I flipped her around. My hand moved protectively to her stomach, as I bent her over the sofa's arm. The tip of my cock slid along her seam and she moaned, half frustration, half pleasure.

"Shh, Poppet. I know what you need. I know what we need." Holding her in place, I started to move inside her. She squirmed, trying to capture me. I smacked her ass lightly and she squirmed and moaned with pleasure.

"Do you like that?" I asked her roughly, smacking the other cheek, my cock twitching at her entrance.

"Yes, please," she cried.

I smacked her ass cheek harder, this time leaving the red imprint of my palm. She writhed, circling her hips against my crown, but I held her steady.

"Why would you want to leave me?" I asked her, something dark overtaking me. I felt the shadows of my past all around me, and for once, I didn't want to keep them at bay. I wanted to show her how far I was willing to go to prove that she belonged to me.

"I don't," she whispered and I spanked her again.

"You said he was cute. Hot," I quoted her.

"X." There was a warning in her voice now. She wanted to play, but she was beginning to suspect this was a different game than when she began.

I wrapped my hand around her hair and yanked

her face up, twisting her at an awkward angle so that I could see it over her shoulder. "I need to know that no one will ever come between us."

She stared at me, her eyes searching for a moment, but whatever darkness she found there, she didn't close herself to it. Instead, she said softly, "No one. No one will ever come between us."

I thrust inside her, abandoning my fear and losing myself to her. Releasing her hair, I wrapped both arms around her torso, holding her to me as I continued to pound deep inside her. A strangled cry of pleasure spilled from her lips. I bent my knees, allowing myself to move deeper, to fuck her harder. I slid a hand between her legs as her cries faded. They tried to close against me, her own climax shuddering to its conclusion. Forcing my fingers past her folds, I spread her sex open and rubbed her clit furiously as I continued to stroke inside her. Her breathing came in pants and fragments of words. I had no idea what she was trying to say to me. I didn't care. I only wanted to feel her come again, to feel her clenching greedily around me, to feel her helpless in my arms. I lifted her into my arms, piercing her to the core and holding her captive. Her body tensed and my own responded, releasing inside her as she broke over me and then went limp in my arms.

I held her there, spent, my dick still pulsing inside her. Finally, after a minute—after an eternity—she whispered my name. I withdrew slowly, unsure what to expect when I faced her. She turned to me and held out her wrists. I untied them, my eyes never leaving hers and the questions reflecting there like a storm over the ocean. I had no answers to give her. I trusted Clara. I loved her. I was doing my goddamn best to be the man she deserved. When her hands were free, I braced myself. The last time I used her so completely, I thought I'd lost her forever. I deserved to.

But there was no slap. She didn't walk away. Instead, her arms encircled my neck, her fingers knitting through my hair and pulling me down to meet her. I knew she had questions. I knew I needed to find the answers. For now, though, she offered me the protection of her kiss and I took it, finding safety there.

CHAPTER ELEVEN

ALEXANDER

The Sovereign Games were becoming a headache. Not only were they a logistical nightmare that required constant attention from me and my staff, but they took up nearly all of Clara's time. Between the games and Elizabeth, we saw each other in passing during the day and sought one another in bed at night. There wasn't enough time in the day for me to heal the damage I'd done to our marriage. Our lovemaking was gentle—tender. Each time I touched her body it was a silent apology. She clung to me after, falling asleep entwined in my arms, as though afraid she would lose me in the dark. But the more space and safety she gave me, the harder it became to tell her the truth.

Unfortunately, when it came to affairs of state there was no choice but to do just that. News of Oliver Jacobson's arrest had leaked to the press. Now

I had a half dozen angry Members of Parliament and the Prime Minister in my offices demanding answers.

I paused outside the meeting room when I saw Prime Minister Clark waiting for me.

"You might have warned me." He sounded tired and cross—two conditions I knew well.

"It would have undermined our investigation." My words implied an apology I wouldn't offer. We had proof that Jacobson had been involved in my father's death. I owed that bastard nothing and I didn't give a damn what any of them had to say about it.

"They're out for blood, Alexander," he warned me in a low voice. "The monarchy isn't as popular with Parliament today as it's been in the past, especially since..."

"I was crowned?" I guessed. "They'll like me even less after today."

"They see it as a breach of contract," he explained. "You've overstepped your bounds."

"Is that so?" I asked coolly.

"In their eyes," he retreated.

I pressed my lips together, tipping my head in acknowledgment of the warning. It was the most he would get from me. My father had turned over an unprecedented amount of functions to the governing body. At the time, I'd considered it a windfall. It would be less for me to oversee when I took his place. Now I saw how it had skewed my position. Parliament believed it was the one with true power. I was merely a figurehead. They were wrong.

There were loopholes large enough to ride a horse through in every assent bill he'd issued. I'd studied them at length. This wasn't the time to reveal that, though. I'd dreaded this moment as much as I'd looked forward to it. Jacobson hadn't been cooperative. He'd offered us riddles instead of information. I suspected that whoever showed up today might be worth looking into further.

"Gentlemen and ladies," I greeted them, unbuttoning my jacket as I took a seat at the head of the table. They welcomed me with glares. This was off to a brilliant start. "You have questions."

"How long has Oliver Jacobson been in custody?" The man on my right asked. At least we were getting straight to the point.

"A few weeks," I said. "I'm surprised you didn't notice he was missing until now." A few mouths twitched, but no one dared laugh. It wasn't a joke but rather an observation.

"We don't meet over the holidays," Alistair May, an aging member of the House of Lords shouted. "It's a mockery to arrest a man over Christmas."

"It's treason to kill a king, but we aren't keeping score." I trained my eyes on him, wondering if he'd rise to my challenge. He was older than the others and the most likely to take offense to my youth. But he fell silent, his beady, black stare meeting mine. He'd been a thorn in my father's side during his reign.

With any luck he would die during mine. He had to be nearing a hundred.

"This won't stand." A fist belonging to an overly boisterous sixty-something MP named Edgar Byrd hit the oak council table. A few of his colleagues had the manners to look offended by the dramatic gesture, but I simply folded my hands and waited patiently. To the others, it was undignified. It wasn't British to lose one's temper, especially in mixed company—and there was no more mixed company than the crown and Parliament.

I, on the other hand, had enough Greek blood in me to appreciate him losing it, because it was about time one of them did. Why had they come, for fuck's sake, if not to shout?

"I assure you that you'll know more when our investigation concludes," I said, speaking at a normal volume. I might appreciate his anger, but I wasn't about to rise to it.

Next to me, the Prime Minister tugged his tie nervously. This was what he had tried to warn me about. They didn't want to talk to me. They were coming for me. Let them try.

"Oliver Jacobson is a member of the House of Commons and a British citizen. He has rights."

"Rights he forfeited when he plotted against the crown," I told him. I leaned back in my seat, studying him closer. Perhaps I needed to be looking into Byrd. "I'm surprised that your sympathy lies with the traitor."

I allowed the implication of my words to sink in.

"I don't think that's what Clark is trying to s-s-suggest," the Prime Minister stuttered. It was too late to defuse the situation. He had already let it get too far. Parliament seemed to be under the impression that they held sway over my decisions. I knew now they'd believed they would come in here, level a few threats, and get what they wanted.

But if they thought they could come in here and intimidate me, they had another think coming.

"We have definitive proof and a confession from Jacobson that he plotted against the crown and took part in the assassination of my father," I said with deadly calm. I almost hoped one of them would challenge what I said. Instead, eyes widened at this announcement, so I continued, "Furthermore, Mr. Jacobson has led us to believe that he did not act alone."

No one so much as breathed. I looked to each of them in turn, wondering if I might spot guilt on one of their faces.

"The man who shot your father died that day," Clark interrupted.

"Yes, he did. But someone supplied the weapon. Someone gave him the security plans. He wasn't smart enough to do it on his own."

"And what proof do you have?" May demanded.

"A couple more dead bodies. A few attempted murders. We sent someone in undercover to find out who was behind this."

"Who?"

"A woman, of course." He didn't need to know more, and I wasn't going to out Georgia Kincaid as my source. I propped my arms onto the edge of my chair, wondering when the interrogation would end. I couldn't tell if disbelief drove his questions or if he was testing me. "She eventually led us to Jacobson."

"And the trail ended with him?" The Prime Minister prompted, sweat beading on his forehead. He sounded hopeful and anxious at the same time.

I didn't blame him for being nervous. Until now, we hadn't shared the full breadth of the investigation's findings with anyone in the government, including the Prime Minister. He had to be doing the math. If we had proof—a confession even—that implicated his government in a way that might permanently damage his reputation. A few of the other MPs seemed to be thinking the same thing. More than a couple had turned their attention to the papers in front of them.

May, however, hadn't backed down.

"Does it matter? Do you seriously believe more of Parliament was involved? This could become a witch hunt," he accused.

"Have you ever studied a witch hunt? Read the findings? Checked the history books?" I asked him coldly. I sat forward, leaning towards him across the table. "A lot of witches burned before anyone realized they were innocent. You would do well to keep that in mind."

"Is that a threat?" he asked, eyes narrowed.

"Just an observation." I settled into my seat again. "This investigation will continue. Jacobson will continue to be held."

"When will charges be pressed?" the Prime Minister asked. "You can't hold him indefinitely."

"I don't plan to. We're within the confines of the law. As for charges, we will levy them when I feel we have explored every possible crime he committed."

"But why keep him longer? Why not charge him now?" A woman piped up from the back. She spun a pencil in her fingers absently. I almost wondered if she was thinking out loud. Of all of the people here, she seemed the least ruffled by this news. If it bothered her that I was holding one of her colleagues on treason charges, she didn't show it.

"As Mr. May pointed out, it was Christmas. I spent it with family. After the attack in Chelsea, we wanted to be certain he wasn't involved."

"And?" Clark asked breathlessly.

"Our investigation has been inconclusive," I admitted, though I hated to do so. It felt like I'd shown them my hand. "I expect we'll file formal charges any day."

He could rot in an unmarked prison cell for all I cared, but I didn't need Parliament calling sessions and demanding a trial. Charges would keep them happy—for now.

"The press is going to have a field day with this,"

the Prime Minister commented as the others filed out of the room.

"The press have a field day when I snog my wife," I reminded him. "Everything is news to them."

"This will be different. It's an international scandal." He studied me for a moment before clapping a hand on my shoulder. "I hope you know what you're doing, your Majesty."

That made two of us.

I PROMISED MYSELF I WOULD NEVER RETURN here. Not until I had the evidence to lock this evil bastard up for good. I wasn't sure why I was here now. The meeting with Parliament hadn't shaken my resolve. More than ever, I suspected others had known about Jacobson's plans. They might not have acted with him, but if they'd turned a blind eye, they were culpable—and they needed to be held accountable. Perhaps they didn't deserve to be locked away like he did and left to rot for the rest of their lives, but their silence had betrayed my family—they had turned away when they should have stepped forward. That couldn't be overlooked.

I didn't bother to have him taken into an interrogation room. I didn't need a guard watching over us or Norris standing in the next room to observe what he said. I considered calling Smith Price, who had even more of an interest in this than I did. But he and I rarely saw eye to eye. I was still surprised he hadn't put a bullet in Jacobson's head before I could arrest him. In the end, I'd gone alone. This was between Oliver Jacobson and me. He had come after my family. He'd allowed a lunatic to touch the woman I loved. He'd set events in motion that had ended in death. This was between me and him.

Jacobson looked up from the bare cot on which he lay. It was the only thing in his cell apart from a toilet and sink. The holding cell was clean, dry, and warm, but that was all it offered. There were no sheets. No pillow. No books. No window. I'd deemed him a suicide risk and refused him anything other than meals and shelter, but Oliver Jacobson would no more take his life than I would. It was another means of punishing him—denying him the smallest shred of humanity. He was a rat, the kind of man who enjoyed squalor and misery. He probably loved it here. Sometimes, late at night, I thought of what might actually break him. I wanted to know. I wanted to know what he loved. I wanted to take it from him. That was why I hadn't come back here. I didn't trust myself to find those answers, not when such a thin thread of sanity seemed to separate me from him. God help both of us if that thread ever snapped.

His head turned, but he didn't rise to greet me. "You took longer than I expected."

"You expected me to come back?" My hands wrapped around the bars dividing us. I'd purposely forgotten to get a key. The cell was the only thing keeping him safe from me.

"You always knew you would come back. I always knew you would. You're desperate for answers, Alexander, and I know you haven't found any." A delighted smile lit up his face. He was insane. He was demented.

He was right.

I wasn't about to let him know that, however.

"You must be uncomfortable here—"

"Is that the best you can do?" He stopped me. "Remind me of how miserable I am, so that I'll beg you for forgiveness? You must be getting desperate."

I was almost glad he hadn't heard me out. I didn't want to give this man anything, even a window.

"We'll skip the pleasantries then," I said coolly. "I want names."

"Parliament is finally leaning on you?" he guessed. "Took them long enough to miss me. I confess I'm hurt that my colleagues weren't more affected by my absence."

"None of them give a shit about you. They don't care if you rot here forever." My hands were beginning to throb and I realized I was throttling the bars and wishing they were his neck. I released them and massaged my ring finger where the band had dug into my skin. It was a painful reminder of why I was here.

He rolled to the side and pushed himself up on his cot. "Someone has to take the fall. You already knew that, though, didn't you?"

"No one is going to fight for you," I said. "You're

stuck here. They are out there. That doesn't make you angry?"

"All great causes demand sacrifice."

My blood ran cold. I wanted to believe he was delusional. Everything we knew about him, about his plans, ended with him. I believed others had known, aiding him or turning a blind eye, but something in the way he spoke led me to believe he was telling the truth. But if Jacobson had merely taken the fall...

He turned his politician's smile on me. "You're a man of duty. I see it in your eyes. You hate this world. You hate being King. Admit it and I'll tell you what you really want to know."

I paused. Was it as simple as that? All I had to do was tell the truth and he would finally give in? It was a trick. But one that couldn't benefit him in any way. He would never leave this cell—unless it was to go to his grave. "Why do you care how I feel about my birthright?"

"Consider it a matter of curiosity. I've always wondered how you live with yourself. Your father— there was a man who didn't care about anyone—but you've surprised me," he admitted. "You love your family. He didn't. I know the secrets he kept. The lives he ruined and the ones he tried to destroy. I know why he sent you to war."

I said nothing. So long as Jacobson talked, I would listen. I wouldn't give him the satisfaction of a response.

"Your dirty little secret isn't as secret as you

thought," he said with a laugh. He looked around the cell, smirking. "You probably feel pretty comfortable down here in the dungeon, don't you? All we need is a whip. Then again, you've got that pretty, innocent wife for that."

"Don't speak of her," I warned him through gritted teeth.

"That's why they'll break you. Everyone can see what she means to you. Your father was ruthless—cruel—but he understood the game he was playing. He gave up his Queen to save his throne."

"My mother died in childbirth." Cold fury broke over me. I wanted to rip the cell door free from its hinges. Instead, I stood and stared, imagining what it would be like to crush the life from him.

"He lost her long before she died. That was one of daddy's secrets. I thought you might know that one." He stood and took a few paces toward the bars separating us. I dared him to come closer, close enough that I could wrap my hands around his neck through the bars. "You know some of his secrets though, don't you? I know them all."

"And how is that?" I called his bluff.

"I'm very well connected."

"It's too bad you'll never see daylight again, then. None of those connections to turn to now." This had been pointless. Another stupid game of cat and mouse. Now that I had caught my prize, it was no fun to play with him.

"Oh, they don't need me." He snorted as though he found this intensely humorous.

I turned, glancing over my shoulder and regarded him for a moment. "You must be lonely to make up allies that don't exist."

"Made up, are they? The threats haven't stopped, though, have they?" He crossed his arms over his chest and tilted his head like an owl, gazing down on smaller prey. "I'll guess something innocuous happened. Something you couldn't pin on anyone, exactly. Everyone will tell you that it was coincidence. There will be no proof. A threat. A bomb. An accident. And a family member in the wrong place at the wrong time. Probably that delicate waif of a wife. It's only going to keep coming. You'll lock her away. You'll drive her crazy. And when we've taken her from you in every way that seems to matter, you will lose her. You will lose everything."

"No one will touch her." My voice was low, deadly. I couldn't be sure he could hear me, but judging from the arrogance shining in his eyes, he had.

"You can't trust anyone, Alexander. Admit it to me. Admit how much you hate being King and I'll tell you."

"Will that satisfy you? Because it's no secret. I hate this life, but nothing you can say will take the Crown from me."

"No, it won't. No matter how much you wish it

would." He turned and went back to his cot, dropping down on it. "Thank you."

"Never thank me." I didn't want even his feigned gratitude.

"But you gave me what I wanted. Now I owe you."

It didn't matter what he had to say. He wasn't going to give me names, and I couldn't be certain even if he did that he wasn't lying. He was a warped, twisted man. Maybe the time in here—alone—had broken him. Maybe he'd always been evil. I didn't care. I'd come here to look the devil in the face and as I left, I felt nothing. No remorse. No fear. Not even hatred.

Then he spoke. "Leaving so soon? But I promised you an answer."

"I don't want your answer," I spit back at him.

"No, you don't. But I so want to give it," he cooed. "By the time this ends, you'll break her heart. Because when she finds out what you've been hiding, she won't love you anymore. She'll hate you."

"Is that all you have?" I laughed, my back still turned to him. "You don't know me, and you sure as hell don't know her."

"When she stops loving you, that will be what breaks you and takes your Crown. But what comes before will be sweet revenge. Your family is nothing but smoke and lies. Secrets kept by you. Secrets kept from you. Those secrets will poison you from the inside out until everyone you've loved, why, you'll hate them as much as they'll hate you. You wanted to know our plans. I'll tell you, because you can't stop us." His voice dropped to nothing more than a whisper, but it echoed in the barren space. "How do you destroy the royal family, Alexander? From within."

CHAPTER TWELVE

CLARA

Alexander grew more distant as my departure for Silverstone neared. I needed to be there to prepare for the opening ceremonies and initial events, which would take place in a week. The rest of the games would run through May.

We'd each been focused on our own agendas for the last few weeks. Alexander had a country to run and I had events to organize. But it wasn't just a full schedule. He'd begun to withdraw from me, particularly in the last week. I couldn't blame him exactly. I'd hoped he would join us when the games officially began, but until then, I would be in Silverstone with Elizabeth, who was too young to be away from me for that long. It was just over a week, but X and I rarely spent so long apart. The last time was before we were engaged. Still, there was no way he could come with me, and there was no way that I could stay here. We were at an impasse. But when I caught him staring, darkness shadowing his eyes, I wondered if he planned to stop me from going. I half-expected it at this point, but the demand never came.

"This one will do it," Belle said as she flourished a loose, cashmere sweater. I took it from her and held it up, studying how the fabric draped in the mirror.

I screwed up my nose. This was impossible. Everything I considered felt plain and uninspiring. Belle, on the other hand, seemed to be transitioning into her pregnancy elegantly. She'd shown up in a loose, linen tunic and leggings that were classy and comfortable. I didn't have anything half as stylish that still fit me. "I feel like I'm fighting a losing battle."

"Maybe you should just make the announcement," she suggested. "Even I told my mother."

I tossed the sweater on the bed and whirled around to her. "You didn't tell me that."

"What's there to tell?" She shrugged. "She's not thrilled at the thought of being a grandmother. Aunt Jane is over the moon, though. Baby Price will have one sane relative."

She rubbed a circle over her belly lovingly, and I smiled. Belle looked curvier these days, but not pregnant yet. Her cheeks were fuller, her eyes brighter. She was actually glowing.

"What about Smith's family?"

Belle shook her head, gloominess descending over her instantly. "He doesn't have anyone. Georgia is the closest person he has to family."

I bit back unkind words. I couldn't imagine what

it would be like to have Georgia as my only family. No wonder Smith was so inscrutable.

"I know, right?" Belle said as if she was reading my mind. "She's not so bad once you figure out whether or not she wants to kill you."

I goggled at her. It sounded like there was a story there, but she didn't share.

"Plus, once you share," she said, switching topics, "I can hook you up with killer maternity clothes."

"I didn't think Bless offered anything like that." I'd had an unofficial subscription to Bless, Belle's fashion start-up, since day one. It was a perk of being the CEO's best friend and her business partner's sister. I hadn't bothered taking out any items in weeks, though, thanks to my ever-larger bump.

"We're expanding." She patted her stomach and added, "in more ways than one. We're about to launch Blessings, a maternity subscription service."

"That's a great idea."

"I figured that pregnancy is one time in a woman's life where she constantly needs new clothes to wear, because"—she pantomimed a big, round belly—"she deserves to feel fabulous."

"I will happily be your test subject," I promised. "But for now, we're stuck hiding this little prince or princess under a coat. I just want to wait until after the first rounds of the games are over," I told her. "I don't want my pregnancy announcement to over-shadow the events. Let them all bet on the races."

There was a knock on the door, and Edward's

curly head poked inside the room. "Mind if I join you?"

"Don't you have anything better to do?" I asked him.

"Yeah," Belle said, crossing her arms over her chest and staring him down. "I thought you were a newlywed."

"Not all of us shag like rabbits," he said dryly. "David and I have known each other for years. We aren't quite the slaves to our hormones some of you are."

"That's sad." Belle and I exchanged a glance.

"Don't do that." He shook his head, wagging a finger at us. "There's nothing wrong with my marriage. I'll have you know we shagged twice this morning."

"That's better," she said with a satisfied smile.

"I can't believe you didn't have me come help you pack," he whined. He picked up the sweater I'd abandoned and looked me over. "What are we going for? Cold weather chic? Down to earth, mom-to-be?"

"We're going for hide the bump at all costs." I plucked the sweater from his hands.

"Really?" He scratched his cheek as he digested this. "I thought..."

"She doesn't want to tell anyone yet, so thank God for coats," Belle said.

"There are more important things than my wardrobe," I reminded them. Both stopped to stare at me and I groaned in frustration.

"My job is to dress women so they feel fabulous," Belle said. "Furthermore, it's my duty as your best friend. What will people think of me? Of my company?"

"And since I came out of the closet, there are certain stereotypical expectations I have to uphold," Edward teased.

"I get it. Wardrobe is important." I threw my hands in the air. These two would be the death of me. "Buy me some time, okay? Let's keep the betting on the games for now instead of a due date."

"About that..." Edward blew air through his lips.

He had something to tell me, but I couldn't fathom what. We didn't keep secrets from each other. What did he need to confess?

"Out with it," I said, dumping a pile of socks into my suitcase. At least I wasn't expected to wear stockings and heels on a race track every day.

"Would it be so bad if people found out?" he asked.

I snorted. He didn't have a clue. Yeah, he'd been photographed every moment of his life, but it was hard to explain what it was like to have people dissecting your reproductive status. "You sound like X. He doesn't understand why I still want to keep it a secret."

Edward opened his mouth, his eyes drooping with a guilty weight, but Belle interrupted him. "Why do you want to keep it a secret? Really?

Announcing it would only boost attention to the Games."

"I don't want everyone to worry about my pregnancy when they should be thinking about more important things. The status of my womb shouldn't undermine charity."

"Is that really the only reason?" Edward pressed.

I stopped and considered it. If there were any two people I could be truthful with about how mixed up I was feeling, it was my best friends. But I hadn't shared how complicated it felt, even with Alexander. It felt wrong somehow to admit that I was more apprehensive than excited. "First of all, I love this baby. I want that to be clear. I will do anything for my little majesty."

"Awww! That's adorable," Edward said, "but it sounds a little ominous."

"Once people know, I feel like they'll just look at me like some gestational machine. I mean, Elizabeth hasn't even turned two yet. I can't even believe I'm knocked up again!" I confessed.

"She's nearly two," Belle pointed out. If that was the best argument she had, I was in trouble.

"It's weird, okay? Having people obsess over when you're going to have a baby. People guessing what you're going to name him or her. Crowds waiting outside the hospital for you to drag yourself out of bed and pretend that you're not in massive pain so you can smile for a picture. I mean, can you imagine if every news source in the world was keeping track on the inner workings of your womb?" I asked her.

"I have a Clara pregnancy tracker app," she whispered.

"You have a what?" Edward and I asked at the same time.

"It tracks my pregnancy in comparison to yours and gives me tips on how the Queen handled pregnancy concerns. There's pictures of you throughout your pregnancy with Elizabeth as illustrations. I got it on the App Store," she admitted weakly, rocking on her heels. "I thought it was funny."

"Oh my god." I couldn't even comprehend such a thing existed.

"I thought it was kind of sweet, too," she added quickly.

"Maybe for my best friend." I buried my face in my hands. My life was too weird.

"But you're right, I wouldn't like that," Belle said. "I think it would drive me crazy."

"And they'll be looking for any signs that something's wrong," I continued. I was on a roll now. I'd tried to ignore all these little things, but they were adding up and wearing me down. "If I wear the wrong thing, they'll say I've gained too much weight. If I go out with makeup, they'll say that I'm trying to hide how sick I am. And God forbid I'm seen without Alexander, then there's trouble in our marriage."

"Is there trouble in your marriage?" Edward asked softly.

I opened a drawer and rummaged through it, unsure how to answer. Was there? I didn't think so. I was as committed to Alexander as ever. I loved him and nothing would change that. But things weren't exactly smooth sailing.

"Clara, you can talk to us," Belle interrupted my thoughts.

"I'm fine!" I slid the drawer shut so quickly the picture frame on top of the bureau toppled over. Picking it up, I looked into Alexander's eyes. It was a photo from the night he'd proposed. Someone—my mother, I think—had given me the frame as a bridal shower present. I'd planned to replace the photo with one from my wedding. But that day had gone horribly wrong, and what pictures existed were a sobering reminder of why there was a strain on Alexander's and my relationship. We didn't have normal lives. It was silly to pretend otherwise.

"We're fine," I said. "I mean, it was never going to be easy, right?"

"Have you ever thought maybe it should be?" Belle asked. "At least a little?"

"So, your marriage is perfect?" I snapped. The truth was I didn't know that much about her marriage. Only what she shared with me. I didn't spend time with her husband. We didn't double date or go out to dinner. And unlike hers, my marriage was the subject of scrutiny. My best friends not only knew what I told them, but they also had an unlimited newsfeed of stories analyzing my life. There was no telling what my best friends had read. I wanted to think they wouldn't believe any of it, but now, as they sat here watching me carefully, I realized they might.

"What do you want to know?" I asked, sinking onto the bench at the foot of my bed. "There are a lot of rumors."

"Does he really forbid you from going out?" she asked.

I blinked rapidly trying to process the question. Why would she ask me that? We'd talked about this on a number of occasions. She'd seen him tell me I needed to stay in or take a security team. They'd both been there when my life had been threatened. "Only some of the time when there's a security threat."

Edward's gaze darted towards her.

"He has a right to be concerned," I said. But even I could hear the excuses I was making for him. I'd had the same argument with Alexander. Now I was defending him.

"Honestly, I don't know how to be a queen. That's the problem."

"I think it's more likely that my brother doesn't know how to be a king," Edward said quietly.

It surprised me to hear him say it. Alexander gave off a firm, unyielding confidence that most people responded to. I thought I had been the only one to see the struggle underneath the bravado he wore for the world. Maybe I wasn't.

"He doesn't lock himself up," Belle pointed out,

"and there has to be at least as much of a chance of something happening to him."

I'd used this argument with Alexander before. It sounded even more reasonable coming from her.

"I'm going to Silverstone without him." It was something—a life raft. Had they forgotten that?

"Are you?" Edward asked.

"What does that mean?" I asked darkly.

He released a heavy sigh that sounded like pent-up frustration. "Have you been online today?"

"No." I didn't wait for him to deliver the bad news. He'd come here for a reason. My heart sped up as I went to my bedside table and lifted my phone from the charger. There had been a lot to do. Preparing myself and Elizabeth to be gone for a week had taken my full attention.

"What's going on?" Belle asked. She'd arrived early this morning and we'd been at it all day.

"Maybe I should just tell you," Edward said, but I'd already opened my YouGram discovery feed. If the royal family was in the news, it would be there. I didn't even have to scroll down before I found exactly what he was talking about.

Another room in the castle is set to be filled later this year. Buckingham Palace announced earlier this morning that the King and Queen are expecting their second child. The Queen, who has been suffering from unusually difficult morning sickness, plans to host the Sovereign Games, which begin later this month. The palace said it was unclear whether Clara's condition would prevent her from fulfilling her duties as host.

I looked up and found Belle gawking at her own phone. At least I didn't have to fill her in on the news.

"You're right," I said to both of them, my voice deadly calm, "my marriage is in trouble."

ALEXANDER WAS IN TROUBLE.

I read through a dozen more stories before I interrogated Edward about everything he knew, which wasn't much. He'd come over expecting to celebrate, not deliver bad news. It was no wonder he'd looked so guilty when he'd first shown up. He'd had to decide whether or not to tell me himself.

Norris stood from his seat outside Alexander's office when I flew around the corner. Folding his newspaper, he dropped it and smiled. "Clara, he's in with the Minister of—"

"I don't care," I said, walking straight past him and into my husband's office.

Alexander was mid-sentence but the words died on his lips, the moment I blew into the room. "Clara."

"Don't Clara me," I warned him.

"Would you excuse us for a moment?" he asked the man sitting opposite him. The gentleman, who'd been watching us both with wary eyes, stood, offered me a small bow, and hurried out of the office like his life depended on it. My husband needed to develop a similar sense of self-preservation.

"You announced my pregnancy," I accused him.

"It was a decision based on increasing media speculation. We needed to get ahead of the story. I had—"

"Don't give me that. Don't tell me you were trying to stop it from leaking to the press. Don't lie to me." I couldn't believe he would try this tactic. Even if it were true, even if the tabloids had somehow found out, there was no way he could justify this.

"I made a decision." He spread his hands on the desk. My eyes darted to a small paperweight, and I saw his throat slide. He picked it up and stuck it in a drawer.

"I'm leaving." It was a low blow—forgetting to add that I would be coming back. But it was worth the panic on his face, even if my satisfaction was only temporary.

"Clara, I—"

"I'm going to Silverstone today," I reminded him. "While you may not think what I'm doing is important, it's important to me, X. If you'll excuse me, I need to go finish packing. It seems I no longer have to worry about hiding my bump."

Alexander leapt to his feet and started around the desk, but I held up a hand.

"I wouldn't come any closer than that," I warned him. "I'll see you in a little over a week."

"But I was planning—"

"No," I cut him off. "*You're not coming.* You can

keep trying to take this away from me, but I won't let you."

He looked hurt. Good. I wanted him to feel as helpless as I did. "I don't want to take anything from you, Clara. I want to protect you."

"From what?" I didn't look back as I opened the door and stepped through, leaving him behind. "You?"

CHAPTER THIRTEEN

CLARA

The atmosphere at Silverstone was festive. I felt anything but. Unsurprisingly, the family had a house not far from the track. No one had visited it in years, but, like the other properties the Royals seemed to hoard, it was maintained and fit to house a small army.

It was a good thing, too, because every hotel and inn nearby had filled up within hours of the event's announcement. Any worry we'd waited too long or that no one would be interested was unfounded—if only everything else in my life was going so smoothly.

I hadn't spoken to Alexander since I'd left London. The last time we had gone this long without talking I'd been in a coma. Other than one text to let him know I'd safely arrived—his least favorite form of communication—I'd handed over updates to Brex. For once, I was glad he and Georgia were assigned to me. Norris had a frustrating habit of helping me see

Alexander's side, and right now, I wasn't interested in psychoanalyzing my husband. I was more than happy to stay mad at him. He needed to sweat this out. What he'd done...I couldn't even let myself think about it without worrying what I'd do.

Plus, there was too much to do before the opening ceremonies to waste energy on it. I had my hands full. Elizabeth was with me, so when I wasn't going over my ceremonial duties or answering questions or preparing speeches, I was with her. It made me feel centered to have her there. It felt less like I'd left my heart behind in London.

When I popped my head into our temporary nursery, I found Elizabeth blinking wonderingly at me from her crib. She held her arms out, her lower lip beginning to tremble. For a terrible second, I saw everything through Elizabeth's tear-stained eyes. Daddy was the one who went to her every morning. He changed her diapers and got her dressed. No matter how busy he was, Alexander never failed his daughter—and I had taken him away from her.

"Oh, sweetie, it's only a few days," I soothed her, kissing her curly head. She nuzzled against me, and I held her closely. She was proof that beautiful things came out of messy situations. "Let's go find Penny."

It took me longer to find the nanny than I expected, mostly because she was clinging to a toilet in the bathroom.

She looked up at me with watering eyes. "I told you the fish tasted off."

"Oh, Penny!" I guessed it was a good thing that I'd had no real appetite for a few days. I'd picked at my dinner the night before, forcing down some bread. It was always harder for me to eat when I was stressed. Morning sickness didn't help. "Can I get you anything?"

"No, ma'am." She tore off a bit of toilet paper and wiped her mouth. "Give me a moment and I'll be in to see to Elizabeth."

"I'll take Elizabeth," I said firmly. "You rest."

She opened her mouth to object and then clamped it shut frantically. A moment later, she lost her argument along with another round to the toilet.

I brought her a seltzer water from the fridge and then considered my options. There was too much for me to do to stay here. I would take Elizabeth with me. It took a few minutes to bundle her up in enough layers to keep her warm. In the end, she looked as squishy as a marshmallow and just as sweet. I took a picture to send Alexander, but then thought better of it.

I could only imagine what he would say if he saw me packing up Elizabeth's diaper bag and preparing to take her down to a racetrack. He'd hear about it, though. There was no way the press wouldn't have a field day with this. I had no doubt the same gossip rags that called me out for attending events without my daughter would declare me a terrible mother for bringing her with me. I was always damned if I did and damned if I didn't.

Georgia, who was waiting in the sitting room, furrowed her brow when she saw Elizabeth.

"Oh good, take her," I thrust my daughter into her arms and rushed to the kitchen for her sippy cup. I returned to find Georgia holding her under the arms and, keeping her far away from her body. She stared at Elizabeth like she was a rattlesnake. Elizabeth let out a screech and kicked her feet.

"I think she's broken," Georgia called over, a frantic edge in her voice. It was almost funny, except I seriously wondered if she was going to drop her and run for it.

"Okay." I held out my hands and she deposited Elizabeth back into them with a grateful sigh. "Don't like kids, huh?"

A shadow passed over her face, but she shook her head and smirked. "All they do is spew bodily fluids. What's there to like?"

"I take it Smith won't be making you a godmother," I muttered, arranging Elizabeth on my hip and shouldering my bag. I usually had more help. If Alexander wasn't with me, the members of our household staff were, or I had a pram. Norris had no issue helping with Elizabeth. He was practically her grandpa. Georgia was clearly the least valuable player when it came to childcare assistance.

"I love that you think he'd want her to have a godmother." She snorted as if this thought was ludicrous. "Besides, I'm sure Belle will choose you. Who can compete with the Queen for that spot?" She snagged the bag from my shoulder and hooked it over hers.

"Thanks," I said gratefully.

"You look like you had your hands full, and my job is to be useful." It was just like Georgia to remind me that she wasn't doing something out of the goodness of her heart. She paused when we reached the front door. "Does Alexander know Elizabeth is coming?"

"He will." I left it at that. I had no doubt he would be getting a briefing on my every movement—probably on the hour.

"Let me rephrase that," she said. "Did you tell him that Elizabeth was coming?"

My lips thinned into a line. It wasn't her concern. "I don't tell my husband everything."

"You really should've taken my advice," she whispered. "I told you he has certain needs."

"Maybe he did," I said, "but people change."

She didn't respond. She didn't have to, because smug was written all over her face. Let her think what she wanted. *That* wasn't my husband's problem.

Our conversation fell away as we trudged out into the cold February morning. My heart pounded as I tried to ignore what Georgia had said. Every time I thought I might be able to stand Georgia Kincaid, she reminded me why I hated her in the first place. Brexton and several others had the cars ready and warmed up, but he did a double take when he saw I had Elizabeth with me.

"Do you need to call him and tattle on me?" I snapped as he opened the door.

"He told me you could handle things," Brex said smoothly.

I doubted Brex believed that. Elizabeth's child-seat was still in the vehicle, thankfully, so I buckled her in and carefully arranged the straps around her coat. Brex opened the other door and doublechecked my work.

"Did he tell you to make sure I knew how to put our child in her seat properly?" I asked coldly. It was going to be a long day if everyone treated me like I didn't know how to be a mother.

He sighed and straightened up. I did the same, glaring at him over the roof of the Range Rover.

"It sucks being between you two all the time," he said. Then he stomped around to the driver's side.

I wasn't being fair. It wasn't Brexton's fault Alexander was being unreasonable. He hadn't been the one to spill the news of my pregnancy to the press. That had been my husband. The trouble was that my husband wasn't here, and I was angry. Between Alexander's actions, Georgia's words, and his hovering over me like a mother hen, I was left to wonder if anyone thought I was competent as a wife, a mother, or a queen. Heat prickled in my eyes and I blinked back angry tears. I wasn't about to let any of them see me cry. That would definitely get back to Alexander.

We rode the few miles to Silverstone in stony

silence. I turned Georgia's words over and over in my head. Was she right? Did Alexander treat me like a fragile creature because he didn't see how strong I was? Our sex life had always been brutal and passionate. I didn't see that there was anything lacking. But I knew submission wasn't about sex. It was about control—me giving it to him. I enjoyed playing. I enjoyed it when he tied me up or spanked me. But I told him once that I'd never be able to give him complete power over my body. Hadn't I, though? I trusted him no matter how hard he pushed me. I could count on one hand the number of times I'd used my safe word. Maybe that was the problem. Maybe I'd kept the one thing away from him that he needed to soothe the beast inside.

I didn't have longer to consider it before we arrived. Brexton turned out to be more helpful than Georgia in the baby department. He gathered Elizabeth from her seat, helped make certain I had everything I would need, and carried her inside.

"There she is," Henry said, darting over when he spotted me. His eyes lingered momentarily on Elizabeth.

"I got her," Brex said. "You do your thing."

I was grateful for the help, until it occurred to me Brex might have seen holding Elizabeth as a security precaution. It was easier to keep Elizabeth safe if he had hold of her. Had there been some other threat? Maybe it had been a mistake to bring my daughter here, and that was why he was sticking close. They probably all thought I was the worst mother in the world. I fell into the fear spiral so quickly that it took physical effort to shake it off. It didn't matter why he was doing it. I couldn't see every situation as dangerous or every helpful gesture as having a hidden motivation.

Brex kept her most of the day, finding me for nappy changes and crying fits only a mother could soothe. We'd adopted a disused office as my temporary headquarters. We needed a place where I could close a door and shut off the fumes from the cars. Brex set up a small playland in the corner on a blanket, producing a surprising number of toys to keep her occupied. I definitely hadn't packed that many into the diaper bag. I decided to go with it.

When Anderson Stone showed up at noon to go over his schedule, he bypassed me and went straight to Elizabeth.

"There's a photo opportunity," Henry said as we watched Anderson drop down next to her on her blanket and start playing blocks.

"We're not using my baby as a photo op." I couldn't imagine what Alexander would say if *that* showed up in his newsfeed in the morning.

"It's probably for the best," Henry said with a sigh. "We'd have uncontrollable swarms of women here as soon as they saw it."

I suspected we would be dealing with that anyway. Anderson looked up at me and winked. I grinned. I couldn't help it. Did he just go around oozing sex appeal and charming women and children? He probably wasn't lonely often. Still, I couldn't imagine being involved with a man who flew around the racetrack in a metal cage at a million miles an hour. I walked over to them, leaving Henry to sort out the latest scheduling crisis.

"She likes you," I said, watching as Elizabeth thrust a block at him with a chubby hand.

"All the ladies do," he said. He put it on the stack they were working on and Elizabeth clapped.

"Well, she is easy to impress," I said dryly.

"That was harsh, but it's always good to keep a man's ego in check," he admitted with a laugh.

Elizabeth's arms flailed, catching the tower and sending it toppling to ruins. Her head fell back and she wailed. I rushed to her, not wanting to interrupt the number of people trying to get their jobs done, but Anderson was quicker. He plucked her off the blanket. Rolling onto his back he held her in the air. "How about we go for a fly, beautiful girl?"

Giggles instantly replaced tears. My heart did a strange little flip at the sight of him zooming her around the air. I could almost see Alexander doing the same thing, except he wasn't here to make his daughter laugh. But her giggles were infectious and I smiled despite the heaviness in my heart. The moment I did, I felt guilty. The feeling settled into my stomach and grew roots there. I didn't know this man. Why was I comparing him to my husband? Because Anderson was here and Alexander wasn't?

Alexander blew raspberries on Elizabeth's tummy and wiped away tears and rocked her to sleep—it wasn't like he was an absentee father. He'd been preoccupied for the last couple of weeks. But what would happen when we had another baby to draw our attention away?

"Are you okay?" Anderson said. I looked down to see his eyes were now on me, his arms still holding Elizabeth in mid-air flight.

"I'm fine. Just tired." It wasn't a lie. I was tired, but sleep wasn't going to do me any good. My *heart* was tired.

"You know, I think they could do without you for a few hours. Maybe you should go take a nap. I'm sure there's enough of us to look after her."

"You want me to leave my baby with a bunch of racecar drivers?" I was more likely to abandon her to a pack of wolves.

"Yeah," he said with a grin. "We can take her around the track a few times."

I reached down and plucked her out of his arms. "I don't think her daddy would like that."

"Daddy isn't here," he teased.

It was an innocent remark, but I flinched. The smirk on his face disappeared as he realized what he'd said.

"I didn't mean anything by it. I'm sorry." He sat up, running his hand through his hair. He paused at the back of his neck, massaging an invisible spot. The movement triggered another wave of guilt in me. He was trying to be nice and I was being crazy.

Elizabeth screeched at being taken away from her new friend. She screwed up her face, her hands balling into tiny fists. "I think we could both use a nap."

"We can manage here."

"Thanks." I meant it. Meanwhile, my daughter was throwing her body toward Anderson. "I think she likes you."

"She just misses her daddy," he said. He pushed onto his feet. He stood and patted the top of her head. "Take a nap and maybe mum will let you go around the track later."

Elizabeth gurgled her approval for this plan.

"Maybe she will," I cooed, "in forty or fifty years."

I helped Elizabeth wave goodbye to Anderson and turned to find Brex. A little quiet time seemed like a very good idea. The next few days would be long ones, and right now my heart was heavy.

Instead of Brex, I found Georgia. She was sitting cross-legged on the desk watching me. Her eyes traveled to Anderson, then retreated back to me.

I forced a smile onto my face and made my way over. "Where's Brex?"

"He's overseeing the crowd control plan," she said.

"Oh." That put a stop to my plans.

"Is there something you need?" she asked.

"I thought I'd take Elizabeth back to the house. I can wait."

She hopped down with enviable grace. "I'll see to it."

She took a few steps toward the door and I breathed a sigh of relief. If Georgia was going to pretend nothing had happened, then I was feeling guilty for nothing. Alexander wasn't here and that was screwing with my head.

Before she'd cleared the office door, she stopped and turned to me. "Word of advice? Tread carefully."

I didn't insult her by asking what she meant. I simply watched her go. Maybe I had something to feel guilty about after all.

CHAPTER FOURTEEN

ALEXANDER

I didn't bother with pleasantries. "How is she?"

It had been less than three days since Clara had left for Silverstone. I'd been in meetings every waking moment, but nothing could distract me for long. My wife and daughter's absence left me feeling disjointed, as though the most important parts of me had simply left. They were my heart—my conscience —and without them, nothing seemed to make sense here.

"She's fine," Brex said. He launched into a report about her daily activities over the last few days. I'd made him wait to make this call. I needed to break some of my bad habits. Clara wanted independence. I couldn't pull back on her security team, especially with Elizabeth there, but I could give her space the only way I had available to me. It was a small gesture toward her wishes—and she wasn't even aware of it.

"Do you want me to call back in a few days?" he asked.

"Why don't you call me tomorrow?" So much for giving her more freedom. In fact, I was going crazy. I'd tried to go cold turkey and it had been too much—too fast. I was addicted to her. I was only half a man without her by my side, and an even worse king. Let Brex think what he would about me. I didn't care.

"I will," he vowed, "but everything is good here, Alexander. I don't want you to worry."

"Is there anything else I should know?" I asked him. Technically, the security briefing should cover more than my family. The opening ceremonies were scheduled for tomorrow and the first racing event for a few days later. They were tying up loose ends, and although I'd chosen not to be there—as a sign of faith to Clara—it was still my responsibility.

"We've got this covered. You worry about Parliament," he told me.

We were supposed to be presenting a united front. Clara was capable of representing our family. My responsibilities rested with Parliament's investigation into the handling of Jacobson's case. If we were going to come out on the other side of these challenges, we would have to work together. I told myself that we were strong. We were undivided. But the truth was, I felt torn in half.

"Humor me," I said.

"There have been very few security incidents. A few people trying to sneak in their own booze in backpacks is about the worst of it. A reporter tried to scale a fence. He broke his camera, so I think he learned his lesson." Even over the phone I could hear Brex's amusement. He probably questioned why he was there. There were more pressing issues to deal with, certainly, but he would never question me outright. He knew that wherever my wife was, my mind was.

"And Anderson?" It was hard to ask about my brother. It felt strange and somehow more clandestine than checking in on my wife.

There was a pause. It wasn't like Brex to hesitate.

"What is it?" I asked. I knew him well enough to know when he was weighing his response. He'd been trained by the military to make snap decisions without thinking, reacting instantly in life or death situations. It was what made him an asset to the team. When he didn't have a quick response, it meant something.

"He seems like a nice kid," Brex said noncommittally.

"And?" I pressed. There was more to this. I could sense it.

"He's thoughtful. He seems particularly considerate of Clara."

Meaning was laced through his words, and I found my hand closing sharply over a pencil. It snapped in half.

My attention had been divided and now the last person who should have been allowed to had gotten close to my wife. Was this a part of Jacobson's plan? He'd said my family would turn against me. But he couldn't know about Anderson. That secret had been well kept. It had taken the CIA to uncover it. How would an MP from the House of Commons discover it?

"He is?" I did my best to sound casual, but it came out strangled.

"It's probably nothing," Brex said quickly—too quickly.

"How considerate is he?" I asked.

"He checks in on her. They talk. He helped her with Elizabeth today."

"He helped her with Elizabeth today?" I repeated, certain I must have heard him wrong.

"The nanny was sick. We all helped."

That didn't make me feel any better. I should have sent Norris instead of asking him to clean up another of my father's messes while everyone was away. It had been a calculated error, but an error all the same.

"And Clara accepted his help?" I asked in a strangled voice.

"She doesn't realize," Brex said quietly. "She doesn't see it. Alexander, her heart belongs to you. He's just a kid."

It didn't matter. He was there, and I was here. He was looking after her, and I wasn't. He had the life I could never have—freedom I had never experienced —and this was how he—how *they*—repaid me?

"I'm keeping an eye on the situation," Brex assured me.

"Let me know if anything happens." I resisted the urge to tell him to stay with her at all times. Clara would notice if he was suddenly clingier. She would ask him why he was suddenly concerned. He could lie to her. Tell her there had been a security threat. But that wouldn't solve my problem and would put undue stress on her while she was pregnant.

I had kept this from her, kept the truth from her, and I was being punished for my sins. Anderson Stone had the life I would never have—and now he was coveting the one thing that belonged to me, the thing that mattered. The one and only thing I would never give him.

CHAPTER FIFTEEN

CLARA

I'd been asked to do strange things since I'd become a Royal, but this was the strangest yet. I stared at the red silk scarf that Henry had handed me a few moments ago. "What am I supposed to do with this, exactly?"

"Have you ever seen a joust reenactment?" he asked.

"In a movie." I couldn't see what it had to do with racing. I turned it over in my hand, looking for a clue.

"At past games, a royal would grant his favor to certain competitors. It was Albert's idea—a nod to jousting."

"So, if Alexander were hosting, he'd be giving Anders the scarf?" I would pay to see that. It would be a touching moment: Alexander acting superior, and Anders glaring at him.

"I believe the honor would still fall to you,"

Henry said dryly. "My mother performed the duty for years."

"Another reason for your mother to hate me." I'd fantasized the games might win her over, but I'd been wrong. Instead of becoming her champion and swaying Alexander to hold the event, I'd become her replacement.

"My mother doesn't..." Henry paused as though he thought better of lying and switched tactics. "It is the Queen's favor—a tradition—and you are the queen."

"It's medieval," I muttered. I was accustomed to being in front of people—I lived my life in front of the world now. But this was different than giving a speech or presenting an award. Something felt too personal. After my talk with Georgia, it felt like sending Anders mixed signals, something I definitely didn't want to do. I couldn't imagine what Alexander would think if he watched the opening ceremonies. I hoped he remembered the tradition better than I did.

"Does it have to be Anders?" A different racer would be a better—safer—choice.

"He is the favorite and I think the press will eat it up," Henry said.

"The press will eat me up." It had been one thing for Mary, the Queen Mother, to perform the ritual. I suspected my participation might be viewed in an entirely different light. I wrapped the scarf around my wrist and sucked in a deep breath. "Let's get this over with."

I focused on the fact that tonight the stands would be full of children. That's why we were doing this. Watching the Queen gift a token to the local hero was going to have a huge impact on them. That's what this was about. The ticket sales and sponsorships we received would go to local schools and health initiatives. At each city we visited over the course of the next three months, kids would have a chance to see their heroes in action. They'd see the men and women they looked up to giving back to their communities. I hadn't always seen eye-to-eye with Albert, but it was a beautiful legacy to leave.

"I thought Alexander might join us," Henry said under his breath as we made our way toward the side of the track for the scarf presentation.

The night was cold and I was glad Edward had insisted I bring along a wool dress coat for warmth and camouflage. I hadn't thought I would need many dressy clothes, but I'd been expected to look the part of the proper English queen this evening. Under the neatly tailored navy coat I had on a boring house dress that wouldn't be winning me any style points.

"I wish he could," I said. I was angry with my husband, but I was beginning to miss him. Being in love had a way of undermining a girl's resistance.

Henry nodded thoughtfully, tucking his Burberry scarf tightly under his collar to ward off the evening wind. "He must have been held up in London. I know he missed the last games while he was away."

"He wanted to come," I lied. It felt like I was

doing that more and more often for him, making excuses for his absence. Being away at war was a good reason for missing last time, this time he was simply avoiding it. "He couldn't be away."

"It was a lovely gesture to do this on his birthday. I'm sure that will make it easier for him."

My stomach twisted into a knot, but I smiled quickly. It was supposed to be a nice gesture. Alexander had ruined it. I hadn't imagined he wouldn't come, especially when I'd given him the dates. He had looked at them and said nothing.

"It feels like we're bridging the old and the new," I said.

"Yes, it does," Henry said. "Alexander's birthday to start and my brother's birthday to end the ceremonies."

That's what I thought. It was carefully planned. I'd suggested the idea when we'd first looked at the schedule. Originally, Mary had wanted to start the games in March. I'd argued it would be a signal of our family's unity to begin on Alexander's birthday, February 26, and end on Albert's, the 25th of May.

"Will your mother be arriving soon?" Mary had been suspiciously absent the past week, which I assumed was an effort to avoid me. In London, she'd come to every meeting. She'd shown no qualms about making her opinion known.

Henry shook his head, dropping his voice to keep his words between us. "The doctor doesn't think this atmosphere would be good for her heart and the travel isn't ideal. I'm glad she's back in London where specialists are available. She's always more interested in the horses anyway. She wishes you all the best, though."

One of those statements was a lie, but it did no good to call him out on it. Henry was trying to be pleasant, which was more than his mother had ever done for me. "At least the equestrian events take place closer to London. So, do I give this to Anders as soon as I see him?"

The closer we came to the actual event, the more nervous I became. I didn't want to admit it, but I wanted to impress those watching. For every person who had accepted and blessed me as their Queen, it felt like there were two who saw me as some kind of Royal Yoko Ono.

"Not quite. Your part comes after the ceremonial lap," Henry explained. "It signifies that we come here in the spirit of brotherhood."

"And tomorrow we come in the spirit of kicking each other's asses?" I clapped my hand over my mouth, horrified I'd let that slip. I backtracked quickly. "Sorry. The philosophy behind competitive sports has always eluded me."

"You really are a breath of fresh air." He waved off my apology with a smile. "Most of my family acts like they have a scepter stuck up their arse."

"Including Alexander?"

"You can't blame a king for being on edge," Henry said wisely, "especially given how young he is.

I do wish you two would have had more time before you had to tackle this responsibility."

That made two of us. But there was no use in wishing. I could only focus on what we did have—a lifetime together. That was all Alexander had ever promised me, and all I could ever want.

Engines roared in response to a marker, and the lap started. The cars zoomed around the track at breakneck speed. It might have been thrilling if my mind wasn't elsewhere. This was what I wanted— what I'd worked for—but part of me wished I was back in London. It was the part of me that had known Alexander wouldn't come.

"They're ready for us." Henry called my attention back to the present. The drivers had returned. Most had climbed out of their cars, depositing their helmets in their seats and were making their way toward us. They slapped each other on the back, laughed, waved—they were having so much fun.

The stands were entirely full, roars of applause deafened me as I stepped onto the track. Anders reached us, his hair mussed from his helmet, wearing a white track suit emblazoned with a bunch of sponsors. He looked like a walking advertisement. He seemed to know that because a goofy grin had replaced his usual smirk. We made our way over to him and I realized he looked a little shaky. I placed a hand over the mic pinned to my coat. It would be turning on any moment.

"Are you shy?" I asked. Maybe putting him in the spotlight had been the wrong call.

"Not if I can help it," he said a bit too smoothly to be believed. His hands were trembling.

Still, there was no mistaking the boyish gleam in his eyes. I wondered what it must be like for him to be here, fulfilling his dream. I had never wanted fame nor fortune. I'd stumbled into this life by accident. He'd worked for this. A lump formed in my throat, a strangely maternal pride coming over me. I really was pregnant. Everything seemed to be sending me into mom mode. I'd probably cry during every race, too.

Next to me, Anders gave me a searching look, his hand landing lightly on my arm. I gave him a reassuring smile. Later, when I wasn't wearing a microphone, I would confess that my hormones were getting the better of me and turning me into a blubbering mother hen.

The ceremony went off without a hitch, even if I felt a bit silly tossing him my scarf. He caught it easily and tied it around his arm. Camera flashes went off all around us as we waved obligingly. At least I only had to do this bit once.

"Are you hungry?" Anders asked as we all made our way to the paddock. "Some of the guys are going out for a bite. We thought we could show you a good time. I mean, not too good of a time." He gestured to the bump visible under my coat. "I don't want to get you in trouble."

"I think I already got myself in trouble." I

laughed as I patted the proof. "That's really sweet, but..."

"But she has other plans," a rough voice broke in.

My heart leapt, already knowing what I would find when I turned. Alexander was dressed down in a pitiful attempt to blend in, but there was no mistaking him. Even in a worn, leather jacket, hands shoved in his jeans, he was a king. My body responded to his presence, drawing me toward him. I locked my knees in place and tried to think. But I didn't have to concentrate for long. Alexander wasn't looking at me. His burning gaze was directed at Anders. X took a step around me and held out a hand. It was a friendly gesture, but his shoulders were rigid. He had his guard up. If Anders noticed, he didn't show it. He took the outstretched hand and shook it as Alexander moved so that his body was between me and Anders. It was a subtle marking of his territory, but one I wasn't going to ignore.

Pushing past him, I stepped between them. Formal introductions were in order before things got less civilized. "Anders, allow me to introduce you to my husband."

CHAPTER SIXTEEN

CLARA

The family estate we were staying in had three wings, sixteen rooms, a stable—and I was pretty sure none of it was big enough to house my husband's giant ego. Security saw us in, parting ways with us to head to the kitchens or to their rooms. No one made eye contact. Not even Norris. I could have sworn the antique portraits lining the corridor walls were studiously avoiding looking our way.

"I can't believe you," I exploded as soon as we made it to the bedroom. That proved to be a mistake because a piercing wail rent the air a second later. I groaned in frustration. Now I'd woken up Elizabeth. Could this get any worse?

"I've got her." Alexander stopped me at the door. He went across the hall, pausing to wave a bleary-eyed Penny back to bed. "I'll see to her."

The poor girl's eyes popped open. Alexander had that effect on women. Of course, I imagined finding the King of England in your hallway when you are half-asleep was a little startling.

I fumed, pacing across the bedroom and trying to think of what to say. I'd left London on bad terms, and I hadn't expected him to follow me here. Now he'd shown up and planted his proverbial flag for all to see. If he thought he was going to get away with it, we needed to have a serious conversation. I made up my mind to tell him that and went across the hall. Peeking into the nursery, I hesitated at the sight that greeted me. Elizabeth was in his arms, one sleepy hand reached out to hold her father's chin. Alexander rocked on his heels, bending and swaying with gentle movements. He was dancing her back to sleep.

I softened instantly. It wasn't playing fair to follow up his spectacular display of cockiness with proof he was an amazing father. Because he couldn't seem to be both an arrogant king and this man at the same time. The trouble was that this was what I wanted. I wanted a husband who rocked our children to sleep. I wanted a normal life. It was something I could never have. I stole back to the bedroom without saying a word. Our argument could wait. Regardless of the troubles Alexander and I faced, I would never allow Elizabeth to be placed between us.

I'd come down considerably by the time he returned to me. My anger had dropped to a low simmer. As long as he didn't up the heat, I wouldn't boil over again.

He shuffled into the room, his eyes cast to the

floor as he shucked his leather jacket and tossed it on a chair.

"You can't hide from me, X," I said when he continued to undress without so much as a glance.

"Believe me, I know that." He pressed his lips into a thin smile, reaching for the back of his t-shirt.

"I don't know why you're getting undressed," I said quickly. The truth was that if he took off his shirt I wasn't sure what would happen. Actually, I had a pretty good idea.

"I was getting ready for bed." He glanced over as if to make sure we had one.

We had one and I knew that because I'd been sleeping in it alone. It had felt too large without him there. My heart ached at the thought of unfolding my body against his and finally getting a decent night's sleep.

Instead, I planted my hands on my hips and forced myself to sound calm. "Maybe you should stay in the guest room."

He blinked like I'd been speaking a foreign language and he needed a second to translate. "I thought most of the guest rooms were taken."

He had me there. Between Penny and Brexton and Noris and Georgia, the house was full. Our group had even spilled over to a local inn. My mind raced, trying to come up with a new objection before my heart got its way. "There's always the couch."

"Poppet," he began.

"Don't Poppet me," I snapped. "You were rude. You were condescending. You embarrassed me."

A muscle in his jaw twitched and he massaged the spot, his hand raking across his 5 o'clock shadow. My body responded to the noise, remembering the times his stubble had scraped deliciously over the skin of my thighs. I hated that I responded so instantly to his presence. I hated that even now, when I was extremely pissed with him, part of me was glad he was here. I'd missed him. No matter how angry I was—no matter the distance between us—I loved him.

"If you want me to go..." He let the offer hang in the air, waiting for me to grab hold of it or dismiss it.

"You should stay," I said, "for Elizabeth. She misses you."

I miss you, too. I kept that to myself.

"I missed her." His eyes caught mine. "I missed you."

"You knew where I was." I hadn't quite forgiven him for acting like an ape to Anderson. Or for outing my pregnancy to the world. Or for a lot of things, apparently. He must have known that, so why had he chosen to show his face today of all days? "Why are you here?"

"It's my birthday." The accusation that should have been there wasn't. Instead, the words were hollow. "You probably were busy."

I swallowed. I'd been caught up in the ceremonies and hadn't called. Or had I been punishing him? "I know. I picked the date. It was supposed to be a surprise. The Sovereign Games should celebrate the Sovereign, after all."

"I don't care about the games." He pinched the bridge of his nose with his thumb and forefinger. "I don't care that it's my birthday. I needed to see you."

"I guess you're supposed to get your wish today."

"You're the only thing I want," he said softly. "I don't need presents or parties. Just you."

"Good, because I didn't get you anything." I crossed my arms, suddenly defensive. I'd been angry and preoccupied. Christ, was I turning into him? Becoming so lost in my work that I forgot birthdays? I was clinging to my anger, because I suspected that if I released it, I'd have to face how horrible I felt.

"I didn't mean to embarrass you," he said in a low voice.

"Is that your way of apologizing?" I could never be sure with him. Alexander had a bad habit of thinking everything he did was justified. It meant that he didn't regularly say he was sorry.

"Yes," he said. "Forgive me?"

"Well, that depends. Are you going to keep acting like a jackass?" But I found myself crossing the room. I stopped short of him, not certain if I should take those last steps. Alexander wrapped an arm around my waist and closed that final distance. My hands slid under his shirt, seeking his warmth and lingering on the hard, muscular plane of his abs.

"If you stop making me jealous," he said. He leaned closer, his mouth temptingly close to mine.

"Jealous?" I raised an eyebrow. "I was doing my job. You didn't want to host the games, so I did."

"That's not what I'm talking about." He traced a finger down my nose to my lower lip before sighing. He shook his head, his mouth twitching with an exasperated grin that looked anything but amused. I wanted to kiss him until he stopped looking at me that way. Or slap him. Both seemed like effective methods. "He asked you to dinner."

"Who? Dinner? What?" I drew back, confused, before I figured out what he meant. "Anders? He's *a kid*."

"He's your age," he corrected me.

"Okay, that might be true. I don't see him that way." He could think whatever he wanted. "Anders invited me out with the guys. It wasn't like that."

"Are you sure about that, Clara?" The words grated from him like he'd turned them over so many times they had left him raw. The question had preoccupied him, I could see that now. The blaze in his eyes wasn't possession or anger. It was fear.

"It isn't," I promised. "He was only being friendly."

He shook his head again, his hand going to his hair and raking through it in a gesture I knew too well. "He wasn't being friendly." His eyes traveled from my feet up until they met mine. "He wants you."

"You are paranoid, Alexander. You have to stop worrying." I pressed a palm to his chest, my skin tingling where our flesh met. "I chose you. It wouldn't matter if he'd asked me to marry him—" This observation was met with a growl, but I ignored it. "My answer will always be no to anyone but you."

"Does that mean..." he trailed away, his hand slipping to the zipper of my dress.

"If you promise to behave." But I was already melting against him. He unzipped me and my dress puddled to the floor. A hand pressed to the small of my back and he bent me over, my body arching into his embrace. The heat of his mouth trailed down my throat to my breasts before closing over my nipple, sucking it roughly through the lace of my bra. I couldn't fight this. I didn't want to.

"Behaving," he murmured, "is overrated."

My eyes had shut tightly, savoring each flick of his tongue and rasp of his teeth, but I squirmed free and pushed him away.

"Promise me," I repeated firmly. Alexander wasn't paying attention, his focus was still on my breasts, so I crossed my arms over my chest defiantly.

"I will behave. I will play nice. I will be your better half." He yanked me to him, before adding, "In theory."

"X." It was all I got out before we collided. There was an urgency to his kiss, but unlike what I'd come to expect after the last few harrowing weeks, it was slow and sweet. It was a kiss that asked for my forgiveness. I folded into him, my hands pressed to his chest. His heart beat rapidly and I relaxed as I felt its steady rhythm. He was what mattered. Every danger we faced, whatever issues we had, we'd battle them together. I had promised him that. I hadn't chosen this life or him blindly. It wasn't going to be easy.

But easy love was for the weak. Easy love gave up. Easy love didn't last. Us? We were forever. It didn't matter if it was harder. I saw past his rough edges to the man he was in his soul. It was a fierce love—a hard love—that had brought us together. That love was worth fighting for.

"I'm sorry, Poppet," he whispered against my mouth. "I wish I could tell you that it won't happen again. I wish I could tell you I deserve you. I wish I could tell you how very much I need you."

I reached up and took his face, tilting his chin so our eyes met, his blue and my gray clashing in a storm of emotion. "Show me."

Alexander scooped me into his arms and carried me to the bed. He laid me down with a gentleness that stole my breath. My fingers fumbled to find the button of his jeans, but he pushed my hand away softly.

"I'll take care of that," he said in a low voice that sent a shiver dancing up my spine. "I'll take care of you tonight."

Tightness constricted my throat and I swallowed hard. The tears came anyway. I shut my eyes against them, but they leaked past my lashes and dribbled down my face. Alexander finished drawing off my pants, but his fingers froze on my ankles.

"Clara," he said my name in a strangled voice.

"I'm okay," I choked out. I wasn't. Not really. I was in love. I was terrified. I was frustrated. I was hopeful. I was everything. He made me feel too much —he always made me feel too much.

"I..." he searched for something to say, but I knew there was nothing to be said. Some truths could only be felt.

"Make love to me," I pleaded, holding out a hand. It was the only answer he needed.

Alexander shed his clothes swiftly and climbed onto the bed next to me, pulling my body to his. He wiped away the lingering remnants of tears with the rough pad of his thumb as he planted a soft kiss on my forehead.

"Clara, you are my world," he murmured, his lips still brushing across my forehead. "I was raised to believe that protecting the world was my responsibility. How could I not protect you?"

"I only need you to love me," I whispered, daring a hopeful glance. Pain flashed across his face and his eyes shuddered against my words.

"I love you. I wish I could go back and tell you as soon as I realized it. I wish I could go back and tell you every time I've thought it since. Your love is a gift I've never deserved. I'm honored to love you."

"I'm honored you protect me." I kissed him softly.

"But X, you can't control everything. You can't control the world. You can't control me."

"I know that." He drew me closer, his strong arms tightening protectively around me. "I won't control you. But I won't stop trying to change the world. You deserve to feel nothing but love and peace. Our children deserve that. If I have to spend every day of my life fighting for it, I will."

I knew he meant it. And I knew this was one enemy he would face on his own. All I could do was give him the strength and faith to keep fighting.

But tonight, on his birthday, he deserved a reprieve. "Let's forget about the world," I urged him, my hand sliding down to grip his length and draw it between my legs.

Alexander groaned, hooking a hand around my leg and moving between my thighs. I guided him to my entrance and held my breath. He paused, allowing me to adjust as he rocked his hips against me, sliding inside me slowly so that I felt every inch of him. He rooted there and stilled, lingering in the sensation of our union. We stayed like that for a few moments, simply together. It was a reminder that nothing could come between us because we were not two separate people, but one. One heart. One soul. There was no Alexander. There was no Clara. There was just us.

When he finally began to move, he drew in and out of me, allowing the ache at my core to build with painful anticipation.

"Promise me I'll never lose you," he whispered. I opened my eyes and found his own full of fear and my heart broke. Even now, with nothing between us, he was afraid.

"What is this about?" I whispered, gasping as he pierced me once more.

"It's about us," he answered with another lingering thrust. "I love you, Poppet."

His words sent me over the edge and I shattered, my heart fracturing and fusing with his. Until he was my beginning and my end. Until he was my everything.

ALEXANDER WAS A CHANGED MAN THE NEXT morning. He'd slept well, judging from the lack of circles under his eyes and the quick smile he flashed whenever he caught me checking him out. I couldn't help looking. It had been too long since I'd seen him so happy.

Everywhere he went, he seemed keen to meet people, to shake hands, to show off our daughter. I wasn't entirely sure what to do with him. In a single night, he'd done a complete one-eighty. I wanted to believe that I had finally laid the fears plaguing him to rest, but I knew it wasn't that simple. Every now and then I would catch a shadow when he thought I wasn't looking. There was more to this and I wouldn't be satisfied until no ghosts haunted his eyes.

"I can take her." I held out my arms for Elizabeth,

but Alexander moved her onto his other hip and shook his head.

"You do too much, Poppet," he whispered, so only I could hear. That was the only trouble. We were surrounded not only by security teams, but everyone who worked at Silverstone. It had escaped no one's notice that the King had come to visit and they all seemed eager to shake his hand. "I'm here to help you, so do what you need to do."

"It's not that simple."

"Why?" His forehead crinkled in concern and he twined his free hand with mine.

"You show up and everyone comes out to see you," I muttered to him. "No one even notices when I'm here."

Except Anders, but I wasn't about to say that after last night's cock-and-bull show.

"They're afraid to talk to you."

"Why would they be afraid to talk to me?" I couldn't see a reason why. I wasn't nearly as intimidating as he was, and no one had any problems coming up to him.

"Because you're beautiful and smart and everyone here sees that." He lifted the hand that he held and pressed it to his lips. "And they probably know that you're taken."

"I wonder what could give them that idea," I said dryly. He had been on his best behavior today, which for Alexander meant only a slight bit of male posturing. It didn't escape my attention that he always managed to be between me and whoever we were talking to. Still, he wasn't displaying any of the primitive behavior that had pissed me off last night. It was a step in the right direction.

All of that changed when Anders arrived at the track. The first race wasn't scheduled until tomorrow, but all of the racers were here, going over important details with their team and running practice laps.

The moment I spotted him, I considered feigning a headache. Maybe it would be better to keep the two of them apart. Alexander had misinterpreted Anders' friendly invitation yesterday. I knew that. My husband didn't seem to, though. Before I could make up my mind on which way to handle it, he'd turned and caught sight of him.

There was a brief pause when both men's eyes met. My husband went rigid like he was about to strike and I placed a comforting hand on his shoulder. He needed to remember that he had nothing to fear. The only way I could help to remind him of that was by staying at his side. Anders forced a smile and ambled towards us, raking his hand through his shaggy blond hair. He stopped and directed his attention to Elizabeth.

"Remember me, beautiful girl?" he cooed at her. "Mum let you come to the track, huh?"

It was a mistake. I knew it the moment he'd spoken. If Alexander was protective of me, then he was overbearing when it came to Elizabeth.

"Anderson's been helpful," I said, breaking in and

hoping I could prevent a fight. "Penny was sick the other day. He helped calm Elizabeth down."

"Is that so?" Alexander asked in a strained voice. I saw what it took for him to stay calm. "Thank you."

I couldn't imagine what resource of self-control he'd drawn on to keep his reaction so even.

Anders' eyes darted between us. Despite Alexander's gratitude, it was clear that my husband was on edge.

"I'm glad I caught you," Anders redirected his attention to me. That was the second mistake. "If your nanny is feeling better, the guys are going out for drinks tonight. You really should join us since you couldn't last night."

So much for Alexander's theory that I was intimidating. I wished he was right, if only so this moment could have been avoided.

"That is..." I couldn't say sweet or nice. I needed Anders to get the message that I could never be one of the guys.

"That's not really appropriate," Alexander said through gritted teeth.

Anders cocked a surprised eyebrow and shrugged. "She's working hard. We thought she might like to have some fun and everyone wants to thank her."

"My wife is expecting," Alexander reminded him.

So much for best behavior. I elbowed Alexander in the ribs, but he ignored me.

"We weren't going to get her pissed," Anders said with a laugh. "We just thought she might like a little time out. It doesn't seem like she gets much of it."

His words were loaded, and it occurred to me that Anders had been reading the tabloids. He had stepped into the role of knight without any clue what he was getting into.

"I go out when I want to." We were no longer talking about a quick walk down to a pub. I wanted to be perfectly clear on this. Everyone—even my closest friends—believed Alexander told me when I could and couldn't leave. But that wasn't true. I'd always chosen when to stay and go. He had never stopped me from leaving. "He usually just sends a security escort behind me."

No one laughed. Tension stretched between us like a taut rubber band. One wrong move and it would snap. Who knew which of us it would hit?

"Clara has responsibilities," Alexander said gruffly, "to this country. To this family. I wouldn't expect you to understand."

"Yeah, what would a poor kid like me know? Who am I next to you, right?" He took a step closer and I moved between them, lifting Elizabeth from Alexander's arms and holding her closely.

"Enough," I hissed. "You have both proven your point."

"Maybe to you." Anders cast a look in my direction before training his eyes on Alexander. "But I suspect he could stand to be taught a few lessons."

"I could stand..." Alexander repeated with genuine surprise. He chuckled slightly at some joke that only he was in on.

"Your men would take care of it though, right?" Anders backed up. He turned from Alexander and gave me a meaningful look. "If you change your mind, we'll be at the Dark Horse in the village. Let me know if you need anything."

"You don't need to worry about my wife," Alexander's voice was as cold as the edge of a knife.

Anders took one more look at me and shook his head. "Nah, but maybe you should."

CHAPTER SEVENTEEN

ALEXANDER

Clara wasn't happy with me. What was new? It was impossible to explain to her why Anderson got under my skin without telling her the truth. And that would change everything for what she was doing here. I could see that now. Still, it was a risk to ignore the situation developing right under my nose.

Anderson Stone was falling in love with my wife. *My brother* was falling in love with my wife. I wasn't blind. Anyone could see it. It was why Brexton had called me here. Maybe Clara could pretend not to notice. She had a frustrating habit of not seeing herself as the world did. If she could, maybe she would understand why I was so possessive of her. Or maybe she didn't want to see it, because then she'd have to admit there was a problem. A really big fucking problem. Anderson might not have crossed any lines yet, but he would.

I knew her heart belonged to me. But would that be the case if a man came along and offered her what I could never give her? Love that came without the price of her freedom? I never wanted to find out.

She fell asleep early that evening, no doubt exhausted by everything that had happened today. I helped her along, making love to her until her eyes drooped closed. As soon as she was asleep, I left the bedroom, shutting the door quietly behind me.

Our security heads were staying in the east wing of the house. I took a chance and knocked on a door, hoping I didn't accidentally wake Georgia. I knew what she would have to say about my plans for the evening. Not that Norris and Brexton were going to be any happier, but they were military men, and, as such, they knew how to take an order. Georgia didn't share that trait unless the order came from someone holding a whip. I wasn't about to go down that path just to get her on my side.

To my relief, Brexton opened the door, his gun in hand. "Everything okay?"

"Stand down, soldier." I held my hands up in surrender. "I thought we could grab a drink."

He hesitated, blinking away confusion before he grinned. "Cool. Let me get my stuff."

His stuff included his gun, shoes, and jacket. For Brex those were life's only essentials. Things had been tense between us the last couple of weeks. I knew he had taken this assignment as a sign of my faith in him, but I hadn't apologized for blaming him for what had happened that day in Chelsea. I also knew he wouldn't accept an apology. That wasn't how it worked with us. When we'd served together, if one of us fucked up, the other held him accountable. And then we let it go. It was how we'd stayed alive.

"Look," I began, "I know you did the best you could that day. Clara can be stubborn. I'm sure she didn't make it easy for you."

"I shouldn't have left her, though." Regret coloured his words and his eyes darkened as he recalled his choice. He shook his head fiercely. "My job is to protect this family. I won't forget that again."

"You saved a lot of people that day."

"Would that have mattered if she'd died?" He was calling my bluff, seeing through the face I wore as King to the heart of who I was underneath.

Because in truth the only life that mattered to me was hers. Admitting that would be admitting that I placed her above everything. Above myself. Above King and Country.

"It's in the past. I trust you," I told him. He needed to hear it. Our friendship had gotten me through one of the darkest periods of my life. Like Norris, he was more than just a member of my team. He was family. I clapped a hand on his shoulder and forced him to look at me. "I mean that."

"She is safe with me," he promised.

"I know."

"So, is there anything to drink around here?" he asked.

I paused. It was a poor show to immediately back him into a corner now that we were mates again. He wasn't going to like this bit. "I thought we would go out."

"Go out? Did you hit your head?" Brex looked me up and down.

"There's a pub down the way. I heard some of the guys talking about it. Might be fun." It was best to leave out the particulars of who would be there. Brex would call it off if he knew Anders was going to be there. I'd pay for it later.

"You don't really go out to bars," he said slowly. It was a lackluster appeal to common sense.

"I used to," I reminded him.

"That was before..." he trailed away.

Before I accepted the crown. When I'd had choices. He didn't need to say it. We both knew it. We also knew that the right thing to do was to scare up a bottle of Scotch and stay put. But I wasn't interested in the drink. I was interested in the company.

"If you're set on this, we should take Norris."

"Yeah, I kinda figured you'd say that."

Norris had even more practice at standing by me when I was doing something irrational, but I hadn't asked him for something this crazy in a long time. Still, when he answered the door, he only blinked in response. At least, he was good at putting on a show.

"This is a terrible fucking idea," Brex told me, as he turned the car into the village. "I want my objections to be known."

"You're on the record," I promised him.

Norris remained silent in the back. I'd refused to sit there and be driven around. I hadn't been entirely upfront with my motivations for going out, but part of me didn't want something normal. I thought back to nights I'd spent at bars and clubs before I'd met Clara. I didn't want that life. But I wouldn't mind feeling like an average guy occasionally.

The Dark Horse was a typical English pub. That is to say, it was built sometime in the last 1000 years, give or take, and hadn't changed much since. The inside was dark and crammed with stools and tables, heavy drinkers and lost souls. I'd added a baseball cap to my ensemble for extra camouflage. I pulled its bill low over my eyes as I scanned the room.

No one bothered to look at us. We were just a group of guys at the bar. Some deeply ignored knot loosened in my gut. I was buying normalcy with borrowed time, but I would take it.

"I'll grab us some drinks," Brex muttered before disappearing into the crowd.

Norris and I made our way through the packed bar, looking for a table. A few passersby jostled us and Norris hesitated, instantly alert. I slung an arm around his shoulder and dragged him toward the back.

"There's one." I pointed to one in the far corner that was conveniently located next to a table full of racers I'd met earlier in the day at Silverstone.

He sighed heavily. I couldn't hear it over the

clamour of the crowd, but I saw it—and I felt it. It carried the weight of deep disappointment. "Is this a social engagement?"

"Happy coincidence," I said, peeking out from under my cap.

He wasn't buying it, but he followed me as I pushed my way to the empty table and dropped onto a stool.

The group from Silverstone was having a good time, judging by their boisterous laughter and the number of empty glasses on the table. I positioned my seat where I could keep an eye on them, watching carefully from under my hat.

"Perhaps, you should talk to him," Norris suggested, leaning close to me so that I could hear him over the rabble.

"Not an option." My curiosity had driven me here tonight. At least, that was probably what Norris thought. Part of me wanted to know more about this stranger who shared my blood. Part of me wanted to assess whether or not he was a threat to me. The truth was that I couldn't wrap my head around any of it. He was my brother. He didn't know that. And yet, fate had thrown us together in this strange way. And then there was the issue of Clara. "He sees me as his competition."

I didn't have to fill Norris in on what the prize was. He'd picked up on Anders's overtures as soon as he'd arrived. It was blatantly obvious to everyone but Clara, and I suspected she was only lying to herself.

"Perhaps you should finally tell her?" This suggestion was less gentle.

"I tried to stop it from coming to this. I tried to keep her away," I told him. "She's happy hosting the games. If I tell her, it will ruin this for her."

Norris seemed to consider this for a moment. "What will happen if you don't tell her?"

"She won't find out?"

"Secrets don't stay buried, Alexander, and they have no place in a marriage." He gave me a hard look that said more than any warning. "It's time for you to let her help you carry these secrets. You've shouldered some burdens too long."

"Burdens?" I laughed humourlessly. "Is that how you view family? I thought it was about loyalty, duty, responsibility." I rattled off the words my father had thrown at me when he'd sent me away to the war. The ones he'd reminded me of when I'd come home. The ones he'd threatened me with before I'd married.

Brex appeared, juggling three pints of beer. I had never been gladder to see anyone in my life. I needed a drink. He handed them off to us one by one, before dropping down to a chair next to mine.

"What did I miss?" he asked.

"We were chatting about our feelings. You're back just in time to braid my hair." I couldn't hide my resentment. Yes, I had come here with an agenda, but I hadn't come looking for a lecture. I downed my beer in one long draught.

Brex didn't say anything. He just shot a disapproving glance at my empty glass. It would take ages to get another one. He looked around, scanning his perimeter and his eyes landed on the table of drivers. More specifically, they landed on Anders.

"Tell me that's not why we're here," he muttered.

"It's a *coincidence*," Norris said flatly.

I hadn't expected them to buy that one, but I didn't need to explain my reasons.

"Look at it this way," I told them, "I could have come alone."

Brex groaned, rubbing his jaw as he continued to eye him. "It's always best to bring close friends when you're going to do something stupid."

"I knew you'd understand." I grinned. He shoved my shoulder, and for a moment, that's what we were. Two old friends, giving each other shit and sharing a pint.

"To bad decisions." Brex tapped his beer against my empty one.

"I'll never understand how you two made it home alive." Norris shook his head. I held up my empty glass and he clinked mine despite his disapproval.

At the table next to us, the noise level rose, and my companions visibly tensed. I, on the other hand, was feeling more and more relaxed. Until one word rose above the ruckus.

Clara.

I twisted, wanting to get closer, wanting to hear what was being said. Next to me, Brex had a hand in his pocket. I placed a hand on his shoulder carefully and gave him a small shake of the head.

"You're saying you wouldn't want to hit that?" A man I didn't recognize called across the table. A few seats down Anders shot daggers at him. Adrenaline rushed through me, setting me on edge. For some reason his reaction made me even angrier. Clara wasn't his to protect.

"She's up the duff, man!" Another one crowed.

"That doesn't matter," the first man cried back. "She's got that look about her. *Like she likes it.*"

"Course she does," another said. "Gold-diggers always like it. They're always on their knees—"

Now I was on my feet.

Anders was closer. He threw himself across the table, grabbing the man's shirt and dragging him to the ground.

"Your Majesty," Norris said under his breath, his hand hooking my elbow.

I shook off his gentle grip, my hand clenching into a fist. There were a thousand reasons for me to turn and walk out of here right now. Some felt more important than others. My wife, for one, wouldn't be pleased if my picture showed up on *The Guardian*'s front page. Neither would Parliament. It was a mark of my true priorities that Clara's anger was more terrifying than my government's. A fight was the last thing the monarchy needed at the moment. I took a step forward anyway. I was tired of being chained by protocol and politics.

"No way, poor boy." Brex hauled me back, handing me off to Norris and jumping into my place as soon as he had a firmer hold on me.

He shouldn't be involved either, but that didn't stop him. He was in the fray before Norris had me out the door. At soon as we stepped—or rather Norris dragged us—into the cool, night air, I jerked away. "I don't need a babysitter."

"You could have fooled me," Norris grumbled. He brushed a few wrinkles from his jacket, not bothering to hide his disappointment.

So Norris was disappointed in me. What was new? That seemed to be his perpetual state of being these days. There was a time when our relationship had felt like that of a father and son. Or what I thought that relationship should be like. Lately, it felt too much like my relationship with my true father. How could I explain to Norris that the responsibility, the endless politics, the constant scrutiny was drowning me? Or that when it came to what mattered most I was powerless to act?

"I wouldn't have hit anyone," I said, hoping that it was true while wishing I could hit someone. One person in particular.

Brex appeared, nursing bloody knuckles and not bothering to hide how he felt about the situation. "How are we going to explain why you got involved with this?"

"I wasn't involved," I exploded.

"Simply being there involved you," Brex shot

back, taking a step closer to me. "I knew this was a bad idea. What happens around you..."

"I'm in charge of the fucking country. There is no separation between man and state. Am I just supposed to sit at home on a throne and not get involved?"

"No one is saying that." Norris was infuriatingly calm, as usual.

"Maybe," Brex ignored him, "if it means you can keep your hands to yourself."

"When did everyone else get to call the shots?"

"When you stopped being able to," Brex said.

My fist flew before Norris could step between us. If Brex had any reservations about me getting into a fight, he forgot them. Knuckles made hard contact with my jaw with a loud crack. Within seconds we were on the ground. I didn't know if I'd brought him down or if it was the other way around. For the moment, we were both giving it everything we had. A fist jabbed my kidneys and I groaned, shoving Brex off and leaping on top of him.

We were too much for Norris to take on alone. This would probably be the last time I was allowed out without a full security compliment. He seemed to take a while to break us up. He probably wished he could be the one pounding my head into the pavement. In the end, Norris got hold of me and someone else pulled Brex away. We glared at each other. Blood leaked from a cut into my eye and I wiped it away, turning my attention to the other party.

Anderson fucking Stone. My knight in shining armour. I had no idea why he'd stepped in. This was what he wanted—to prove to Clara that I was a fuck up.

"Everything okay?" Anders asked. He had pulled Brex off while Norris barely contained me. His own nose was bleeding, but he didn't seem to notice.

"Brilliant," I grunted, pulling free of Norris. My shirt was covered in dirt, I'd just been caught brawling with my friend, and I didn't give one fuck. I levelled a glare at Anders. This had started with him. If he'd had the decency to live a nice quiet life, none of us would be here now. Instead, he'd unwittingly placed himself into the spotlight.

"We should be going," Norris urged in a low voice.

"What is your problem?" Anders asked.

Brex laughed, spitting a wad of bloody saliva on the dirt. He knew exactly what my problem was.

"You." I growled at him.

"You should get him out of here," Anderson said, taking a step away. "Before someone sees."

Hate rolled through me. He didn't get to play at being in charge. "You don't presume to order me around!"

"Maybe someone should." Anderson moved closer to me, getting in my face. Neither Brex nor Norris tried to stop him. There seemed to be an unspoken agreement. Anders might not know he was my brother, but he was a member of the royal family.

Whatever was about to go down, they shouldn't intercede in a family matter.

"What does that mean?" I asked.

"You order them around. You order Clara around. It might do you good to be on the receiving end."

"Do you think you know her? Because whatever fantasy you've concocted in your head. She is my wife. She belongs to me."

"Belongs?" he repeated with wide eyes. "I shouldn't expect any better from someone like you. But Christ, do you hear yourself?"

"Stay away from her." I jabbed a finger into his chest, knocking him back a few inches.

"Clara might put up with that—and God knows why—but I won't. I don't care who you are," he warned me.

"You should."

Brex moved behind him, waiting for one us to move. Apparently, there was a line they wouldn't allow either of us to cross. I turned away, keeping my fists at my sides. "I'll see you around."

Anders shook his head as he strode back to the pub. "I'm looking forward to it."

CHAPTER EIGHTEEN

ALEXANDER

By the time we reached the house, I already regretted what had happened. Mostly, because I hadn't gotten in a few more drinks before the fight. Now I was sober, bruised, bleeding, and I had to face my wife. No one had spoken on the ride back, but Brex stopped me at the door.

"I'll tender my resignation in the morning." He didn't meet my eyes as he spoke. I wasn't certain what I'd find if he did. Hatred? Shame?

"Why would you do that?" I asked him in a rough voice.

"It's generally poor form to hit the person you're protecting," he said.

"I didn't ask you out tonight as my bodyguard. I asked you as my friend."

He snorted and I thought I saw the edge of a smile, but he held it back. "I feel I should tell you it's poor form to hit your friends, too."

"Not if they deserve it," I told him. "But to be clear, I'm still pissed at you."

"That makes two of us."

"But you're not resigning." As far as I was concerned, that was the final word on that.

I made my way to the kitchen, grabbing a bag of frozen peas for my hand and digging a bottle of Scotch from the cupboard. Norris slid me a glass. He still hadn't spoken.

"Care to get one more shot in?" I asked him, pouring a drink. I slid him the glass and took a swig out of the bottle. It burned down my throat, a reminder I'd made my own hell.

"I think you'll get yours soon enough." He sounded tired. If I had to put up with me, I would be, too.

"Time to face the firing squad." I took another long drag from the bottle and abandoned it on the counter.

Neither of them followed me into the west wing of the house. With any luck, Clara would be asleep. Not that facing this in the morning would be any better. I had no hope that word of my indiscretion wouldn't spread through Silverstone by morning. I had no idea who had seen, and I couldn't imagine that Anderson would keep my secret. Not when he so clearly wanted me out of the picture.

If only he knew what I'd given him. An opportunity for a normal life. Yet, he was here rubbing that sacrifice in my face. It was unfair to judge him for it.

He didn't know better. But that didn't stop me from hating him.

Clara sat up in bed the moment the door opened, rubbing her eyes.

"X?" she called out.

Busted.

"Go back to sleep," I said in a low voice.

She was already flipping on the bedside lamp. Her eyes landed on me, taking in my sloppy appearance. Dirty shirt. Bruised face. She zeroed in on the cut still oozing blood on my eyebrow. So much for putting this off until morning.

"What happened?" The question was full of awe and a fair bit of righteous anger. She was giving me the courtesy of not jumping to conclusions, although she clearly had.

"The guys and I went to grab a drink." That was true. I wasn't lying to her. I was just leaving some things out.

"The guys and you went to grab a drink?" She repeated as though I had been speaking another language. "*The guys and you went to grab a drink?*"

"That's what I said." I made my way to the bathroom and flinched when I saw my face in the mirror. No wonder Clara was upset. Soft footsteps padded across the floor and she appeared behind me. She took one more look at me, sighed in frustration, and started opening drawers. She slammed them shut, until she landed on one that held first-aid supplies.

"Your hands," she said in a strangled voice.

"I had a little accident," I told her.

"With someone's fist?" she guessed. It wasn't exactly hard to deduce. Scotch on my breath, bloody knuckles, and dirty clothes—the evidence was there.

"Brex."

She relaxed a little. It was probably better news than she was hoping for, given my state. At least I'd been pounding on a friend. "How does he look?"

"He's still pretty if that's what you're asking," I said, sucking in a breath as she doused my knuckles with rubbing alcohol.

"That's going to hurt," she said flatly.

"Thanks for the warning."

She reached up and took my chin, moving my head from side to side to check me out.

"Did anyone see this fight?"

I shrugged.

"Alexander Cambridge," she said, no longer holding back her fury. "You are the King of England. Did anyone see this fight?"

"It's hard to say." I plastered my most charming smile on my face, but the expression on hers didn't change. "A lot of people were fighting."

She dropped her head into her hands, shaking it slowly. "And you're worried about me being out in public."

Fury rolled off her in waves. I could swear that if I reached out I would feel its heat. I followed her—at a safe distance—into the bedroom. She strode across it, going for her phone. It'd become instinct to check the news. That was what Norris would be doing. Perhaps Brex, too. I stopped her before she reached it.

"This is under control," I told her.

"If you believe that, then you're more out-of-control than I thought," she said. "Where did this happen?" If she couldn't look up the details, she'd get them from the source.

"A pub," I said in an offhanded way. Her eyes narrowed as she connected the dots.

"Would it have been the Dark Horse by any chance?"

"I thought you weren't interested in his offer," I said through gritted teeth. The fact she remembered the name of the pub told me she'd been paying attention.

"You're unbelievable." She smacked my chest. "You show up here with bloody knuckles, fresh from a bar fight, and you have the nerve to act like I did something wrong."

She had a point.

"This one's on me," I admitted.

"This is going to be a mess."

"Nothing I can't handle."

"Why did you come here?" she asked.

"I missed you," I said.

"The real reason, X."

So she wasn't buying it. I tried to imagine the mental gymnastics she was going through, trying to figure out what was going on in my head. I reminded myself that now wasn't the time to tell her. She had enough on her plate. Now she not only had to worry about hosting the games, she had to think about what would happen if the media got ahold of this story.

I was cocking things up left and right.

"I came for you," I repeated gruffly. Advancing on her, I pushed her against the wall. That part was true. How could she question that? Clara ducked out from underneath my arms and put a healthy distance between us.

"Are you testing me? Because that doesn't seem like a very good idea."

I made my way closer, prowling like a panther across the room. She knew better than to expect me to heed her warning. In fact, I thought that might be the point. Of course, that could also be the Scotch thinking. I caught Clara in my arms and lifted her off her feet. Taking her to the bed, I dropped her on it, recalling how the previous evening we'd made love. That wasn't what I wanted now. I wanted to possess her.

"This isn't going to change anything," she breathed as I pounced on top of her.

I bit down on her shoulder, pushing aside the strap of her nightdress while I reached down and undid my fly.

"Believe me, Poppet, I know that." Shoving up the gown, I pushed inside her with the one thrust. Clara let out a breathy cry, her fingers sinking into my back, raking across the fabric of my shirt, as I began to pound inside her. I needed to make her mine. I needed to remind her that she belonged to me. No one would question that. Not even her. She panted, groaning with every sharp jab of my hips. My hands sought hers, lifting them over her head and pinning her against the mattress until she was helpless beneath me. A strangled moan spilled from her, releasing me and I came with a violent shuttering burst. A moment of relief quickly swallowed by regret. I stared down at her, but there were no tears in her eyes tonight. Instead, they were full of challenge. The flush of satisfaction on her cheeks deepened into a furious red.

"Clara, I..." But I could find no words. I lowered my mouth, needing to make this okay. Needing to show her that I was sorry. But before our lips met, she whispered one word.

"Brimstone."

My reaction was instantaneous—involuntary. My hands released hers and I recoiled, falling back onto the bed, and staring at her. Why had she let me take it that far? How had she felt? I was a monster. She sat up, pulling the straps of her nightgown up to cover her breasts which had spilled over.

"What is this about?" she demanded.

"I was drinking," I said, trying to find the right words to apologize. "I don't know what's wrong with me."

"You're lying," she accused. Before I could respond, she continued quickly, "I know you're lying.

I've known you were lying—for weeks. I thought you would tell me the truth. I thought if I gave you space." She pushed off the bed and made her way across the room, disappearing into the closet.

"It's complicated," I called after her. Where was she planning to go at this hour? I couldn't stop her from leaving, not after she'd used her safe word. That was the deal—the one promise I would never breach. If only I'd been able to keep myself from crossing other boundaries.

"It really isn't." She stuck her head out the door. When she reappeared, she was carrying my bag.

"I think it's time to go," she said.

"I'm glad you agree. We should go back to London. We can work this out. Away from all of this—"

"No," she said firmly. "You should go back to London."

"Clara, I'm not leaving you here."

"You don't have a choice. I'm staying. You're going. End of discussion."

I opened my mouth to argue with her, but I didn't get another word out before she threw my bag at my feet.

"Get out," she repeated before she turned and walked into the bathroom. The lock clicked behind her.

I hadn't brought much with me to Silverstone. I'd only planned to stay a few days, so it only took me a few minutes to pack up my belongings. Clara didn't reappear. I paused at the door, considering my options. Part of me wanted to knock. Another part of me was willing to plead with her to see my side of things. The other part of me wanted to break down the door and drag her out. I couldn't allow myself to do any of those things. Not when she'd made her wishes so clearly known. Instead, I listened for a moment until I was certain that she wasn't crying and then I made my way downstairs.

Brex and Norris were still sitting in the kitchen. Norris hadn't touched the glass of Scotch I'd poured for him before I left. I raised an eyebrow. Brex blinked rapidly. He had clearly thrown a few back.

"We thought you might be needing us?" Norris said. He'd known exactly what was about to happen.

"Plus, it sounded like the house was about to come down. You two were so loud." Brex finished his glass and poured himself another.

"If you're going to keep drinking, call Georgia and let her know she's on point tonight," I barked at him.

Brex sat back, took one look at me, and took another drink.

"I'm quite capable of handling matters," Norris began, but I held up a hand.

"We're heading back to London." I didn't explain further. I didn't have to. If either of them were surprised, neither showed it.

"I'll let Georgia know," Brex said. "Any other instructions?"

"Keep an eye on her," I ordered him, opening the door that lead to the garage. "Make sure no one gets too close to her."

"Is that all?" he asked.

"No, keep an eye on him, too."

CHAPTER NINETEEN

CLARA

I avoided my mobile when I woke up and focused on damage control. My eyes were swollen and puffy from crying, I had no appetite, and sadness had shifted to righteous indignation overnight. I wasn't hurt anymore. I was furious. I'd worked my anger into apoplectic levels by the time I was dressed.

Checking in, I found Penny changing Elizabeth. My heart sank and I tried to ignore its traitorous plunge. I'd told Alexander to leave, so I couldn't be disappointed that he had. I wasn't certain what I would have done if I'd found he'd stayed. Still, it seemed like his husband barometer was off. He had a tendency to leave when he should stay and fight. Or ignore me when I needed him to listen.

Penny handed Elizabeth to me, her eyes sweeping over me. "I thought His Majesty might be here this morning."

"He had to leave for London." I forced a brittle smile.

"I thought he might," she said in an offhanded way.

My blood ran cold, and I clutched Elizabeth so tightly that she squawked in protest. "Why would you think that?"

Penny turned a shade of scarlet darker than her hair. "No reason, ma'am. It's just that I saw something on the news."

I didn't have to ask what she'd seen on the news, because I had a damn good idea what it was.

"Penny," I said in a strangled voice, "we have a race today, so I think it's best if Elizabeth stays here. It will be too loud there and I know I'll be distracted. I'll check in this afternoon and I'll have my phone."

"Of course." She sounded relieved that I wasn't going to press her for answers.

I excused myself and grabbed my phone. There were dozens of notifications, but I didn't bother to check any of them. Instead I went straight to trending news. There he was.

Alexander thought no one would single him out last night, but he was wrong. Someone had gotten a photo. It had gone viral.

I didn't have the stamina to deal with the fallout from this as well as my duties to the games. Alexander didn't want to tell me the truth, which meant this wasn't my problem. The trouble was that no matter how hard I tried to sell myself on that, I couldn't. I'd signed up to deal with all his troubles when we'd gotten married. I was pretty sure whatever was going on still fell under the whole 'for better or for worse' thing.

Choosing not to respond, I went downstairs and forced myself to eat some toast. I had no idea if my queasy stomach was from morning sickness or stress. But I needed to eat, so I stuck with something I could keep down. Brex joined me in the kitchen and eyed my toast without comment.

I slammed a cabinet door and he winced, rubbing his temples gingerly. It looked like he had a hangover. I didn't bother to ask him what had caused it. I knew exactly where it had come from. Instead, I kept my commentary to a disapproving scowl until we reached the track. Brex continued alongside me, but I turned on him.

"I think I'd rather have Georgia with me today." It wasn't his fault he'd gotten into a fight with Alexander. I imagined my husband deserved it. Hell, I probably would have sided with Brex. But I suspected the fight has started over whatever Alexander was hiding. If that was the case, then Alexander trusted him more than me. I couldn't stomach the idea. It didn't matter how long they'd been friends. I was his wife.

And the fact that Brex might know tempted me to bring it up. Would he tell me if I asked? That wasn't how I wanted to find out.

Brexton didn't argue with me. Instead, he waved Georgia over. She appeared, studying her nails. The perk of having her beside me was that she blended into the crowd more easily. She didn't feel the need to wear the stock uniform of the rest of the bodyguards. There were no suits. No ties. Her hair hid whatever earpiece I assumed she wore. Instead, she was dressed down in jeans and a leather jacket. It was a bit more casual than my wool peacoat and skinny black trousers, but next to each other we looked like friends. We were about the same age. It wouldn't be a stretch. But we weren't friends, and I couldn't imagine a scenario in which we would be. For a moment, I recalled the first moment I saw her. It seemed like a million years ago. Maybe I should've paid more attention to her then. Maybe I wouldn't be in this mess now.

"I need to make a few calls," I said to her. She followed me while I looked for an empty office and didn't argue when I went inside and told her I'd be a few minutes. The fact was that I'd woken up to half a dozen text messages from pretty much anyone who had my direct number. It wasn't just my friends wanting an explanation, it was the world. I'd start with my friends.

I bypassed my mother's calls. I didn't have the strength of character to deal with her right now. Then I went up the list in ascending order, starting from the person I assumed would demand the least amount of time. Lola answered on the first ring.

"Need a publicist?" she asked.

I sighed and shook my head. It was just like my

sister to switch to business mode. Alexander would have probably been better served with her as his wife. At least she would know how to deal with it when he fucked things up. "I'm sure there's a half dozen or so sorting this out right now."

"Need to talk?"

"No, I have to call everyone before people start coming down here and demanding answers," I said. I appreciated the offer, but my sister and I had never been close. We got along. We just weren't tight. Lola didn't press me for more information. At least one member of my family seemed to respect my privacy. I hung up with her and I called the next person on my list. Belle was spitting angry when she answered. "He's really lost it, hasn't he?"

"You have no idea," I said with a sigh.

"What happened?"

I filled her in on the little details I knew. By the end, she was even more angry.

"Maybe you should go to London, grab him by the bollocks, and explain that if he ever does anything that stupid, he's never shagging you again."

"I don't think that's the answer," I said dryly.

"Powerful men only respond to threats," she advised me.

"You think I haven't threatened him?" I whispered, afraid my voice would break.

"Oh, Clara. I'm sorry. Do you want me to come out there? Smith won't mind."

Belle knew what these games meant to me. But I

couldn't stand the pitying tone of her voice. I didn't need one more person in my life to coddle me. I also wasn't certain I could face her.

"No, I can handle it," I told her. "But I should go. I need to call Edward."

"Okay, but call me back. And let me know if you need backup."

I knew that offer always stood. Belle would be there without question the moment I asked her. But she had her own responsibilities now. I had to sort this mess out on my own.

Before I could call him, Edward called me. He was the person I most needed to talk to because he knew Alexander in a way that even I didn't. They were brothers. They had shared the same past and the same tragedies. He was my last hope of getting answers if Alexander wouldn't give them to me himself.

"How are you holding up?" he asked.

"Terribly." I didn't feel the need to lie to him. There was no point in hiding from everyone. Someone had to be on my side. Someone who could still be sympathetic to Alexander and mad at him at the same time. Belle didn't have that capacity. She was clearly Team Clara. Lola didn't know him. Edward was all I had. "What's going on with him, Edward?"

There was silence on the other end.

"Do you know? He's keeping something from me," I pressed him. If Edward knew, he had to tell me. I wanted to believe he would. Maybe it was asking too much of him to confide in me if he did.

"I don't know," he said at last, dashing my last hope. "But I've been looking into it."

It was relief to hear that I wasn't the only one who thought something was wrong. I wished it was more. "He's been acting oddly for weeks. I don't think it's just the attack. There's more to it."

"I think so, too. But I promise you, Clara, he hasn't told me anything."

"I figured," I said, slumping against the desk.

"What are you going to do?" he asked me after a few seconds of silence.

"You know what they say," I said through gritted teeth, "the games must go on."

The Games *were* going on, as it turned out. Despite my husband's faux pas, nearly everyone at Silverstone acted like nothing had happened. I suspected they had been briefed on how to approach me. But I knew that outside the security perimeter, the press would hold no such reservations. They owed nothing to me or my family as far as I could tell. They'd certainly never showed me a shred of decency when it came to my personal life. I managed to steer clear of Anders for the day. I could only imagine what he thought about Alexander's behavior. There was no way he hadn't heard about it. It was plastered over every news source in the world. Even with tonight's upcoming race, he would know. He hadn't hidden his concerns about my marriage. What must he think now?

And that was the problem. What must they all think? Somehow, it seemed less important than what I thought. Or what I felt. I'd kicked him out. I'd turned my back on him—something I had promised never to do. But Alexander had promised me no more secrets. We were supposed to be in this together and he had breached that contract. I was his wife—his partner—but I was not his welcome mat. He couldn't walk all over me and expect me not to fight back.

"Do we have a problem?" Henry asked in a low voice when he found me mid-afternoon.

"Do we?" I asked in a weary voice. I couldn't be entirely certain if we had the same problem, but I didn't want to call attention to my problems with Alexander.

"Anders has a black eye and my nephew is all over the news."

Alexander hadn't mentioned Anders last night. My anger, which had been simmering since he came home, boiled into a seething rage. That's what this was about? His stupid, unwarranted jealousy? Even if Anders had a thing for me, which I seriously doubted, why would it matter? I loved Alexander. He knew that. Or I thought he did. Nothing seemed clear anymore.

"I don't think they were fighting." Not physically, at least. Unless Alexander had simply left that part of the story out.

"It doesn't look good, though." Henry exhaled heavily then offered a weak smile. "I'm sorry to bother you with this. I'm certain, you have enough concerns."

Like my out-of-control husband and a fresh scandal to maneuver? "It is my responsibility when it involves my family."

"Your family?" Henry scratched his chin for a moment.

"Alexander," I said slowly. "His behavior is my concern."

"Ahhh." He nodded as if this now made sense. "But it is not your responsibility. Don't confuse the two."

When I spotted Anders a few minutes before the race, I fixated on his black eye. How the papers hadn't picked that fact up, I didn't know. But it was obvious to me now what had happened.

That was why Alexander had wanted me to leave with him. It hadn't been a simple fight with Brex. Anders had been involved. Now I understood. Maybe Alexander saw Anders's invitations as crossing a line. Maybe his paranoia had finally warped his brain. I had to face facts. Alexander believed Anders was a threat to our marriage. It hurt he would believe that. It didn't matter that Anders was only a friend. Alexander should have taken me at my word. Why couldn't he trust that things were innocent? Why did he always have to jump to irrational anger?

Henry found me as the announcers began their commentary. This afternoon, we'd be in a box. I was grateful I didn't have to face Anders on the track. I would apologize for Alexander's actions. But no excuse I could come up with would make up for the fact Anders was right about Alexander. He was controlling. Maybe he did need to be taught a lesson.

"You're awfully quiet," Henry said. A dozen or so other people were in the box to watch the race, but I found a quiet spot by the window so I could be alone with my thoughts. "Will Alexander be joining us this evening?"

It hadn't occurred to me that others might notice my husband's absence or expect him to be here. "I forgot to mention that he left for London this morning. He couldn't stay."

"That was probably wise." He gave me an appraising look as if to ascertain how I felt about it.

"I thought so," I said pointedly.

"He has my brother's temper," Henry said, his words full of regret. He placed one hand over mine on the railing. "Albert was a hard man to love. Elizabeth always told me that."

My eyes flashed to his, searching them as though they might hold answers. "Albert talked about her like their marriage was perfect."

Henry loosed a low laugh and shook his head. "Their marriage was like any other marriage, except more demanding. Liz felt stifled by him at times, crushed. In the end, their love became more about duty than genuine affection."

"I've never heard anyone call her Liz before. Not even your brother."

"We were close—united by our love for Albert as well as our concern for him. We were a two-person support group. Not unlike you and Edward, it seems. Liz needed allies. I imagine you will, too. She told me once that it was impossible to love a king, because she loved Albert as an equal and he saw her as a subject."

My throat closed at his words, tears threatening to give away my own fears. Albert had told me once that Elizabeth had understood her duty. I thought that meant she was obedient. Now, I realized it was a warning. She had been expected to fall into line. I would be expected to as well.

"I don't know what's going on anymore," I admitted. "Alexander's changing and..."

"It scares you?" Henry guessed.

I nodded, my eyes on the track as the cars began to fly across the pavement. I hadn't even realized the race was starting. I owed myself more than this, allowing myself to be distracted from the work I'd chosen by Alexander's behavior. "I don't even know where things have gone wrong. It wasn't supposed to be like this."

"The course of true love never did run smooth." Henry squeezed my hand.

"Shakespeare could do a lot with this story," I muttered.

"He could do a lot with this family," Henry said conspiratorially. "If there's anything that I can do..."

He left the offer hanging. I wanted to trust him—to open up to him—but something held me back. He was still Mary's son. Albert's brother. But wasn't that the problem with this family? Everyone believing that everyone else was beholden to a destructive pattern of behavior—their entire lives choreographed for them from birth. Alexander and Edward had tried to change that. Didn't I owe it to all of them to push them harder in that direction? What other way would things finally change?

"He seemed on edge here," Henry noted. "It made me wonder if..."

I waited, wanting to finish the sentence. "Wonder what?" I pressed.

"But it would be impossible." He shook his head, muttering to himself. "How would he have found out?"

"Henry," I said, trying to draw his attention back to me. "What is it?"

His pale blue eyes turned to me and stared through me. He looked so much like his brother, but the tentativeness on his face was his own. "It's just that if Alexander knew that—"

A metallic roar shook the glass windows. Everyone in the box flooded toward us. I pressed to the glass, panic crashing through me. This time it wasn't a bumper that had been clipped. A car had flipped over, landing upside down on the track. My stomach turned at the sight, my body remembering the accident I had tried to forget. I clutched it, willing my food to stay down and felt an unmistakable flutter. I held the place where my child grew protectively, feeling as helpless to keep him safe as I did to help now. Teams rushed onto the track, followed by paramedics, battling through the smoke pouring from the wreckage. Every second seemed to last an hour, and I couldn't turn away from the number displayed prominently on the car's backend. I'd never remember every driver's number, but there was one I wouldn't forget.

Anderson Stone made an impression.

CHAPTER TWENTY

CLARA

Anders' car looked like a crumpled tin can. From a distance, it was impossibly small, less than half the size it was supposed to be. No matter how much I stared, the whole scene was surreal. The only thing that seemed to make sense was that this was not simply an accident.

Next to me, Henry had gone into crisis mode, but I couldn't process what he was saying. It wasn't until he touched my arm that I even realized he was speaking.

"They're going to have to cut off the doors to get to him," he said. "They've ordered the other drivers into the pit."

Henry's words stuck in the cloud that fogged my brain. Was this how Alexander felt after arriving to my accident? Because I felt helpless, like nothing I could do would matter.

Then I remembered I wasn't powerless. I was the

most powerful woman in the country. I snapped out of my daze, my eyes scanning the room for Brex and Georgia.

"Brexton," I called when I spotted him. "Send our teams to clear the streets. I want emergency vehicles to be able to get through quickly."

"They'll probably need to bring in a helicopter," Henry said softly.

I nodded, but this time I said what I was thinking. "Other people will still need to get to the hospital. See if his family's here. He said his mother was coming, make sure she can get to him quickly."

Brex reached me first and lowered his voice. "This is not really our job."

"It is now." He was accustomed to taking orders from Alexander. It was time he learned to take them from me. "Once you've gotten everyone going, let's get the car and head to the hospital."

"I think it would be better—" Brex began as Georgia joined us.

"That's an order," I said, leaving no room for further discussion. Brex looked like he was struggling to follow my command but Georgia yanked him away.

Amidst the chaos around me, my mind strayed to Alexander and to my own car crash. I tried to remind myself this was different. I didn't know how fast Anders had been going, but it had been fast enough to destroy half of his car.

I'd been too distracted to see what had led to the

crash. Henry filled me in on the way to the hospital. I listened without speaking as Brex navigated us through the streets. My eyes on the empty streets that we'd cleared. The drive there felt like its own race, but one that had life and death stakes.

Another driver had lost control while going around the corner heading into the straight. When that car began to spin out, it crossed in front of Anders. This left Anders with two choices: he could let the other car slam him into the wall, or he could try to cut inside the other car, even though he was going too fast to turn that sharply. In the end, Anders waited too long. By the time he tried to cut inside, he could no longer avoid clipping the other car. As soon as he hit it, his car went airborne and tumbled nearly a quarter mile down the straight.

I couldn't bring myself to ask if he would survive.

Everyone around discussed details as they came, but I blocked them out. If he wasn't going to make it, I didn't want to know. I'd told Alexander he'd been worried needlessly, but now I realized how dangerous these games were.

What was Anders doing racing cars? He was playing with fire. That wasn't what the Sovereign games were supposed to be about. It was supposed to be about bringing people together, not destroying lives. All the belief I had in the good I was doing drained away. If Anders died, it would be my fault. *I* had pushed the games to go on.

The waiting room was packed, full of Anders'

team and other drivers. We'd halted the race. It made me sick to know that usually a race would continue, even if someone's life hung in the balance. But no one here appeared unshaken by the tragic turn in tonight's event. Everywhere I looked, heads were huddled and people were speaking in hushed voices.

Henry had tried to convince me to go to a private area, but it felt wrong somehow. I'd spent the last few weeks getting to know these guys. My place was here. Henry had kept up a steady stream of conversation, no doubt in a bid to distract me. I hadn't heard any of it until he called across the room. "Rachel!"

I looked up to see who he was talking about and caught sight of an older woman with sandy blonde hair. My heart plummeted into my stomach. She was slight, not nearly as tall as her son, but the terror on her face gave her away. It was Anders' mother. It had to be.

I didn't know what to say as Henry introduced us. Rachel took my hand, hers shaking slightly, and shook it.

"It's an honor to meet you," she said, her voice hollow. She was going through the motions, her mind elsewhere. I couldn't blame her. If it was my child I wouldn't be able to think straight, let alone politely introduce myself to someone.

"Rachel used to work in the household," Henry said as he placed a comforting arm around her shoulders and drew her close.

I didn't know what to say. She was going through

her worst nightmare and Henry was taking a trip down memory lane. I wanted to offer her some solace. Although Henry might be right by distracting her. "You worked for Elizabeth?"

"Yes, before she died," she said. "It was a long time ago. I didn't think anyone remembered me."

"Nonsense. You must be so proud of your son. When I saw his name in our files, I knew it must be him."

"I was thrilled when he was asked to participate," she said, managing a difficult smile. "But I've been avoiding the track. It makes me nervous."

"He's going to be okay!" I blurted out and instantly regretted it.

Rachel shook her head and then nodded. "I know you're right. These things happen. It's not the first time he's crashed."

"It isn't?"

"Oh heavens, no. I should have more faith. He's a good driver." A small sob rose through her body. "It's just that he's all I have. Look at me," she said, dabbing her eyes. "Anders would be so upset if he saw me raising such a fuss. You can't mention I did."

"Of course, I won't, I promise." It was the least I could do. "It's my fault he's here. I wanted the games." It slipped from my mouth thoughtlessly, but Rachel grabbed my hand, shaking her head vehemently.

"Don't think that. He would've been racing somewhere. It's in his blood."

"I imagine he does take after his father. Todd was always a daredevil," Henry said. He looked over her shoulder to answer my questioning look.

"We served together when we were younger," Henry explained. So, like most Royals, Henry had been a member of the armed forces. "I've been telling Anders stories about what his dad was like before he was born."

"Before he died," Rachel added quietly. My heart broke all over for her. I hoped she was right and the accident wasn't that bad. The problem was I had seen it, and it did look that bad. I would do everything in my power to make certain Anders walked out of here.

Then I would try to knock some sense into him. He had no business racing if he was the only family his mother had left. Why hadn't Henry told me this? I'd been too preoccupied with Alexander's misplaced jealousy to learn about Anders' past. I made a mental note to ask Henry for details later.

A doctor walked into the room, pulling a mask from his face. He looked tired, worn down by years of delivering bad news. Instantly everyone was on their feet, crowding him.

"Just a moment. Where's his mother? Rachel?"

She took a tentative step forward, a path clearing between her and the doctor.

He smiled reassuringly, and I felt a wave of relief wash over me. "It's not too bad. A broken arm and a couple broken ribs. Nothing we haven't seen before with him," he said with a smile.

Rachel flung her arms around his shoulders and hugged him tightly. "Thank you, Dr. Wilson."

All around us everyone cheered. They might've been through this before, but I imagined it was always a relief to get good news. I wondered for a dark moment what it would be like to get bad news. How many more times would Anders' mother wait for Dr. Wilson to deliver it?

"He's resting comfortably. I want to limit visitors for now. But he's asking to see you."

He dropped an arm around her shoulder and leaned in to whisper something. Rachel started and then turned to look directly at me. She said something to Dr. Wilson, and he nodded. I chewed on my lower lip, suddenly wishing I hadn't come here. A nurse took Rachel through a set of double doors and she disappeared down a long corridor. Dr. Wilson rounded and scanned the room. When his eyes landed on me, he did a double take.

He came over and spoke in a low voice, "Anders asked to see Clara. His mother assumes he means, um, you."

My head tilted, trying to puzzle out why I would be the person he wanted to see right now. "He's probably worried about the games, but he shouldn't be. We can talk later. Maybe he wants to talk to his team?"

"He was quite adamant he needed to speak with Clara. Is there a Clara on his team?" Dr. Wilson asked with the delicacy of a doctor delivering bad news.

"No." My mouth felt like I'd swallowed a handful of cotton balls.

"Then would you speak to him?"

I couldn't speak past my dry tongue so I tipped my head in quick agreement, hoping no one had seen this exchange.

"This way." He led me through the double doors to a recovery room.

I froze at the door, my eyes falling on Anders and his mom talking. She was hovering over him, brushing hair from his eyes and shaking her head as she spoke. Anders replied and she pulled back sharply.

"Your Majesty?" Dr. Wilson prompted, his hand on the door handle.

"I'll wait," I choked out. I had no business here, no matter what he'd asked. This was a private family moment. Any business I had with Anders could wait. I was about to ask Dr. Wilson to relay this message when Rachel came bursting out the door.

She halted in her tracks and gave me a long, appraising look.

"He wants to talk to you," she said flatly. She didn't wait for a response.

"I'll give you two some privacy," the doctor said before disappearing after her.

I took a deep breath, steeling myself to see him. But

the sight that greeted me wasn't that bad. There were bandages and a few cuts, but Anders was sitting up and alert. His face lit up when I entered the room, but when he tried to lean forward to beckon me in, he winced. His hand went to his torso, his face twisting in pain.

"Are you okay?" I rushed to his side, my eyes checking the monitors for signs of distress.

"I'm fine." He waved off my concern. "Broken rib or two."

"That doesn't sound fine." Guilt washed over me. Those broken ribs were my fault.

"I've had worse. Trust me."

"That accident. I can't believe that you're..."

"Alive?" A smirk carved over his face. "It takes more than bad luck to kill a Stone."

"Was that what it was?" I asked quietly.

A muscle twitched in his jaw before he finally shook his head. "No. It wasn't bad luck. I was distracted. This is my fault."

"No, it isn't," I said fiercely. I'd been right. His fight with Alexander, the last few days of tension were to blame. "Whatever was on your mind—"

"You," he cut me off. "You were on my mind."

"I know that Alexander showing up made things..." I struggled for the right words, trying to ignore the implications of his. He couldn't mean that.

"It wasn't him I was thinking about. It was you," he repeated. "I know so many things are cocked up right now, and this is the worst timing, but I can't pretend—"

"Don't," I stopped him. "Anders, you're confused."

"I may have a concussion," he said, pausing for a second to ruffle his hair. "Actually, I do have a concussion, but that isn't the point. I'm thinking clearly, Clara. I have been since the moment I met you and you're the only thing that's been on my mind. I can't stop thinking about you. I've fallen in love with you."

My mouth opened, but nothing came out. There was no way to defuse this situation. Someone was going to get hurt. Anders was going to get hurt and I was going to lose a friend.

"I know you're married," he said quickly, "and it may seem like it couldn't work, but—"

"It doesn't *seem*," I interrupted him before this got any worse, "It won't. You and I are friends. I care about you, but I love Alexander. I am in love with Alexander."

"You think you love him, but you're scared of him." His heart rate monitor jumped up. "He's not good for you."

I wanted to tell him he was wrong, but the problem was that in some ways he was right. I did love Alexander, but I didn't know if he was good for me anymore. All I could do was admit the truth. "He has always scared me," I said in a quiet voice. Anders went rigid and I went on before he got the wrong idea, "*Loving* him has always scared me. He's from a different world than we are. It's like loving the sun—dangerous, unknown—but impossible to deny."

"And likely to burn you," he muttered.

"I belong with him," I said. It was a simple fact. I wasn't certain of much anymore, but that was still true.

"He acts like you belong *to* him." Anders usually bright eyes darkened with hatred.

"And he belongs to me," I said wearily. "I need you to accept this. I am—and will always be—Alexander's."

"So you'll stay with him and let him push you around?" he asked harshly.

"I'll stay but you overestimate him. I make my own choices. I hope you can understand that."

Anders didn't say anything and after a few more moments of awkward silence I left him to his thoughts, wondering how we'd ever get past this.

Alexander had been right. I'd refused to see Anders' feelings for what they were. Now I'd hurt them both. I made my way back to the waiting room. I needed to talk to Henry. I needed to leave and sort out this mess. I needed to figure out where to start.

But when I got back, Rachel Stone intercepted me.

"Can I have a word with you?" she asked me.

Henry hesitated, his hand lightly touching my elbow. "Perhaps, it would be better if..."

"It will only be a moment."

"It's okay," I reassured him. Rachel stepped away and I followed her, my pulse ratcheting up.

"Is Anders okay?" I asked as soon as we were out of earshot. "If there is anything I can do..."

"There is. You can leave Silverstone." Her voice was cold. She was no longer a trembling, anxious mother but a lioness. She didn't fear me or my title. I didn't mind that, but what I couldn't understand is why she wanted me to go.

My brain spun on her words. "I can what?"

"Anders told me that he met someone, but I cannot believe—"

"I think you have the situation confused." I stopped her, aware we might have stepped to the side but that hardly made our conversation private. "He must have meant someone else."

"The last time my son was in an accident, he'd been dating a local girl for months. He didn't even call to tell her he'd been to hospital," she said harshly. "He's never asked for anyone but friends or me."

"I'm his friend." It was taking a lot of effort to remain calm with her voice so full of accusation. This was hitting too close to home after what Anders had said to me. "Nothing more. I can understand why you're upset, but—"

"You're married, which is only one of many good reasons for you to leave before this situation blows up in all of our faces—your husband's included."

"That sounds like a threat," I said coldly.

"A threat. A warning. Call it whatever you want. Just leave."

I took a deep breath and focused on finding the right words. She had just faced her worst nightmare, it was understandable she was lashing out. That didn't mean I had to just take it. I could, however, be understanding. "Let me talk to Henry. My family can—"

"Your family has done enough," she spit out. "We were happy. Anders was happy before you came into our life with Albert's self-indulgent games."

I could guess why she'd left the household. Her opinion of my late father-in-law didn't appear to be very high. "Your son chose to participate."

"Anders makes his own choices." She crossed her arms over her chest as if daring me to contradict her.

"So do I," I said defiantly.

She stopped and studied me for a moment. We stood there, weighing each other. Would either of us win this battle of wills? Probably not. Because we weren't fighting over what we wanted. I wanted to forget what Anders had told me and move forward. She wanted her son to forget me. But Anders was part of the games now and I doubted that either of us could convince him to quit. We were at an impasse. We were fighting different battles.

"Then make the right one," she said softly, lifting her fierce demeanor to reveal a vulnerability that made my heart ache. "Leave here before you break his heart."

Maybe she saw I was tired of being commanded. Maybe she saw I'd never wanted any of this to happen. It wasn't a demand anymore. It was a plea— mother to mother.

"I've seen the papers. Anders has said some things on the phone," she spoke hesitantly, waiting to see how I reacted. When I didn't bite her head off, she continued, "Your husband needs you. You should go to him. Go to your family. Leave me mine."

CHAPTER TWENTY-ONE

ALEXANDER

Clara wasn't answering her phone. The only information I'd received since the accident had routed through my people on the ground to my people here. At first I couldn't bring myself to watch the footage. Car crashes triggered me too severely. One accident had changed my life forever, another had shown me what was important. That was a lesson I'd clearly forgotten, because my brother had nearly died tonight without ever knowing the truth. I didn't know how to feel about that until I forced myself to watch the footage from Silverstone. Seeing it filled me with a white-hot rage that only Scotch could drown.

I was pouring myself another when Norris entered. He took in the glass without comment as he moved to the chair opposite mine. We sat for a moment, the only sound in the room the comforting crackle of the fire in the hearth. For some reason, despite its heat, I still felt cold.

"I assume you have something to tell me," I said when I grew tired of the silence, no matter how companionable it was. I swirled the amber liquid in the bottom of the glass, wondering if I would have a third.

"Have you spoken with her?" he asked.

"I'm drinking. What do you think?" I downed the remains of my drink and reached for the bottle.

"Will that help you cope with her absence?" Norris didn't move to stop me, although he probably should have. It didn't matter which one of us was the so-called ruler. Only one of us was being responsible at the moment.

"I'm not coping," I corrected him, continuing to pour. "I'm surviving."

"You might want to survive on one."

"This is my third." There was no point hiding it from him.

He frowned. "Stop at two then. Your wife is on her way home."

"Why didn't you lead with that?" I abandoned the Scotch and switched into crisis mode. The last time I saw Clara I'd been drinking. I didn't want her to come back and find me in the same state. Even though we'd been apart, I had actually been attending meetings and to business.

"I thought I'd give you the opportunity to do the

right thing for the right reasons." He shrugged. Norris hadn't pretended to approve of my choice when we'd left Silverstone, nor had he been happy to learn I still hadn't told my wife about my connection to Anderson Stone.

That was about to change.

"How long before she arrives?"

He considered for a moment, as if adding time and distance together. "Another hour or so."

"Call Edward and ask him to be here in two." I'd been delaying the inevitable. I couldn't risk avoiding the truth about Anderson any longer.

Norris's eyebrow curved into a question mark.

"It's time." I didn't need to say more. I would take an hour with my wife before I told her the truth. One hour to win her back before I risked losing her forever.

Her knock was tentative, so unlike her that I paused and studied the door that separated us. One slab of wood that stood between me and my whole life—me and my future. But it was more than a physical barrier, it was a choice. Once I opened that door I was committed to this path, and it wasn't going to be an easy one.

I turned the knob and made my decision.

Clara had turned but she stopped when the door opened, her back still to me. Her dark, glossy hair was piled messily on top of her head, as if she'd been in a hurry. She was wearing a t-shirt and loose, grey pants.

As she glanced over her shoulder, her face was pale and tired, but, Christ, was she beautiful. Her full lips trembled as if stuck on what to say. This wasn't the Queen of England. This was Clara Bishop. For a second, I saw her standing lost in a hallway on the day we met. She was in a club dressed in a t-shirt and jeans, looking irresistible as she said no to me. She was crying as I asked her to marry me. My life flashed before me in glimpses of her. She was the girl I'd fallen in love with despite swearing I'd never do so. She was the girl who'd stumbled into my life and changed everything. She was my beginning, my end, and every breath in between.

"Poppet," I murmured. I didn't care where we'd left things. She was here and that was all that mattered. I crossed to her, hesitating only a moment before I caught her hand and pulled her into me. She belonged to me—with me. But somehow that fact felt more fragile than before, as though one wrong word could shatter the bond between us.

She didn't resist but rather crumpled in my arms. Her body shook with silent sobs and I held her. It was torture having her so close, but resisting the urge to kiss her—to carry her away. I buried my face in her hair, breathing in her scent and reminded myself that she wouldn't walk away. We'd been through worse. We'd lived through it. We'd fought through it. Now it was time to fight again, not with each other, but *for* each other.

"X, I fucked up." She pulled back, her confession

trembling from her, and my heart stilled. Regret shadowed her grey eyes like storm clouds, and something
dark twisted inside me. She belonged to me. She
always would no matter what she'd done.

I thought I'd known what I had to lose, but seeing
her now, I realized that I'd pushed her away—forced
her to defy me and led her to another man. I hadn't
lost her. I'd taken her for granted. Maybe I didn't
deserve her at all.

"I'm s-s-sorry." She turned into me and clutched
my shirt, hiding her tears, but I felt them. I heard
them, even as she tried to stifle her anguish. It jolted
me to the present. I had taken her for granted, but I
could stop. I only had to make the choice.

I hooked my index finger under her chin and
directed her face to mine. "You don't apologize
to me."

"But I—" she began.

"Don't apologize for my mistakes. What has
happened was because of my choices. My mistakes
aren't your burdens. "

"Everything you are, I am," she breathed. Despite
the tears swimming in her eyes, they were full of fire.
We were a marriage of opposites. One gave meaning
to the other. "Your mistakes, your sins, your secrets..."

My breath hitched as she spoke. I had secrets—
we both knew it. But there was no demand in her
words now, only an offer. Or rather, a reminder. The
secrets I carried with me were no longer mine. They
were ours.

"I know," I promised her. How could I not? "You are my life. Always."

"I don't—" She shook her head, her fingers sinking into my chest as if trying to hang onto me.

"Nothing will change that," I said firmly and meant it. "Nothing."

"I should have listened," she said, "and now everything is ruined."

I sighed, wondering how she couldn't see what I could. "I don't want you to obey me."

She was still crying, but this earned me a rueful snort. "You could have fooled me, X."

"I love *you*. The you that is headstrong and reckless and opinionated and intelligent. Stop me if I'm rambling." I allowed a small smirk to sneak onto my face.

"You can keep going." She bit back a smile of her own.

I cupped her chin, brushing tears from her cheeks with my thumb. "You are everything I've always needed and more than I ever hoped for."

"Can I quote you on that the next time you're ordering me around?" There was a hopeful edge despite her sharp tone.

"I deserve that," I admitted. "Every day, I want to be better for you. I try, but I know that choosing me meant giving up a life you could have had and—"

"This is the only life I could ever want," she cut me off. "For better or worse, remember?"

"I do. Do you?" I didn't know what had brought

her here tonight. But I'd lived my life with secrets weighing on my soul. I wouldn't allow Clara to carry that same burden.

She hesitated, then tipped her head toward the office. She wanted privacy for what she needed to tell me. We'd been standing here, baring our souls. Whatever came next needed to be said behind closed doors. Blood roared in my ears as my heart pounded with panic. Nothing would change between us, even if...

I swallowed against the anxiety clawing its way from my chest to my throat. I thought I'd lost her before. I'd faced a world without her. In those moments, I'd operated automatically, allowing instinct to kick in and handle what my mind couldn't. But that wouldn't work today. I'd lied. I'd broken my vows to her. I'd sinned. Now the devil had come to collect.

"You were right," she said softly as I closed the door. "About Anders. About me and him. He's... he's..."

"In love with you," I finished for her. I'd seen it. I'd recognized it, because it had been like looking in a mirror. I had seen the love in his eyes—the eyes that looked like mine, but strangely not like our father's. Was it some trick of genetics? Or some strange, inexplicable magic? My father and his brother shared the same watery blue eyes that felt as infinite and unknowable as the sea. But Anders's eyes blazed like mine—the brightest tip of a flame. We were explosive, uncontrollable, and determined—and when we finally saw what we wanted, we couldn't hide it.

Clara perched on a chair and clasped her hands in her lap. She was waiting for me to say something more, but for once I knew I needed to listen. I took up a familiar circuit of the room, trying to focus the frenzy building inside me.

"He told me he loved me," she confirmed in a voice barely louder than a whisper.

"He does love you."

"He thinks he does," she corrected me.

"He does," I said flatly. I stopped in my tracks, only a few paces from her chair.

"I don't know why I let myself..."

"And?" I braced myself for the worst of it. She'd come here full of regret. There had to be more.

"And what?" She blinked rapidly, trying to process the question.

"What happened?"

"He told me he loved me," she repeated this like it was news. "He wanted...I'm not certain what he wanted."

I barked a laugh, my chest relaxing so I could breathe freely again.

"Are you laughing?" she asked in a strangely high-pitched voice. "A man I barely know thinks he's in love with me and I've spent the last two hours trying to figure out how to tell you that I somehow led him on, and *you're laughing*?"

I closed the short distance between us and sank to

my knees at her feet. "I can't fault a man for falling in love with you. I certainly can't fault you. Poppet, you have no control over how bewitching you are."

"He doesn't know me," she said, displaying the stubborn streak I loved.

"It doesn't take much. I fell in love with you the moment you warned me about the dangers of smoking."

"It took you long enough to tell me," she said dryly. I'd be righting that wrong for the rest of our lives. "So you aren't mad?"

"At you? No."

"I thought you couldn't blame Anders," she pointed out.

I pressed my lips into a thin line. "I can't blame him for feeling the way he does, but he shouldn't have told you."

It was going to make telling her the truth more difficult to bear. I propped my head on her knee. Now that I'd faced the firing squad, I felt a familiar desire taking root in me, but I fought it, knowing that I hadn't escaped danger entirely. There were other truths to confront tonight. My eyes flickered to the clock.

"Have somewhere to be?" she asked.

"Checking the time." I kissed her knee and she shivered. "I should look in on Elizabeth."

"She's asleep." Clara sighed and checked the time herself. "I sent Penny in with her. I didn't know how this would go."

"It's fine," I said, waving off her apology. Someday, my wife wouldn't feel the need to apologize to me for every goddamned choice she made. I would make sure of it. "I'll peek in on her later. Besides, that leaves me and you time."

Forty-five minutes to be exact, but I left that detail out. I couldn't be positive I'd seen to all her needs until I'd seen to all her needs—and I was determined to do that before I told her the truth. Waiting for Edward was important and a ready excuse to be selfish now.

"We could go to bed," she suggested.

"Too far." I shook my head. There wasn't time for a change of location and any horizontal surface would do—or vertical for that matter. Hell, no surface at all. I just needed my mouth on her. "I've been patient, but it's been forever since I tasted you."

"It's been *days*." Her words snagged as I pushed her legs apart and knelt between them.

"As I said: *forever*." I tugged at the waistband of her pants and caught the elastic of her underwear, urging her to lift her ass to accommodate my efforts. Pulling them off her, I chucked them to the side before reaching up and yanking her ass to the edge of the chair. My palms slid up her silky thighs and pushed them open wider. A fine covering of downy hair dusted her pretty cunt, but above me Clara looked away.

"I've been a little preoccupied and I haven't—"

"Don't apologize to me, Poppet," I reminded her.

There was no need. This was my favorite present. I didn't mind how it was wrapped. I was more interested in playing with what was inside. I brushed a finger down her weeping sex and she gasped. "I think it missed me, too."

Pushing between the folds, I massaged her with my thumb, relishing her soft wetness and the greedy way it swallowed my finger. Spreading her, I lowered until her taste danced across my tongue.

"Yes, please." A delicate hand grabbed ahold of my hair and tugged me closer.

"So demanding," I teased, still close enough to breathe her in, "but since you asked nicely."

"Oh...my...God..." she groaned as I caught her swollen clit between my teeth and sucked on it. I could stay here forever and listen to her make those noises—the sharp, breathy intakes, the loud, joyous moans and every sound in between. My cock could, too, judging by its hardness.

Clara's hips rose to buck against my mouth and I grabbed hold of her ass, rocking her against me, urging her toward release. Her muscles tightened and I clamped down, fucking her with unrelenting strokes as she fell apart. Her hands released me, clutching at the sides of the chair as she continued to grind against me through the last aftershocks of pleasure.

I pushed her back on the chair, blanketing her leg with kisses as I sat back on my heels and watched her eyes close and her body melt into the seat. She peeked down at me. Her cheeks were flushed and her eyes bright. I worshipped her. I needed her to see that so I slowly ran my tongue over my lower lip before bringing my fingers to my mouth and sucking her taste from them.

Her eyes clenched shut and she shook her head. When she finally spoke, her words were strangled but demanding. "Get off your knees."

"My place is at your feet." I meant that. If I could give up my crown and turn my back on the world, I would happily spend the rest of my life right here doing what I'd just done.

"Up, X." There was no room for argument.

I stood but before I could lean down to kiss her, she'd pushed out of the chair to kneel before me.

"Clara, you don't have to." That wasn't what this was about.

"I know that." She looked up at me with a wicked smile. "I want to, X, because this is my place." Her hand gripped my cock through my pants, stroking it, as the other worked to loosen my belt. I reached to help but she batted my hand away. The message was clear: she was claiming what was hers. When she pulled it free, she shoved my pants to my ankles and began to press hot kisses through my boxers until I was painfully hard. I fought the urge to lift her up and fuck her as she continued to tease. Instead I placed a steadying hand on her head. Clara seemed to understand that I was struggling to stay under control, because she finally drew down the last barrier between me and her sweet, little mouth. Her tongue met my shaft as I sprang free, drawing up it until her lips popped over the crest of my cock. I groaned as warm heat surrounded me and began to suck with lapping, thirsty draws.

"Fuck, Poppet," I ground out as she took me deeper with long, drawing pulls. "You are the most beautiful thing I've ever seen."

It was true. Clara was always beautiful, but there was something about the sight of her kneeling before me with my cock in her mouth that lit a flame inside me. As much as I was enjoying it—and I was fucking loving it—I needed to be inside her.

Still, it wasn't easy to pull away. Not with her eager mouth protesting. My erection bobbed in the cool air and I felt my balls ache. Reaching down, I guided her onto her feet.

"X," she said in a disapproving tone, but I stopped her objection with a kiss that effectively silenced any complaints. Clara dissolved into me and my hands slid down to knead her ass.

"Do you know why I love when you disobey me?" I asked against her mouth.

"Hmmm?" She was half here, half in a dream. I loved seeing her like this—undone and willing.

"Because it gives me an excuse to spank you." I smacked her ass with a hard thwack and she startled out of her daze. I winked as I rubbed the skin still hot from my palm. "I'm mostly kidding."

"I don't think you're kidding at all."

I raised an eyebrow. She might be right about

that. I was about to admit that, but her lips crushed against mine again. I allowed the kiss to deepen as I reached down and stroked my cock against the soft skin of her lower belly. After a few minutes, she drew back and glared at me.

"Are you going to use that?" she asked impatiently.

"You want this?" I smirked. I loved hearing her say it—hearing her beg for it.

"I'm not groveling for what's mine." She grabbed my cock as if to make her point. I scooped her off her feet and dropped her on the edge of my desk. Sweeping aside papers and pens and photos, I pushed her onto her back and thrust inside her before she could continue her argument. Clara's legs wrapped around my waist and I gripped her hips as I pounded until my balls began to tighten.

It was raw and real, but unlike the last few times we'd fucked, she was with me—giving and taking. We needed this. We needed to feel each other.

"I want to feel you coming on my cock," I urged her, moving a hand so my thumb could press to her overworked clit. The reaction was instant. She rocketed up, her fingers sinking into my chest for leverage as my own orgasm exploded inside her. Her hips circled, milking me until we collapsed against one another.

IT TOOK EFFORT TO GET CLARA DRESSED

without telling her that Edward would be here any moment. I wanted a few more moments with her before our world shifted on its axis, which was made trickier by the fact she was a boneless heap who seemed quite content to stay half-naked on my desk forever.

"I thought you wouldn't mind," she said dreamily, rolling to the side and pulling her legs up.

"Believe me, I wouldn't," I said, rubbing her back and considering the offer, "but it would make taking meetings harder."

She smiled, dropping a hand to her belly. "By the way, you woke someone up."

"What?" I said, forgetting for a moment that we were running out of time. "This early?"

"I'm past four months," she reminded me.

"Can I?" I asked.

"Probably not yet, but I doubt it will be long," she said dryly. "I think he's going to be strong like daddy."

"Him, huh?"

"This time I'm sure." Clara had been convinced that Elizabeth was a boy until a sonogram had revealed otherwise. "Care to make a wager?"

I leaned down and kissed the place where my child grew. "Why bother? You're having my baby. I win either way."

A loud knock shattered the domestic glow and Clara bolted out of her position, pointing to her pants frantically while running a hand up to discover her loose bun had fallen out. She twisted it frantically into place. "Are you expecting someone?"

"Just a moment," I called, hoping Edward heard and didn't let himself in. "Edward's here. We need to talk."

"I'll get out of your way." She shimmied into her pants.

I took a deep breath. "Actually, we all need to talk."

She abandoned her efforts to fix herself up. "Why?"

"It's easier if I tell you both at the same time."

Her eyes narrowed.

"No more secrets in this family," I explained softly. I lifted her hand to mine and kissed it before going to the door.

Edward was leaning against the wall and he rolled into the doorframe, studying us both with eyes that laughed over the rim of his glasses. "Are you two ever not shagging?"

"Thank you for coming." I forced a smile. I wasn't exactly looking forward to wrecking both of their nights.

"Hey," Clara greeted him with a smug smile and flushed cheeks. "It's my marital duty."

"Duty fulfilled." He crossed to her and pointed to her stomach as proof.

He kissed her cheek and she squeezed him in a tight hug. My chest tightened at the sight of the two of them. Sometimes I was jealous of Clara's relationship with my brother. It was easier than the one we had. It had been my job to be a role model, a position I'd extravagantly shirked for years. Now it felt like I hadn't earned his respect, but couldn't afford a close friendship with him, either. It might risk what he had with my wife, and I didn't want to divide his loyalty. Someone in this place had to consistently be on her side, since I couldn't always be counted on to fulfill that duty.

Edward turned a mock glare on me. "My God, man. She's already pregnant. You can't get her *more pregnant*."

"That won't stop him from trying," she said in a conspiratorial whisper. "I think he's trying to produce his own small army."

"An army of miniature Alexanders?" Edward crowed. "The monarchy won't survive it."

"When you two are finished." I rolled my eyes, trying to appear like I was enjoying the good-natured ribbing. On any other evening, I might. But if I was going to stick to my plans, this couldn't wait any longer.

Norris slipped into the room quietly, and the smile ran away from Clara's face. Her bright eyes, so happy moments before, darkened. I tipped my head to him, catching the attention of Edward. He glanced between me and my head security guard.

"What's going on, Alexander?" he asked quietly.

I gestured for them to take seats. They both hesitated before choosing to sit next to each other.

Strength in numbers. I was glad they had each other now. Edward wouldn't be nearly as upset as Clara but he would be angry for her. Clara? I didn't know how she would react.

"I need to tell you something," I began.

"Like why you've been acting the part of a cave man?" Edward guessed and I saw Clara elbow him in the ribs. "Ouch! It's true!"

She made a zipping motion with her fingers and then gave me an encouraging, but brittle, smile. "Go on."

"I told you both that we discovered our father had a secret son a couple of months ago."

"Yes." Clara's throat slid on the word.

"We now know who he is." I dared a look at Norris, but he made no motion to correct me. I'd called them here to tell them the truth. I could try to soften it—but what was the point? "Actually, we've known for some time."

"I know," Clara said to my surprise.

"You know?" I repeated in a strangled voice, my eyes darting to Norris. How had she found out? If she had known the whole time, why had she allowed Anders to get so close?

"I knew that you knew," she rushed to clarify. "I've just been waiting for you to tell me."

"You knew the whole time?" I said weakly.

"It was pretty obvious," Edward jumped in unhelpfully. Maybe it wasn't such a good idea to have him here.

"Do I need to bother, then?" I asked, running my hand through my hair and beginning to pace. Clara's head cocked to the side as if she was studying me.

"Who is it?" she called softly.

"I don't know where to begin."

My brother and my wife shared a look.

"How about a name?" Edward suggested.

I was making them nervous. That was understandable. Why I'd kept this from them was less so. I cleared my throat and then fell silent. I couldn't erase my father's choices any more than I could hide from them. I closed my eyes and found my voice. "We tracked him down. His mother used to work in the household after Mum died."

"Yes," Edward said encouragingly. I dared to open my eyes. But where Edward's face was blank, Clara's eyes had widened.

She knew. Somehow she knew. She didn't speak and we both waited, frozen in horrified realization, until Edward coughed.

"Is this some weird married thing I have to look forward to? Do you read each other's minds now?"

This time there was no laughter. Clara didn't even crack a smile. Edward reached a hand out to her and she grabbed it like he'd offered her a life preserver.

"Who is it, X?" she whispered. Edward had faded from the room. It was only her, waiting for me to say what we both already knew. A name. But not that of the stranger she'd expected.

How had she figured it out?

"She worked on the staff and then moved outside London to give birth. She's lived there with her son —*our brother*—ever since. Her name is Rachel and her son's name is—"

But Clara stole the name from my lips. "Anderson Stone."

CHAPTER TWENTY-TWO

CLARA

Going to cry at my best friend's house used to involve a smaller security detail. I'd taken Elizabeth with me, though. Even I had to admit that warranted more concern. Someday, my baby would take the crown her father wore. It was a heavy responsibility, not only protecting her now, but also figuring out how to give her as normal a life as possible. That was something Alexander had never had, which was why we were in this mess now.

For the moment, I needed to sort through the mess in my brain, and I couldn't do it alone. I wasn't sure what I was going to tell Belle. Somehow the truth seemed so strange I didn't know where to begin.

"We'll be out here," Norris assured me as I did my best to avoid the photographers that had arrived shortly after us and had set up camp across the street. They tailed us from Buckingham. I knew Norris had it under control, and I was grateful he was here.

Alexander had insisted when I'd told him I wanted to see Belle this morning. I'd agreed, which was pretty much where our conversation had ended.

It wasn't that I *wasn't* speaking to him, but rather that I was avoiding him. I'd listened to his rationale and half-hearted excuses when he'd told us the truth the night before. But none of it accounted for why he'd continued to keep the truth from me. I needed to clear my head and talk it through.

Belle pried open the door and shooed me inside, flipping off the photographers for good measure.

"They're going to love that," I said, shifting Elizabeth to my other hip and dropping my diaper bag in the foyer. It was getting harder to maneuver her with her little brother or sister growing so quickly.

"One of us has to behave, and thankfully it's not me." She held out her hands, and I passed Elizabeth over. She grabbed Belle's face and giggled in approval. Belle put on a sing-song voice that didn't mesh with the women who'd just flipped the Vs at a dozen paparazzi. "Uncle Smith is ready for your play date."

"Smith is home?" I hadn't expected that. Then again, I'd never been exactly clear on what he did.

"He's retired from law and become a proper gentleman," she informed us, still cooing at Elizabeth.

"Did I hear you call me a gentleman?" Smith asked distastefully as we entered the parlor. He was lying on the floor, surrounded by cushions. He pushed up from the ground, displaying impressive biceps that strained against his t-shirt. So that was what Belle saw in him.

"In all the ways that count to anyone but your wife," she told him reassuringly.

"Good. Don't sully my reputation." He gave her —what seemed to me—a rather chaste kiss on the cheek. Belle held out Elizabeth and he hesitated, turning to me. "May I? Belle said you two needed to talk."

"Of course." I swallowed back my anxiety. There had always been a dangerous edge to Smith Price, but if Belle had chosen him, I trusted him.

Elizabeth studied her new handler before smacking him on the nose.

"Lizzie!" I said, unsure whether there was a point to reprimanding her at this age, but feeling compelled to do so. Smith only laughed.

Looking around, I realized that he'd arranged a cluster of pillows into a makeshift baby fortress. He waved us off. "Go talk. I'll call up if I need you."

"Is he going to be okay with her?" I asked, my nerves showing themselves.

"He's been dying to practice since we found out we're expecting. It's adorable, really," she whispered as we headed up the stairs. Her eyes moved wistfully toward the first floor, but she shook herself as if clearing cobwebs from her brain. "Office or bedroom?"

"It doesn't matter." I just needed to talk. I didn't need a prime location.

She surveyed me for a moment. "Bedroom. I think the office will stress you out."

The bedroom, as it turned out, was the least stressful place on the planet. Belle had decorated in cool shades of white and pale wood tones that practically glowed in the light of late morning. It felt like stepping into a luxury spa, but I really didn't feel relaxed until I joined her on the bed.

"Is this an actual cloud?" I asked, sinking into the layers of fluffy down. I felt like I was in heaven.

"This is my sanctuary," she confessed. "I'm totally at peace here."

I could see why. "I'm not sure Alexander would go in for this. Our bedroom isn't very...peaceful."

"I used to share a wall with you. I know," she reminded me. "Believe me, I don't mean peaceful in that way, either, although I do find sex very relaxing."

I raised an eyebrow. We clearly had very different taste in men. There was nothing relaxing about being with Alexander. He was a force of nature in the bedroom, and I wouldn't have it any other way —even when I was angry with him.

"Spill," Belle ordered, and I realized I'd been silent for far too long.

"Alexander has a secret brother," I blurted out. I'd been trying to think of the most delicate, mature way to tell her so that she would understand why this was a secret. I had clearly failed to deliver on that goal.

"A what?" she repeated. "Did you say *secret brother?*"

"Christ, it sounds even more clandestine coming from you," I said, rubbing my temples as a sudden headache began to form. "Yes, he found out a few weeks ago that his dad had a son with someone after Elizabeta died. Basically, he paid for the woman to go away."

I was oversimplifying the situation. Now that I knew the truth, I couldn't help but wonder if that was the real reason Rachel Stone had wanted me to leave Silverstone. Was she worried I would discover her secret? She knew Anders was Alexander's brother—but did he?

"When did he tell you?" Belle asked shrewdly, twisting a blonde lock around her finger as she considered my story. She may have pushed me toward Alexander in the beginning, but she'd had her reservations about our relationship ever since.

"Right away," I said, "kinda."

She gave me a *that's-what-I-thought* look.

"He told me about the brother, but he didn't have a name at the time."

"And when he did?"

"Belle, it's Anderson Stone."

Her mouth fell open. She didn't even try to shut it.

"Surprise," I add weakly.

"Anderson Stone is Alexander's illegitimate brother?" She seemed to be having trouble processing this information. "And you didn't know?"

"Not until yesterday," I grumbled.

That was what was eating away at me. The whole time, Alexander had known Anders was his brother. He'd admitted as much. Instead of telling me, he'd allowed me to go and make friends with him. I couldn't figure out why.

"I don't understand it," I confessed to Belle. "Why wouldn't Alexander have told me as soon as he found out that I'd met him?"

For once, she wasn't spitting with rage over his actions. Instead, she pursed her lips. "Does Anders know?"

"Not yet."

"So if you had known, you would have had to keep that secret from Anders or decide to tell him that he was dumped as a baby by the Royal family," she pointed out.

A lightbulb went off in my head, care of Belle's astute observation. "Oh."

"You know I'm not always Alexander's biggest fan, but I think he did it for you. I mean, what would you have done if you'd known?"

Acted strangely? Pretended not to know? No, there would have been only one course of action. "I would have handed the games over to someone else."

"There you have it. I think he was actually trying to do something right," she said softly. "It pains me to admit it."

"He's not that bad."

"Really? So you aren't angry at him?"

"Oh, no," I said, shaking my head. "I'm pissed. He should have told me."

"In his own *incredibly* twisted way, I think he was doing it for you." She tucked her legs under her chin and sighed. "What are you going to do?"

"What can I do?" That was my problem. I didn't know how to react.

"Will you leave him?" she asked bluntly.

"No!" My mouth hung open even considering her question.

"I figured that was only a hypothetical question," she said dryly. "But I had to ask."

"Why? I mean, it's a big deal, but it's not really leave-your-husband material."

"You left him before," she reminded me gently.

"Look how that turned out." The memory tumbled in my mind, and my stomach lurched. I covered my mouth to be on the safe side. Just the thought of leaving him—truly leaving him forever— made me sick.

"Clara, you're okay." Belle wrapped an arm around me and I dropped my head to her shoulder. "I was just trying to make a point that this time it's different, right?"

"I left the first time because I thought he didn't want me or the baby. I thought he didn't love me," I said, working through the painful memories. "He pushed me away then, but this time he's trying to keep me close—maybe a little too close."

"Oh, he's an overbearing arse," Belle confirmed and I couldn't help but laugh at her matter-of-fact tone. "But he never stopped loving you. It's hard to love a stubborn man. Believe me, I know."

"Is Smith bad?"

"He makes Alexander look like a wallflower."

"How do you do it?" If that was true—and I doubted it—she made it look easy, somehow.

"I don't let him get away with it. When he pulls that alpha male crap, I remind him I'm in charge," she teased, dropping her voice to add, "Except in the bedroom. I don't mind being at his mercy there."

"Ms. Price," I said, pretending to be shocked. In truth, I was a bit.

"Don't act like I've offended you. Every girl needs to be tied up once in a while. It reduces stress. Less stress equals less wrinkles. It's good for the skin."

"How scientific." Giggles spilled from me and I drew away to eye her carefully. She did look incredible. I'd thought it was all pregnancy glow. "So that's your new skincare regime?"

"Oh, love," she said, winking at me. "Submission is the new Botox."

We laughed for a minute before my thoughts drifted back to my own husband. He was trying, which had to count for something. That didn't mean I was going to go easy on him.

"You're going to get through this," Belle murmured, sensing the shift in my mood.

"I just need time, and"—I patted my stomach—"I have other things to worry about."

"Have you been feeling any better?" she asked sympathetically.

"Much better. I think hitting the halfway point helped."

"Twenty weeks already? No wonder you're showing so much more than me." She frowned as she studied her flat stomach. "I'm only ten weeks."

"You'll be big as a house soon," I promised her. Twenty weeks meant I was due to see Dr. Ball. I hadn't really thought about it since I'd gotten back from Silverstone.

"Hey." Belle smacked me on the shoulder. "You disappeared again."

"Sorry. I'm due for a scan, and I guess that means I'll be making up with Alexander sooner rather than later." There was no way I could face that alone.

"I'll go," she offered. "Smith can drive us. Your *entourage* can follow. Just give me the details."

I hesitated, wondering if I needed more time away from Alexander, or if I was just punishing him. In the end, it didn't matter. "It's on Wednesday."

I was getting nowhere with Brex.

"You don't need to come. I want Georgia there." I planted my hands on my hips and wondered how to get through to him. He wanted to send half an army to the doctor with me this afternoon. I hadn't told him I was having an ultrasound, because I didn't want it to get back to Alexander. As far as anyone needed to know, I was going to a routine exam.

"I need to run it by Norris."

I was getting somewhere, but that was the last thing I wanted. "I'll tell him."

Brexton tilted his head to the side, his lips flattening.

"I will," I promised.

"I should come," he said, shaking his head.

"You don't want to come. It's going to be Vagina City."

"Now I definitely want to come." He smirked and glanced toward Georgia, who had stayed out of the argument.

She raised her hands. "It's up to you."

"Talk to Norris," Brex said firmly.

"I will." Norris could be reasoned with. He'd been there when Alexander had revealed the truth about Anders, so he would understand why I needed some space now.

Georgia followed me as I went to look for him, making tiny impatient noises. Finally, I spun on her. "Spit it out."

"Why do you want me there?" she asked coolly. "I'm not exactly the type to hold your hand."

"Because I'm going with Belle, and Smith is driving. I'd rather that not get back to my husband."

She blinked in surprise.

"I don't have to tell Alexander everything," I said.

"Not if you want to punish him," she said softly.

I stared at her, realizing what should have been obvious. "You knew. That's why you warned me about Anders."

"Professional courtesy," she said with a shrug.

"Did everyone know before I did?" I exploded. The revelation solidified my choice to do this without my husband. I stalked off to find Norris.

He was in the kitchen, having a cup of tea, and he looked up, his face remaining blank, as I stormed into the room. A few cooks paused to curtsy, but I waved them back to their work.

"I have a doctor's appointment. Georgia is taking me," I announced.

"Alexander will want to—"

"No," I stopped him, painfully aware that this was how palace gossip got started, but somehow not giving a fuck. "I just want to have a normal, stress-free exam. Alexander's busy anyway."

"He is never too busy for you," Norris said gently.

I snorted. If only that were the case. "I'll fill him in later."

"Clara, he would want to know."

"Really? Maybe he should get a taste of what it feels like to be kept in the dark." I left before Norris could try to reason further with me. I wanted my husband there, but he needed a less-than-subtle reminder that he'd screwed up.

"Punishing him it is," Georgia muttered as she followed me to the garage.

I ignored her.

THE PERK OF LETTING SMITH DRIVE WAS THAT NO one bothered to follow us when we exited Buckingham, which meant, for once, there wouldn't be a write-up of my day posted on every tabloid site in the world. We passed a bunch of bored-looking photographers lingering outside the gates, and I shrank into the seat.

"Don't worry," Belle said, pointing to the heavily tinted windows. "They can't see you."

"Not that they'd miss this car," Georgia said dryly from her passenger seat.

"What's wrong with my car?" Smith demanded.

"It's not exactly subtle."

It wasn't. Belle had warned me that Smith had finally won out and gotten a family car. I'd expected a classic Range Rover or a terrible estate car, but I'd been surprised to find a shiny Mercedes monster waiting for me on the grounds.

"I told him: only dictators and pop stars drove G-wagons," Belle whispered, "but he insisted."

It was nice, if a little glossy for my taste. She continued to tell me about its safety features and various amenities, but my mind was elsewhere. In particular, it was on the phone that kept buzzing in my purse. The third time it rang, Belle groaned.

"I better get that before he calls in SIS," I said flatly, annoyed that Norris hadn't kept his mouth shut. But when I pulled my phone from my bag, it wasn't Alexander. I flashed the screen at Belle.

"Brace yourself," she warned me as I answered.

"Hi, Mom," I said.

"I have been calling you all morning." My mother's voice was so shrill I held the phone away from my ear, and Georgia twisted in the front street, startled by the noise.

"I've been busy."

"What if there had been an emergency? I could have been dying." Somewhere in the last few years, my mother had shifted from pressuring me about my future to obsessively reminding me how little time she had left on the planet. I suspected this was said to encourage me to answer the next time she called. The guilt trip continually backfired, though, since I tended to ignore her calls as long as possible.

"I'm sorry," I said dutifully.

"I called to ask about your appointment. You haven't been keeping me up-to-date."

"I've been preoccupied with the Games." Among other things she didn't need to know about. "And I'm on my way to the doctor now, so nothing to report."

"Is Alexander with you? Maybe *he'll* remember to give me an update." My mother had taken to fawning over my husband and appealing to his sympathy whenever possible. Christmas had been full of special moments like this.

"He had a meeting," I lied. "It's really not a big deal."

"You're halfway through. They must be doing a scan."

"Not this time." Talking with my mother always reminded me how easy it was to lie to someone you loved. "I will let you know how it goes."

"Yes and we need to do dinner soon. We missed celebrating Alexander's birthday—"

"I'll ask him about it. I have to go. I'm there." I hung up the phone after five more promises to make concrete plans soon.

We had missed Alexander's birthday. I'd opened the games as a ceremonial gesture, but I hadn't even gotten him a cake. It hadn't occurred to me to plan a party or host a dinner. I'd been focused on the games while I ignored my real life. Was that where everything had gone wrong?

"Does your mother know where your doctor's office is?" Georgia asked, calling my attention away from my self-flagellation. I shook my head. "Thank God, or she probably would have shown up."

"Let's get this over with, just to be sure," Belle teased as Smith pulled into a carpark.

"Around the corner." Georgia directed him to a secluded spot and Smith shot her dirty looks.

"Who taught you how to drive?" he asked her.

"The same person who taught you," she admitted, "but while you've been roaming the streets in your flashy sports cars, I got better at it."

"They're always like this," Belle said under her breath.

The doctor's office was empty, a courtesy I was definitely grateful for. Right now I didn't feel like having my photo taken or eyes follow me through the clinic. Belle was the only one allowed into the exam room with me. We left Smith and Georgia bickering outside.

A round-faced nurse bustled in and cheerfully took my vitals, asking me questions about how I felt, like I was any other patient who might walk through the doors. It was a nice change of pace.

"This is different than I expected," Belle told me when the nurse left to call the doctor.

"What happens at your appointments?" I settled against the exam chair.

"The exact same thing," she said.

"I'll make them call me *Your Majesty* for the rest of the exam if you like," I said dryly.

Doctor Ball entered the room scanning my chart, and his brows crinkled with concern. "Your blood pressure seems high."

"I just spoke with my mother." Madeline Bishop should come with her own side effects disclaimer: *May cause sudden increase in blood pressure, heart palpitations, feelings of depression and homicidal urges.*

"I suppose I can't tell you not to speak with your mother until after the baby's born," he said.

"I wish you would," I said with a bitter smile.

Doctor's orders might be the only thing to keep her at bay.

"Leave her to me." Belle patted my hand.

"Let's keep an eye on it," he suggested. "Are you ready to see your baby?" He glanced around as if realizing something was missing. "Will your husband be joining us?"

I forced a brittle smile. "He couldn't. I brought my best friend."

"Oh lovely." He stuck out his hand in introduction. She took it and his head cocked to the side. "And how far along are you?"

"Ten weeks." Belle practically vibrated with excitement because he'd noticed. He must have had a sixth sense when it came to pregnant women, because she still looked the same to me.

"Now let's meet the new addition," he suggested.

The ultrasound gel was cold as he applied it to my bump and I craned my head to see the monitor, holding my breath. I was still only feeling the baby sporadically, and I was a little nervous. But then: there he was, dancing on the screen. I exhaled as a gentle peace washed over me, followed instantly by guilt from keeping Alexander away.

"So, are we finding out?" Dr. Ball asked.

I hesitated. Part of me wanted to keep it a surprise. The other part wondered if Alexander wanted to know. One of my favorite things about being pregnant last time was the ongoing debate we'd had about whether the baby was a boy or girl. "I'm not sure."

"I'll make a note in my files and I can tell you later if you decide you want to know."

I nodded. That seemed like a perfect compromise.

"I'm going to check some measurements and make sure we're where we should be. I'll send you with pictures to share with your family."

I murmured a thanks, my eyes never leaving the tiny life growing inside me. Belle squeezed my hand and I saw she had tears in her eyes.

"He's perfect," she told me.

"He, huh?" It was good to know she was in my camp on the gender debate.

"Or she," she teased.

"I can't wait until you have yours. Are you finding out?" I asked her.

"I bloody well will be," she said. "I have a lot of shopping to do!"

"Is the placenta okay?" I asked Dr. Ball, worried that we would have a repeat of my pregnancy with Elizabeth.

Dr. Ball looked up, startled, and stared for a moment, before quickly nodding. "It's anterior. You won't have felt much movement, I expect."

That explained it, but it didn't explain why he looked so worried.

"Is something wrong?" I asked, no longer caring about the placenta.

"I'm not certain," he admitted. He spent the next few minutes moving the wand around and zooming in on the baby. With each second that passed, my panic ratcheted up a level, until he finally swiveled around. "I'd like you to see a specialist."

"What's wrong?" I pressed. Belle's hand tightened over mine and I clutched it like a lifeline.

"There's a slight irregularity with the baby's heart. It might be nothing, but it should be looked into."

Tears swelled in my throat, and I choked out the one question I needed answered. "Is the baby going to be okay?"

"The baby is healthy. It might be nothing, but I'd rather be cautious. I can make a few calls and get you in to see a specialist."

"Can I go after hours?" I asked softly. "I'd rather not have people speculating..."

"I understand. I know a doctor who will see to your absolute privacy," he reassured me. He paused and offered me a warm smile. "I don't want you worrying about this. I see nothing to suggest we have a serious concern."

"What if it is serious?" I wanted to face the worst case scenario now rather than imagine what it could be. "What could we do?"

"Medicine has come a very long way. If surgery is necessary, we can perform it immediately upon birth. Believe me, knowing what, *if anything*, is wrong will make a difference."

I stared at the monitor where our child moved freely, oblivious to the world waiting for him, and wished I could keep him there, safe and protected. "Can I have a minute?"

"Of course. I'll need to..."

I nodded that it was okay and said a silent goodbye as he shut off the monitor. He reached down and handed me a few printed pictures. Hesitating at the door, he turned, "It's really quite normal to have little abnormalities pop up during a scan and then discover it was nothing."

I pressed my lips into a grim smile. It wasn't always nothing. The second the door closed, the tears I'd been holding down broke free. Belle moved to sit next to me and circled me in a tight hug. She didn't try to calm me down with empty words or reassurances. She just let me cry. Sometimes that was all a best friend could do.

CHAPTER TWENTY-THREE

ALEXANDER

I was in no mood for political drama. I'd spent the last few nights sharing a bed with Clara in a frustratingly puritanical fashion. She was asleep when I turned in and gone when I woke up. Her meals were spent with Edward or Belle or alone. We'd barely spoken more than twenty words to one another since I'd revealed the truth about Anders. I was determined to give her space, but if she appreciated it, I didn't know. She certainly hadn't told me. Meanwhile, I had the fucking privilege of sitting through unproductive meetings and accomplishing nothing. I was trapped in a cycle of doing nothing and saying nothing, which left me feeling bloody hopeless.

"The Prime Minister has arrived," Norris informed me.

"You aren't my secretary," I snapped. "Shouldn't you be protecting someone?"

"At the moment, the only person in danger is you," he said in an even voice.

I placed the bait on the hook and dangled it, angling for a fight. "Oh really?"

"In danger of making an ass of yourself." He tugged at his suit jacket without blinking. "Shall I show the Prime Minister in?"

"Please," I said through gritted teeth. Norris wasn't going to fight with me and, in my experience, Prime Minister Clark was more likely to roll over and take it than defend himself.

The whole situation left me feeling twitchy. I'd tried to do the right thing and give Clara what she wanted. I'd fucked up plenty, but it wasn't as though I was keeping a secret to hurt her. It was the opposite. I'd accepted she would be angry with me when I finally decided to tell her, but her silent show of disappointment was so much worse.

The Prime Minister showed up in my office looking as though he'd swallowed a rotten egg. I wasn't fond of these meetings either, but this was extreme. He took a seat across from me and cleared his throat ominously.

"What's happened now?" I asked wearily. There was always some new economic crisis or terrorist threat. The sky was always falling, and yet, we were still sitting here breathing.

"Parliament has called a special council to discuss the treatment of Oliver Jacobson," he informed me.

It was the last thing I expected. "He's been formally charged."

"Yes," Clark hesitated before continuing, "but there are some members of Parliament who feel the crown has overstepped its bounds in this case."

"I bet I could pick those members out of a line-up," I said darkly.

Clark winced as though I'd struck a sore point. "In addition, they're calling for his release."

My fingers dug into the arms of my chair and I stared at him, waiting for the punchline. "You aren't serious? We have a signed confession."

"Some are saying a man will confess to anything after being held—"

"Stop being a politician for one goddamned minute, Clark," I ordered him, rising from my seat, "and tell me what you think."

His jaw tensed as he stared up at me, the only proof that he was anything but calm. "I think its bollocks. I've seen the evidence. It's damning."

"Then what are you going to do about it?" I turned and gazed out the window, wondering how anyone could be so blind.

"I can't do anything. They're calling for action and for legislation which will severely limit the powers of the monarchy," he explained in a low voice.

"They want my crown," I muttered with a laugh as I stared at the grounds of my palace. It was ridiculous. I never wanted the damn thing in the first place. I'd been forced to take it to protect my wife from a man who wanted to destroy me, no matter the cost. It was a twisted, unending cycle, and I was trapped. I whipped around to face Clark. "Maybe you should be King."

"That's not really how it works," he said slowly, missing the joke.

"I'm not looking for a lesson in government." My whole life had been one: shaking hands, enduring endless hours of political discussion, parties, paparazzi, lies, secrets, and impotent compromises.

"I wanted to warn you." He paused as if weighing what he would say next. "I think you might have more enemies in Parliament. I only pray they don't come after you like Jacobson."

"Let them." I leaned down, clutching the edge of my desk. "Let them come for me. They've mistaken me for my title, but I'm flesh and blood and I'll fight like any man for what's mine. They think I'm some powerless figure that they can control—that they can frighten into bowing to them? I bow before no man."

NORRIS APPEARED AS SOON AS CLARK LEFT, white-faced and apologetic. He smiled tightly as he shut the door behind him. "That went well."

"So I don't need to catch you up?" The perk of having an advisor trained to eavesdrop constantly was that I didn't have to rehash the sordid stories. Now that Clark was gone, I collapsed in my seat, feeling the fury that had fueled me moments before leak away.

"I'm having our people look into who is behind this legislative action."

I rested my head against the back of my chair, closing my eyes. "It will be interesting to see where it leads."

"I spoke with the nurses and everything is fine," he reported. It was a needless reminder of my responsibilities.

"I assume you'll tell me if that changes."

"I thought you might like to know."

I filed the information away. There were more important items to consider: Clark's warning for one, and my wife's studious avoidance of me for another. I pinched the bridge of my nose and sighed.

"You've done all you can," Norris began, "so I think you should take a day off."

"I get a break from ruling the country? Brilliant. I thought it was a full-time job." I rubbed at my jaw and wished I was talking to Clara. Being with her was the only thing that could grant me a moment's reprieve. But I was being punished; I had to take my medicine and like it.

"Do you even know what day it is?" he asked, finally taking a seat. "Burning the candle at both ends only leaves you in the dark."

"I'm afraid I've been in the dark for a while," I admitted. "That's how it always feels when she shuts me out, but this time I can't pretend I don't deserve it."

"Clara doesn't want to hurt you."

"She's doing a damn good job despite that," I said with a rueful smile. "She needs time."

"She needs you."

I wanted to believe him, but right now, it felt like I was the last thing my wife needed. She certainly didn't need me to burden her with any more trouble. What would I tell her if she was here? Nothing would come of the parliamentary council except an increase in editorials calling for the end of the monarchy. Personally, I might welcome an early retirement. It was best to give her the opportunity to process things, even if I would rather she was here distracting me with her perfect body.

Instead, I had Norris, who was good company, but not half as sexy.

"What day of the week is it anyway?" I asked.

"Wednesday," he said pointedly.

"And that's important because?" I didn't have the energy to decipher the hints he was dropping.

"It's less the day of the week so much as the date."

"Just tell me," I begged. "What am I forgetting?"

He considered for a moment before taking pity on me. "A rather important doctor's appointment."

I was on my feet before the last syllable left his mouth.

"Keys," I barked.

"I'll have the car brought 'round." Norris stood, straightening his jacket with excruciating care. Sod his goddamn suit when I was wrecking my marriage —again!

"Keys, Norris," I said, hoping to make myself clear.

"Alexander, I can't allow you—"

"There is nothing more dangerous than failing her right now," I said in a low voice. I needed to be there not as a king but as her husband. "Some things a man has to face alone."

His wife was one of them.

CHAPTER TWENTY-FOUR

CLARA

I peppered the doctor with questions for the next hour and refused to leave until we had an appointment with the specialist arranged within the week.

"You can exercise, eat normally, have sex," he reassured me. "Anything that reduces your stress will help the baby." He tacked on the last bit with a sort of forced hopefulness. We both knew there was no avoiding stress in my life. It was a given.

But I could try to de-stress, and I would do whatever it took to see my child safely into the world.

Dr. Ball paused outside the exam room door and placed a hand on my shoulder. "It's going to be okay, Clara. You have an army of specialists at your fingertips."

"Dr. Ball," I didn't know where to begin, because there was one more question that haunted me. "The placenta with Elizabeth and now this—I'm not very good at being pregnant."

Belle, who had kept a firm hold on me throughout, hugged me around the shoulders.

"It has nothing to do with you," he said, but he didn't sound sure.

I couldn't press him further. Since Alexander had become a father, it had changed him. The man who had never wanted a baby would happily see me barefoot and pregnant for the rest of my life. Having a child had done more to help him become a better man than I ever could. Even he had acknowledged it. He'd also made it clear he'd happily fill every empty room in the palace. I couldn't imagine telling him I was damaged goods—unfit to bear his children—when he wanted them so badly.

Before we reached the waiting room, I pulled Belle aside.

"Don't say anything, please."

She searched my face for a moment. "Clara, we're all here to support you and you're going to need that more than ever."

"But I don't need pity." I couldn't expect her to understand. My every move was already watched by security teams and tabloids, even my own husband. The thought of them analyzing me, judging me—or just feeling sorry for me—was too much. No one else could carry my burden, just as no one else could carry my child.

"I won't say anything," she promised, "but you are telling Alexander."

"I don't know," I admitted.

"Clara, I know you're upset with him, but—"

"It's not that," I interrupted her. "I'm not upset anymore. All of it feels so inconsequential compared to this. I'm the only one who can save this baby. He can't do any more than I can."

He would feel helpless and Alexander didn't do well with that.

"You have to tell him."

I grabbed her hand. "He already treats me like glass, Belle. If he knew, he wouldn't touch me for months. I'll go crazy."

"This is about sex?" Her hand dropped mine.

"No." I shook my head. "It's about needing to be in control of my life—of my body. If he knows, it will be worse, not better. If he's worried it will stress me out..."

"But what if," she trailed off, as if finishing that sentence was too painful.

"I am made of glass?" I finished softly. "He won't be surprised if I shatter." He seemed to always expect it. At least, he would be prepared.

"You won't," Belle said with a sudden ferocity that ignited my own.

"I know that." I did. After the tears dried, I'd confronted the fear churning inside me, and I hadn't turned away.

"I won't tell." She might have believed I was

strong enough, but it was clear she wasn't certain of this decision. I knew she would respect it, though.

I felt better knowing I would have at least one person I could talk to about this. I'd have to ask Dr. Ball to keep the information private from Alexander, as well. I was sure the doctor wouldn't be thrilled, but he'd have to respect my wishes as his patient.

"Do I look like hell?" I asked her. "I don't want Georgia tattling on me."

"You might be surprised at how understanding she is, if you let her be," Belle advised me, "and you look fine."

I'd never told Belle about the past Georgia shared with my husband, so I couldn't tell her why I'd have to take her word for that.

"Truly fine? Or fine for having spent an hour crying fine?"

"A little camouflage might help," she admitted. She dug in her purse and found a lip gloss and under-eye concealer. I took it gratefully, desperate to erase any remnants of tears, even if it meant hiding behind make-up. I stepped into the waiting room with a half-assed excuse for why we'd taken so long.

But it wasn't Smith and Georgia waiting for me.

Alexander waited in a chair that was too small for his powerful body. His dark head was in his hands, but he looked up hopefully when he heard us. He was on his feet in an instant. His tie was undone, hanging loosely around his unbuttoned collar, and he'd abandoned his suit jacket. He hesitated for one agonizing second before he crossed the space in two great strides and took me in his arms.

Belle murmured something I was too dazed to hear and disappeared.

"Poppet." He pressed me to his firm body and I melted against him. "You should have told me."

I fought the tears that threatened to betray me and forced my gaze up to his. "I didn't want to bother you."

It was a lie. It was the truth. It was the complicated reality of our lives.

"Christ," he muttered and I tensed, waiting for him to explode. Instead, he kissed my forehead. "I'm sorry. For missing this. For everything." He glanced down and caught sight of the pictures I clutched. "Did you...?"

"Yeah," I said shyly. "Want to see him?"

"Him?" he repeated.

"I think it's a boy." It felt good to slip into the debate — a moment of normal as my world spun out of control.

"You didn't find out?"

"And miss a chance to argue with you for a few more months?"

I handed him the pictures and he studied them with awe. His nostrils flared as he saw his child for the first time and he shook his head, turning briefly away from them and from me.

"I should have been here," he said in a strangled voice.

I couldn't tell him I was glad he hadn't been. Maybe all of these mistakes had served a purpose. It had kept him from being here today. It had given him a few months of excitement. I didn't know what the future held, but I could give him that.

"I will be here," he vowed, "every step of the way."

I brushed a palm down his cheek, wanting to erase his regret. "X, you are always with me."

I rocked Elizabeth until she passed out in my arms, counting her fingers and thanking God she was healthy. It felt selfish to wish for another perfect baby, but I couldn't help it. The doctor was right. I had resources that others could only dream of. In the end, I was simply a mother who would do anything for her child.

The door to the nursery cracked open and Alexander appeared. He lingered there, watching us. It was one of the only times he looked at peace: in those small moments when he was just a man and a father, not a king. After a few minutes, he crept over and lifted her from my arms. Her weight evaporated from my chest and a bittersweet sadness took its place as Alexander gently lowered her into her crib.

He held a hand out to me and guided me to my feet. We reached our bedroom and he stopped inside the door. Reaching up, he unpinned my hair and let it fall to my shoulders. Gathering it in his hands, he held me captive as he lowered his mouth to mine. His kiss was hungry but restrained. I couldn't stand that he was holding back, but I knew it was an offering— an olive branch. I could push him away or stay in his arms.

"Let me run you a bath," he murmured when he finally pulled away.

I shook my head. "I'm too tired. I'll fall asleep and drown. Maybe a shower?"

I wanted to wash this day and its stress away—not soak in it. Tomorrow I'd do as Dr. Ball ordered and take a hot bath. Tonight I wanted to go to bed with my husband.

Alexander led me to the bathroom and slowly undressed me, his eyes drinking me in like it was the first time. He always looked at me like that, and when he began to take off his shirt, my heart faltered for a moment. I'd never been able to tell him what it meant for him to give his body to me. The perfect, carved abs that narrowed into an invitation, and the roped scars that twisted across his left torso and up over his heart—my heart. Every time I looked at him I believed in destiny a little more. He could have been taken from me on the night of the accident that had given him those scars. Fate played a hand and saved him for me.

He turned on the water and stepped under it. I joined him, enjoying the way the water snaked in rivulets over his muscles. Alexander turned his face up to it, and I wondered briefly if he was washing today away, too. After a second, he looked down, his mouth cocking up in a lusty grin that made my knees weak. He reached for the soap and began to lather it over my body, kneading my shoulders and then continuing to the rest of me, as though he could erase the time we'd spent apart. His hands slipped down to my breasts and he grinned as he took an extra long time there.

"I think they're clean," I teased him softly.

He shushed me and continued. "I'm very thorough."

But it wasn't until his hands slid lower, stopping on the swell of my stomach, that tears stung my eyes. His gaze met mine, blazing with unrestrained love, as he dropped to his knees. Alexander lowered his head and rested it there, his arms circling my waist. Water showered over us, mingling with my tears and washing away the evidence. His arms protected me—*protected us*—and I protected his heart. We were an endless circle—unbroken and unbreakable.

Alexander stayed there holding me, and when he finally pushed onto his feet, his eyes were wet. He didn't hide from me. He'd stripped to his soul. Nothing could separate us. We were bared to one another: body to body and soul to soul. He took my face in his hands, his mouth angling to capture mine. The kiss started sweetly, but it deepened until his breath was my own. His heart beat in my chest. My fingers tangled in his hair, holding him close as we whispered promises of forever in a language only we spoke.

His body backed me against the tile and we continued to press together. I was barely aware of our bodies fighting to close every last inch of space between us. There was only him and his taste on my lips. When we finally surrendered to one another, he lifted me from my feet and pushed inside me with agonizing tenderness, allowing me to envelop his cock completely before he began to move. His hips rolled slowly, winding me tighter with each stroke. I pressed my forehead to his, savoring the pressure building inside me.

"Always," he ground out, brushing a kiss over my lips. "Always, Clara."

His words stole my breath and I splintered apart, coming with his name on my lips. Alexander anchored me as I fell apart and rebuilt myself around him until he was my world. My always.

CHAPTER TWENTY-FIVE

ALEXANDER

It was a press conference, and my bastard brother had shown up in a t-shirt and jeans, with devil-may-care hair and an attitude to match. Anders and I stayed on opposite sides of the room. I'd promised Clara I'd be on my best behaviour, but it was difficult to do while staring at the man who'd tried to steal my wife. Judging by his glare, he wasn't any happier to be near me. The number of press allowed inside the White Drawing Room was limited by the room's size. Each of them seemed more interested in Anders than in me, but I caught a few looking between us. That was my cue to excuse myself.

I wanted to slip away through the secret door hidden behind the mirror in the corner, but before I could, Clara caught me.

I allowed myself a moment of wonder. She was beautiful, her glossy hair cascading loosely over her shoulders, her pregnancy on full display in a fitted, cream dress. Without thinking, I lifted her hand to my lips, forgetting we had an audience. There was a murmur of approval throughout the room, followed by the sound of cameras.

"Trying to charm them, X?" she whispered as I placed a hand on her back and followed her to the front of the room. "Or trying to escape?"

"Which am I more likely to pull off?" I asked so only she could hear. I paused before we reached my uncle and Anders.

"Aren't you coming?" she asked, her gaze darting to me.

"They're here to see the Queen." This was about the Sovereign Games, not me. Clara deserved a place outside my shadow. "I'll be waiting."

I took a few steps away, joining Norris and Edward to watch.

My brother leaned toward me, lowering his voice. "Do let me know before you lose it and rip off his head."

"I'm in complete control," I assured him. As long as Anders behaved himself.

Clara smiled widely as she took a seat next to Henry. She crossed her legs at the ankles and waited for the room to quiet. "Thank you for coming. I know there has been speculation about the next round of the games, given that we chose to end the first round early. We're very pleased that Anders was feeling up to joining us. I know there has been concern about his recovery over the last few weeks."

A number of hands shot in the air and she tipped her head to one. "John?"

She was a natural at this. I'd spent my whole life resenting obligations like this and somehow I'd found a woman who made it look easy.

"Will you complete the auto racing event?" John asked.

"I believe that's a question for Anders," she said, looking to him, one hand coming to rest on her belly.

My shoulders tensed at the insignificant gesture. I hated that he was nearer to her than me.

"She can handle this," Norris said in a low voice.

I knew that. The truth was that Clara held all the cards. Mostly because she held all of our hearts.

"I'm game once I'm out of this." He gestured to the sling on his left arm, grinning. "The doctor might prefer I wait until my ribs are healed."

"That's not going to stop you, is it?" someone called.

"It hasn't yet."

"Am I that insufferably smug?" I asked Norris.

"Yes," he said without a thought.

So much for loyalty. "Whose side are you on?"

He shifted his hands behind his back, shaking his head.

"We plan to return to the races this spring," Henry announced. "It is our sincerest hope that Anders will be able to join us when we return to Silverstone. For now, the games will move on to the equestrian events."

"Will that conflict with Her Majesty's pregnancy?" John asked. It was a clever question meant to get at the more popular question about my wife's due date.

"It will be cutting it rather close," she said with a laugh, not giving anything away.

Clara's eyes darted to mine, something unreadable there and I shot her a reassuring smile. I'd promised her that we would make this work. The last two weeks had brought us closer than ever before. We'd picked out baby names, visited a number of our patronages, and enjoyed private family time. There had been a fair bit of sex, too. When the issue of how to proceed with the Games had come up, I'd made it clear I was completely behind her, even if it meant she would be working with Anders.

"Actually," she continued, "given that there is significant travel involved with the May rounds and a return to Silverstone in June, I regret that I will not be continuing as host of the games."

A low murmur spread through the audience and I stepped forward. Norris grabbed my arm and kept me from interrupting her. I wanted to stop her. Across the room, Anders had found me, his eyes blazing, as though he was thinking exactly what I was. She was quitting for me. But what he didn't know was I didn't want that. There was no need to give this up. A June round would likely conflict with the baby's birth but she could easily attend the London rounds.

"Will Alexander be taking your place?" someone asked.

That was a good question. These were the Sovereign Games. But she shook her head. "These games are King Albert's legacy, so they will continue to be a family effort. With Henry and my brother's help, we will honour his memory and the sacrifice he made for us."

I froze at the mention of brother, until Edward dared a glance at me, then moved to join her. He stood behind her seat and placed a hand on her shoulder.

"I'm delighted to help. After all, my sister is working harder than all of us at the moment." His joke came off well, painting Clara as the blessed Madonna of the family.

The conference continued, but I checked out. Why hadn't she told me what she'd planned? Why had she gone to Edward instead?

When the audience ended and I no longer had to smile politely for the cameras, I escaped into the Royal Closet.

"Give me a moment," I barked, hearing the sound of someone follow me in.

A hand grabbed my shoulder and jerked me back. I spun around, coming face to face with Anders. It was like looking into my own eyes—the same color and the same anger. I wondered if he saw his own reflecting back at him.

"You can't lock her away," Anders growled.

"You're on dangerous ground," I warned him. "Leave."

"I don't take orders from you, unlike the rest of the puppets here."

"Anders!" Clara's voice broke in sharply.

Neither of us moved. We were inches from each other and it was taking a considerable amount of restraint not to tackle him.

"Clara, my love, please give us a moment," I gritted out.

"That was polite." Anders spat the words. "I didn't expect please to be in your vocabulary."

"I have a rather impressive vocabulary. Ask me how many words I can come up with for how petulant you're being," I said coolly.

"Petulant? Fancy. Where I'm from we stick with calling a wanker a wanker."

"Fine," I said, taking the bait, "you're a wanker."

"You forced her to quit," he accused.

"Clara makes her own decisions." I didn't bother to add that this was one she hadn't bothered to run past me. More people filtered into the room. Norris moved closer, giving us room, but staying near. I spotted Henry and Edward over Anders' shoulder.

It wasn't until Brexton entered that anyone commented on the scene playing out before them. "Oh bloody hell," he said. "You're on your own, Poor Boy."

"Don't worry. I have this in hand," I said without looking away from Anders.

"You would think that," Anders muttered.

"Try me," I dared him.

He had one good hand and it flew at the same time Clara stepped between us. I reacted instinctively, covering her body with my own. Anders's fist bounced off my shoulder. I sheltered my wife, throwing a murderous look at him.

"Get him the fuck out of here," I ordered.

Anders didn't resist as Brexton grabbed his shoulder and dragged him toward the door.

"Clara, I'm sorry," he called, ashen-faced. "I would never hurt you."

"No, you won't, because you're *never* coming near her again." It didn't matter if we shared the same blood. Anderson Stone was dead to me.

CHAPTER TWENTY-SIX

CLARA

Everything had happened so fast. From the moment I'd met Alexander, he always positioned himself between me and the world. He'd been there to carry me away from the paparazzi. He'd stepped in front of a bullet for me. It wasn't his protection that surprised me. It was Anders' recklessness that did. I peeked over Alexander's shoulder, feeling torn as Brex dragged Anders away. It was hard to think with the stifling amount of testosterone in the air, but I knew kicking him out wasn't going to fix whatever was broken between them.

Only the truth could do that.

I ducked free of Alexander. "Stop!"

"Clara, he nearly hit you," Alexander said, a dangerous edge to his voice.

"But he didn't," I said.

"Semantics." Alexander jerked his head. "Get

him out before I show him what a real punch looks like."

Anders moved toward the door without a struggle, Brexton behind him.

"For fuck's sake," I said, finally losing it, "you are brothers!"

Betrayal flashed in Alexander's eyes, but he covered it quickly. Lifting his head, he met Anders' confused gaze. Anders looked between us, then to everyone else in the room.

"What are you talking about?" he demanded when no one spoke.

"Albert was your father," I said gently. I took a step toward him, glanced at Alexander's strained expression, and thought better of it.

"Todd Stone was my father." Anders's face hardened into stubborn refusal. I recognized the look. Alexander wore it often.

"She's telling the truth," my husband said. He came to my side and looped his arm around my waist as though he needed my support to get through this. "After my father died, we discovered he'd been taking care of an ill...another child—a son none of us knew he had. I began to investigate and it led me to you." He cleared his throat, but his words were thick as he added, "You're my brother."

Anders looked around the room, his jaw unhinged. His mouth clamped shut, a muscle twitching in his jaw. "You're telling me this is my family."

"Yes," I said. "I know it's a lot to process. I had a hard time when he told me."

"And when did he tell you?" Anders rounded on me. "Did you know the whole time?"

"I told her after your accident," Alexander said.

"That ashamed of me, huh? You probably wish the accident had finished me off."

"How can you think that?" I asked.

Anders threw his head back and released a shaky laugh.

"I'm sure you have questions." Alexander was doing an impressive job of keeping his head. I took his hand and squeezed it.

Anders zeroed in on our clasped hands. He looked up and shook his head. "No, I don't."

"You must want to know about your father," Alexander said.

Anders leveled a glare at him that sent a chill shivering up my spine. "Todd Stone was my father."

He turned and strode out of the room. I started after him, but Alexander held me back.

"Let him go."

"No, X." I pulled free and ran after him.

I caught Anders in the White Drawing Room.

"Stop," I begged him, unable to keep up with his long strides in my heels.

"Why?" He whipped around to face me. "You've made it clear that there is nothing between us and now..."

"This isn't about—"

"What is it about, Clara? Am I supposed to hug you and call you sis and show up for Easter brunch?" He moved closer, leaving very little space between us, and lowered his voice. "Am I supposed to join the family and pretend that I'm not in love with you?"

"You aren't." I swallowed, praying Alexander hadn't followed us.

"I am. Christ, I might not know much, but I know I'm in love with you."

"Then you should go." My voice trembled and he pulled away.

"I guess we won't be one big happy, family after all." He choked back a bitter chuckle, turning his face away. "Goodbye, Clara."

"Goodbye, Anders," I said in a small voice.

Before I could stop him, he leaned forward and brushed his lips over my forehead, lingering a moment too long. "Sorry," he said, straightening up. "I had to kiss you just once."

And then he was gone.

I watched him leave, knowing Alexander's eyes were on my back—knowing he'd seen the whole thing. I was always acutely aware of his presence, but now I felt his gaze raking over me possessively. Sucking in a breath, I turned to face him.

Alexander's stony face might have been unreadable to some. I recognized it as his battle mask. He was fighting to stay in control, the war raging within him. Norris appeared at his side along with Edward, and the two began to speak in low voices as my husband listened without a word.

They would need to strategize, of course. The information had been controlled and I'd just spilled it to an outsider they couldn't keep quiet. I thought about telling them Anders wouldn't say anything, but it didn't matter. The boys would withdraw to the proverbial war room to plot.

"Just a moment," Alexander said, cutting them off.

He crossed the room in four great strides and pulled me into his arms. His thumb brushed away a tear I didn't know had fallen.

"X, I'm sorry," I murmured, turning my face into his palm.

"Don't apologize for my mistakes, Poppet," he reminded me

"I shouldn't have told him. It wasn't my place—"

"It wasn't your job to keep it a secret." He kissed me swiftly. "I would, however, have liked some warning about you quitting the Games."

"I knew you wouldn't let me," I admitted softly.

"I won't exactly mind having you home, barefoot and pregnant." He glanced behind him. "They'd like to discuss a few things."

Security things, no doubt. They needed to plan what to do when my slip blew up in their faces. I nodded. "Not too late. I don't want to sleep alone."

"I won't let you be alone or sleep," he promised

with a grin. He disappeared with a kiss, taking my heart with him.

I stood in the empty room, small and humbled. It was easy to feel that way under the gold leaf and chandeliers. But it was a symptom of something else. No matter how hard I tried, I didn't seem to fit into this life. I was the insignificant nobody playing at being a Queen, and I was messing up at every turn.

"Fancy a walk?" a gentle voice asked. "Everyone's gone off to worry about King and Country."

I looked up to find Henry, hands shoved in his pockets and ascot undone. I'd never seen him looking quite this ruffled.

"I could use some fresh air." I paused and reached down to pry off my heels. I sighed with relief as my toes sank into the plush rug.

"Someone will pick them up," he reassured me.

At last count, nearly eight hundred people worked here, so he was undoubtedly right. "I never quite feel at home here," I admitted to him, eyeing the shoes. "I can't even leave my things lying around."

"Maybe you should," he suggested, offering me his arms. "The gardens?"

I nodded at the suggestion. It was early evening and not overly cool for March. The days had begun to lengthen, and so a few minutes later we found ourselves under the purple dusk of twilight.

"Will you be cold?" Henry's forehead wrinkled as he looked at my bare feet.

"I have my own little furnace." I patted my stomach. "I'm always too warm."

We walked in companionable silence for a few minutes. It was early spring and the flower beds were barren, but there was something magical about the quiet. The grounds were dry, but the smell of rain hung in the air. We were in the middle of London and a world apart.

"Henry," I asked, putting to words a question that had bothered me since Alexander had revealed the truth about Anders, "that day at the track, before the accident, you said something about it being impossible—that Alexander couldn't know. What did you mean?"

"I think you already know." Henry patted my hand with a sigh. "It's nice to have it out in the open."

"Is it?" I wasn't sure that was true. A year ago, Alexander hadn't known a thing about Anders. Now he had another family member to worry about, one who wouldn't make it easy for him.

"It may not seem like it, but trust me, secrets are poison. They change you." His eyes took on the same distant quality they had the day of Anders' crash.

"So you've known Albert's secret the whole time?"

"I knew *all* my brother's secrets."

"All?" I repeated.

"A King is burdened with many worries. Albert turned to me often." He said this as if it were no big deal to cover up illegitimate children and God knew what else.

"I wish he would have talked more with Alexander," I admitted. "I guess everything was different after Sarah died."

His brows knitted together as he considered this. "Everyone believed Sarah's accident broke Alexander's relationship with his father. Albert broke it himself, just like he destroyed his relationship with Liz."

"You said that before." My mind drifted to Alexander and me. Albert had loved his wife. He'd spoken of her with a passion I couldn't deny. Maybe her loss had shown him what he'd taken for granted, but Henry spoke like it was something more. "What drove them apart?"

"The thing that sets a sovereign apart. Power." He looked down at me, his eyes narrowing. "You're worried about your relationship with Alexander."

I swallowed on the lump of uncertainty in my throat before I tipped my head.

"He kept the truth about Anders from you. I can't say I approve."

"You said secrets were poison. Sometimes I think my husband doesn't know that," I admitted. I wanted to believe we'd put that part of our relationship behind us, but could we ever, really? I was keeping something from him now, because I believed I was protecting him. He had done the same for the same reasons. "It's difficult to know what to tell and what to keep buried."

"Secrets don't stay buried in this family," he advised.

"Then I hope we've dug them all up."

His lips twisted into a rueful smile as he looked across the grounds of the palace. His eyes were full of memories.

"I don't care what this family's done," I said fiercely. "Alexander and I are going to change it all. Anders was the last secret that will come between us."

"Oh, Clara." Henry turned and patted my hand like he was soothing an innocent child. "Do you know how many estates this family has? There are lots of rooms to bury secrets and even more closets to stash skeletons. I'm afraid your husband hasn't been as honest as you think."

CHAPTER TWENTY-SEVEN

ALEXANDER

It was dark before I sent everyone home. When I'd failed to appear for dinner, Clara had appeared. She circled around my desk and grabbed the arms of my chair. Spinning me to the side, she leaned down and covered my mouth with hers. A curtain of hair fell around my face, surrounding me with her sweet scent. My hands went to her ass, drawing her closer.

"I thought you were coming to bed," she murmured, taking her lips from me.

"Too far," I grunted, shoving her skirt to her hips.

"You have a one-track mind." She wiggled away from me, but didn't push it back down. Instead she hoisted herself onto my desk, allowing her legs to fall open. Her stockings stopped at her creamy thighs, held in place by garters.

"I do." I wasn't ashamed of it. I rolled my chair between her legs and hooked a finger under the fabric

bunched at her waist. Lifting it, I discovered a lace
garter belt slung low under her belly. My cock, which
has been following recent developments, stiffened at
the sight of her sex on display, her body rounded with
the life she carried for me. "Fuck, Poppet. We are
definitely not making it to the bedroom."

"How was your meeting?" she asked, playing
with a strand of hair in an expert display of coyness.

My eyebrow arched, a low rumble growling in my
chest. "No business talk."

I gripped her hips but before I could yank her
forward, she placed her palm on her chest. "We said
no more secrets, X. Tell me how it went."

"As expected. Brexton thinks we should get in
front of this and out Anders. Norris seems to think he
won't tell anyone." It was hard to concentrate with
her so near and so naked.

"I think Norris is right," she said as though she'd
considered this, too. "Anders doesn't seem interested
in getting dragged into this family."

"The first smart move he's made," I muttered.

"Try to think of how he feels," she urged.

"Yes, Poppet. You're right. He's had his whole life
paid for without any responsibilities. I must consider
his feelings." He raced cars. He was reckless. He was
everything that my father had tried to stamp out
of me.

"Don't be an ass." She smacked me on the shoulder. "What else?"

I blinked. "What do you mean?"

"You were in here for ages. You can't have spent all that time worrying about Anders."

"Nothing much." I settled into my chair, my eyes never leaving the temptation in front of me. I blew air through my lips. She was determined to have a conversation. "Is this some torturous new form of foreplay?"

"Huh?" She glanced down and her eyes widened. Crossing her legs, she smiled sheepishly. "Sorry, X."

"Now I wish I hadn't said anything." This was definitely not an improvement.

"What else did you talk about?" she pressed.

I hesitated. I hadn't told Clara everything that had been going on lately. She'd had enough on her mind, but she'd asked for no more secrets and I could give her that moving forward. "There is an issue with Parliament."

She tilted her head, her eyes narrowing as if she was trying to get a better read on me. I did my best to look unconcerned by this news.

"It will come to nothing. A few people are upset that we arrested Jacobson, but there will be press coverage."

"When is there not?" she asked, suddenly looking tired.

"Do you ever wish"—I searched her face hoping to find the truth—"that you had a normal life? Away from all of this insanity?"

"Don't you?"

"I'm serious. Sometimes I hate myself for taking

away your choices in life." I meant every word. I thought about it more often than I liked to admit, because considering it forced me to imagine a life without her.

"You gave me the chance to make the most important choice of my life," she said softly. "You let me choose you."

A wide smile carved over my face. "I think you're a better statesman than I am. You always have a good answer."

"It's the truth." She pushed her hair over her shoulder and leaned forward to hook her arms around my neck. "I chose all of you. Nothing you could tell me will ever make me regret that. No mistake. No secret. I need you to know that."

"I do," I said, sweeping a kiss over her lips.

"I need to know that you'll stop keeping secrets. I can handle it."

"I know you can." I nuzzled her nose with mine. "In the spirit of being honest, I suppose I should tell you that I'm finding it hard to think, knowing what's under that dress."

She didn't laugh. Instead, her eyes bored into me.

"Promise me." Her voice broke on the request.

"I promise." I would do everything in my power to keep that vow. She deserved that much. Every time I thought she was fragile, she reminded me how strong she was. "God, I love you."

Her head tilted, tears filling in her eyes. She tried

to blink them away but they clung to her dark lashes. "I love you, too."

She gulped, but she couldn't swallow away her emotions. There was only one way to set her free from her worry. My hands sank into the soft flesh of her hips and drew her to the edge of the desk. Clara responded, opening her legs so I could lift her onto my lap. Her arms coiled around my neck as she kissed me hungrily.

"Oh, X," she whimpered, burying her face against my neck.

"I'm right here," I said in a hushed voice.

She released my neck, her hands going to my pants. "I need to feel you."

I considered carrying her to the bedroom, but the thought ran away from me as she unfastened my belt and slid a hand down to grip my cock. I groaned as her delicate fingers stroked my shaft. If she wanted all of me, I definitely wanted all of her. I reached up and found her zipper and drew it undone. Lifting her dress over her head, I unhooked her bra, allowing her full breasts to swing loose.

Clara moved against me, her hand still manipulating my cock, as I bent to capture her dark, pert nipple. I sucked it, watching as she slowly came undone, writhing against me. She was primal and beautiful—my very own goddess.

I moved to the other breast, my hand reaching to knead and plump the one I'd abandoned.

"Yes, please," she whimpered as I drew the soft

furl into my mouth. I would never have my fill of her, but I would never stop trying. Our story was only beginning, but she was every word, every page, every chapter.

I felt her hands undoing the rest of my pants and a cool breeze as my cock met air. She planted her palms on my shoulders and lifted her body to hover over the wide crest of my cock. My eyes never left hers as she eased, inch by inch, over me. Hers started to close, but she fought the urge, her irises rolling slightly as she moaned.

"That's right," I said, rubbing her back as she adjusted to the deep position. The dazed pleasure on her face was nearly enough to make me come. "Is this what you need?"

"Yes," she whispered, her teeth sinking into her lip and she began to circle her hips. "I need you—all of you."

"You have me."

She tightened against me, her channel contracting around my cock as she slowly rode me.

Her face fell forward, burrowing against my neck. A small, anguished cry escaped her mouth as she began to roll her hips in desperate circuits. I rocked my hips, urging her there faster. I needed to feel her come. She clung to me as a violent spasm surged through her. I held her through it, joining her in the end. Then I carried her to our bed and proved she had all of me.

CHAPTER TWENTY-EIGHT

CLARA

I waited until Alexander's breaths slowed into a peaceful rhythm before I slipped out of bed. I let him make love to me for hours because I'd known what faced me when he finally stopped. When I was with him, I was lost to his mistakes and his secrets. I couldn't avoid them any longer. Pausing by our bed, I watched him sleep. In a few hours he would wake. By then I needed to know the truth. Having this hanging over my head had kept me awake with a racing heart. The doctor told me I needed to keep my stress level down. There was no way I would be able to do that if I tried to ignore this. Because, after everything, I was certain: I was done with secrets. If there were skeletons to uncover, I would find them. I wouldn't allow anything to come between us—not even him.

The trouble was, I didn't know where to begin. Any hope I had that he would come clean had been dashed by his stubborn silence. But Alexander had a

warped perception of truth and lies. Given his family's twisted politics and power plays, how could I
blame him?

Grabbing clothes from the closet, I made my way
to the lower apartments. I dressed quickly in my
private office and then started rifling through the
papers on my desk as my conversation with Henry
replayed in my mind. Most of the files on my desk
pertained to the Sovereign Games. I ignored the pang
that shot through me as I stacked them in a neat pile
and dumped them into a drawer. The rest of my
papers were an odd collection of letters and notes. It
took forever to dig out what I was looking for.

When Alexander had given Clarence House to
Edward, I'd folded the list up and forgotten about it.
Now, smoothing it open, I stared at the list of royal
residences I'd brought to him weeks ago. All the
names were antiquated and ridiculous, and I thought
back, trying to remember the ones that I'd pointed
out to him.

I'd wanted Edward close while still giving him
some much-needed distance from the London press.
My finger ran down the list until I reached Windsor
Castle. Windsor would have been the perfect place, I
argued then. Close to the city, but apart. But the
castle itself wasn't what I'd suggested. I followed the
list down to an attached property that sat several
miles away in a secluded hamlet.

Windsmoor House.

Unacceptable. That's what Alexander had said.

He'd called it practically condemned.

Now I saw how stupid I'd been. The Royal family didn't leave estates to rot to nothing. If there were skeletons to be found, I needed to search Windsmoor's closets first. I folded the sheet in half and stuffed it in my pocket. There was no way I was leaving the grounds on my own without someone alerting Alexander. I considered my problem and realized I only had one choice. I dialed the number and cut her off as soon as she answered. "I need your help."

To her credit, Georgia Kincaid showed up in record time. She'd once told me her loyalty was flexible, and I could only hope that was still the case. She didn't speak as I joined her in the garage.

"I need this to stay between us." It was better to cut to the chase with her. We were both busy women. I had to figure out if the secret at Windsmoor was a danger to me or my family. I had no idea what Georgia did with her free time, but I assumed it was something along the lines of thwarting terrorism or meeting up for a quick dungeon date. It was impossible to say which.

"I don't work for you," she reminded me.

This was already off to a great start. "If you work for Alexander, then you do. We're partners, after all."

Her lips twitched but she revealed no other feelings on the matter. "What do you need, exactly?"

"You told me once that you were discreet." I fought the wave of nausea this memory induced.

"I am," she confirmed. She'd arrived here in her usual black, but her face was absent the usual crimson lipstick and coal-rimmed eyes. Barefaced, she was breathtaking and somehow even more intimidating.

I reminded myself that I had no other choice. If I was right, then Norris most likely knew about Windsmoor House. Brexton was totally loyal to my husband. I needed someone with a certain moral flexibility. Georgia had always struck me as that type. Of course, I'd met her after she'd been hired to kill my ex-boyfriend. That might have colored my perception of her.

"I need to visit a family residence," I told her. "I'd like you to drive me."

"Why?" she asked, crossing her arms over her chest.

"Does it matter?"

She studied me for a minute before she shook her head with a laugh. "If you've come to me, then Alexander has no idea what you're up to."

I didn't say anything. I'd only incriminate myself.

"So why do you want to go there? Or should I call Norris and ask him to take you?" she asked, calling my bluff.

"Because Alexander doesn't want me to go there." It was a hunch, but I was sure I was right.

"He loves you," Georgia said, her words coated

with a surprising layer of concern. "When he decided to marry you, I thought he was sending a 'fuck you' to his father. I didn't consider it was because he loved you. I didn't think that was possible."

"Why?" For two years I'd carried the burden of her thoughtless words. Now she was taking them back?

"Because I've been on the other end of his whip and I have the scars to prove it," she said blackly. "If you had been, you would only see his darkness, too."

I had seen his darkness lurking when he fucked me. I'd given him my body in every way and watched him chase ghosts. But I'd also made love to him when no shadows clouded his blue eyes. Alexander clung to the shackles that imprisoned him. It was up to me to set him free.

"Clara, are you sure?" she asked after a moment. "You might not like what you find."

"Yes." I'd given him everything and he'd promised me all of him. It was time to collect.

IT WAS A SHORT DRIVE TO WINDSOR SO EARLY ON a Sunday morning. Georgia left me to my thoughts, and I was grateful for the silence. There was no way to prepare for what I might find. As the city gave way to countryside, the roads narrowed until we turned down an unpaved road that wound past Windsor Castle and into the untouched lands of the estate's park. Trees clustered along the path, blocking curious

eyes from view. It was oddly serene, with no sign of
cameras or guards. They were focused on Windsor, I
assumed. But before we reached the house, a guard
station came into view.

My heart sank. It was the first proof Alexander
had lied. Until that point, I'd begun to wonder if
Windsmoor really was abandoned.

A guard ran into our path, panting, like it had
taken real effort. Georgia slowed the car and sighed.

"We can still turn back," she muttered. But we
both knew that wasn't true. The guard rapped on the
window and she rolled it down, putting on a sweet
smile that didn't suit her.

"This is private property, miss. I'm s-s-sorry," he
stuttered, no doubt taken aback by finding a gorgeous
woman behind the tinted window.

"It's her property," Georgia said in a voice so
sugary I nearly gagged. She pointed to me and I
resisted the urge to sink into my seat.

"Hi," I said in a small voice.

The man's eyes bulged out of his head when he
saw me. Meanwhile, Georgia pulled out a badge that
identified her position with royal security. He
glanced at it, his eyes continuing to dart to me.

"I'm sorry," he said, beginning to wave us on.
"We don't get many visitors out here."

I started to ask him why that was, but Georgia
pulled past him. Trees lined the way, shading the
path as we continued toward the house. When they
ended, the drive opened into a large, circular drive

and Windsmoor came into view. It towered ahead, sprawling in every direction. The brick estate was half fortress, half country manor.

There was nothing remotely run-down about its appearance. The house was well-kept, the grounds tended, and, more significantly, it was huge. I gulped, considering the number of closets I might have to search.

Georgia pulled up to the front door and shut off the engine.

"Not very inconspicuous," I said.

She raised an eyebrow. "First, you own this place. Second, they might as well know they have company. Or did you want to skulk around and hope we don't get caught?"

She was right. There was no point sneaking around, since the guard had seen us. If Alexander hadn't noticed my absence by now, he would probably be alerted to my arrival at Windsmoor very soon.

I climbed out of the car with a hand on my stomach. The baby began to flutter around, and I took a deep breath, reminding myself that I needed to stay calm, no matter what I discovered. I rubbed my belly, silently promising him that everything was going to be okay.

Georgia didn't rush me. She stood to the side, an odd expression on her face as I took a moment to consider the needs of my unborn child. When I finally started toward the house, she startled, as if waking from a dream, and joined me.

"Do I knock?" I asked her when we reached the door.

"Alexander wouldn't," Georgia said dryly. Before I could open it, she stepped in front of me. "Let me."

She tried the knob and it turned. "Great security."

I peeked around her as she stepped inside. The house was dated—a time capsule. Some of it was traditionally Royal, with tapestries and paintings and overly ornate furniture. Nothing looked like it had changed for at least twenty years. But the space was clean. There wasn't a speck of dust to be found.

We looked to one another.

"What the—" But Georgia was cut short by a robust woman bustling into the entry. She had on an old-fashioned nurse's uniform and a shocked expression.

"We weren't told there would be visitors," she said curtly, but the moment the words left her mouth, she froze.

One day I would get used to being recognized like this, but it wasn't going to be today.

"Sometimes my husband forgets to share things." I searched for an excuse for our presence other than that I'd come to snoop around. "We're sorry for the intrusion. I came to—"

"Visit," Georgia broke in, shooting me a meaningful look.

"Of course. I do wish His Majesty had warned us about the visit. Not that there's much to prepare," she chattered as she led us through the labyrinthine halls. Georgia and I fell back a few steps.

"Visit?" I hissed under my breath.

"Look, I don't think Alexander got into medical kink," she whispered. "If there's a nurse, she's caring for someone."

I held my stomach tightly as we followed her, my mind spinning in every direction but finding no answers. Finally, we reached a long, paneled hallway. Forgotten family portraits smiled in welcome from the walls, as if pleased to finally be seen.

"This way," the nurse chirped. She didn't stop to wait for me as she ambled toward a door at the far end.

I started after her and Georgia grabbed my arm, stopping me.

"I'll be out here," she said softly.

"Come with me," I said, tugging her on, but she shook her head.

"Alexander kept this from everyone, even you. Part of being discreet is knowing when to turn around. He wouldn't want me in there, and I'm beginning to like my job," she added.

"Your job is safe," I promised her. She released my arm and gave me a small smile. That was the most encouragement I could expect from her.

I turned back to the door, considering what she'd said. Alexander had kept this from me. What was I risking by walking through that door? But it was what I stood to lose by not opening it that spurred me on.

CHAPTER TWENTY-NINE

ALEXANDER

I woke up alone. My hand swept over Clara's side of the bed as if it hoped to find her hiding in the sheets, but her spot was cold. Stumbling to my feet, I rubbed sleep from my eyes as I checked the clock on the nightstand. It wasn't even seven, which meant she must be with Elizabeth. Heading into the bathroom, I splashed water on my face and washed up, determined to relieve her from parental duties. I'd kept her up late. It was my turn to play daddy.

When I opened the door to the nursery, Penny sat quickly up in the chair. Her eyes dropped when she saw me standing in nothing but my pants. I hadn't thought to get dressed.

"Sorry, Sir," she called in a low, embarrassed voice. "I dozed off."

"Not to worry." I glanced around the room, but Elizabeth was the only other soul present. "Is my wife..."

Penny tiptoed across the room, her eyes still glued on the floor. "She called me in."

"Did she say why?" I asked in a strained voice. It wasn't unusual for Penny to come in if we had other engagements, but it was Sunday, the day we reserved for family.

Penny shook her copper head. "She did mention that you would be here, Sir."

"Of course," I murmured. I was out the door and across the hall, mobile in hand before her words struck me. Clara hadn't told her to call if she was needed. Instead, she'd shifted the responsibility to me. It wasn't like my wife. I dialed her number and it went instantly to voicemail.

I tore through our private apartments, my panic ratcheting higher with every empty room I found. When I reached her study and found it deserted, I called her again. But the photo of her, caught in a private moment while she slept, was the closest I came to reaching her.

A pit opened in my stomach, threatening to swallow my heart. I forced myself to dial another number. Norris answered immediately.

"She's gone," I mumbled, the words foreign to my lips. "Clara's gone."

"Did she say anything?" Brex pressed. "Did you two fight?" He had asked the question at least a dozen times.

I shook my head, still numb. Brex had arrived with Norris nearly an hour ago. My answer hadn't changed, but he still didn't seem satisfied. We stood in my bedroom, the last place I'd seen her. We'd yet to find any clue as to where she'd gone. "Something's wrong. Someone took her."

"Alexander, no one could have taken her. We would know," he said gently.

"Goddammit, I was making love to her a few hours ago. She didn't leave," I exploded, finally putting to words what everyone else thought.

I sank into a chair, collapsing under the weight of her absence. If only I knew she was safe. If there was a note. But there was nothing. She wasn't answering calls. I'd called Belle and Edward. Now they were worried, too, and I wasn't any closer to having answers. A dark thought occurred to me, one that sent my heart racing in my chest, but I forced myself to confront it.

"What's his number?" I asked Brexton. I didn't have to say what I was thinking.

He shook his head, dismissing the idea outright. "Alexander, there's no way."

"His number," I barked.

It took a few minutes for Norris to dig it out of a file. I'd never called him before.

"'Ello?" Anders' sleepy voice greeted me.

"Is she with you?" I forced myself to ask him, squeezing my eyes shut as unwanted visions of Clara in his bed swam to mind.

"What? Who is this?"

I didn't have time for this. "Is Clara with you?"

There was a pause and I died a million times in the silence. "What's the matter, brother? Lost your wife?"

I suddenly understood why so many monarchs executed their siblings. I didn't care what he was to me or what I'd promised Clara.

"So help me God, do you know where she is?" I growled. "Tell me or there will be a security team ripping your house apart in ten minutes."

"I haven't spoken to her," he said harshly. "I can only hope she scraped together the last bit of willpower she had and left your miserable ass."

I ended the call without another word. I didn't care what he thought about me or my marriage. Only one thing mattered to me now.

Brexton threw his mobile on the floor and cursed.

"What is it?" I swallowed, expecting the worst.

He bit his lips as if struggling with what he was about to tell me. "I can't reach Georgia."

"Georgia?" I repeated.

Clara wouldn't leave with Georgia, not given my past with her. But that only left one other possibility. Had I let the devil in through the front door?

"Georgia wouldn't," Brex said fiercely.

"Are you sure about that or are you too in love with her to see straight?"

"She wouldn't," he said again, stepping in front of me.

I grabbed his shirt and yanked him closer to me. "I don't care what you believe. Find them."

Georgia was a mercenary. I'd always known that. How had I let her close to my family? Her loyalty could be bought—but who had purchased it?

Brex hurried out to consult with our security teams, leaving me alone with Norris.

"We'll track her mobile. The men discovered a car is gone from the garage. They've turned on its tracking system." He paused and leveled a serious look at me. "We will find her."

It took an eternity to get a lock on the car. Brexton finally reappeared, and, without meeting my eyes, held out a tablet with a map. Tension tightened his jaw, but despite his obvious anger, he looked confused. "The car's outside of London. Not far from Windsor."

I took the extended tablet and stared at the screen.

"We're looking into it," Brex continued as Norris came to look at the map over my shoulder.

He stiffened but didn't say a word.

That was up to me. "There's no need."

I knew where she was. It was the why and how I lacked. I glanced to Norris and our eyes locked. He cleared his throat. "We have it from here."

"What?" Brex said, jerking back in surprise. "Are you fucking kidding me? What's going on, Poor Boy?"

"We have it from here," Norris repeated.

The door slammed behind Brexton and I wondered briefly if I'd finally driven him away for good. I trusted him with my family and my secrets, but I could never trust him with this. Norris was already on his own. He spoke in a low voice as I paced through the room. I watched as his expression shifted from grim to slack-jawed.

I stopped and clutched the mantle, searching for strength now that I had my answer. There would be questions later—mine and hers. For now, I needed to figure out how to face this.

"We have confirmation. Clara is at Windsmoor House," Norris said finally. "She arrived a few hours ago with Ms. Kincaid."

I closed my eyes, but my relief quickly transformed into dread.

"There's more. Something happened. *She's awake.*" His voice was gentle, his tone one he usually reserved for delivering delicate, but unwanted news.

It took a moment for Norris's words to sink in. When they did, my eyes flashed to him. I'd heard him wrong. "She?"

"It's a miracle," he said softly. His eyes drifted from mine to an old photo on the mantle next to me. The picture was of a family that didn't exist anymore —one that might never have existed as far as I knew. In it, my father was smiling, his arm hooked around a mother I didn't remember. Three dark-haired chil-

dren clustered at their feet, laughing, innocent to
what the future held.

The air left my lungs as though I'd been knocked
off my feet. I couldn't remember how to breathe. It
wasn't possible. I'd been told it wasn't possible. I'd
believed it wasn't possible. And a miracle? Miracles
were in short supply. "What are you saying?"

I didn't need Norris to answer. I didn't need my
old friend to repeat himself. Norris responded
anyway. "She's awake."

Unwanted family portraits lined the wood-
paneled corridor, which narrowed, then narrowed
again until it reached a single door. I took each step
dreading the next. I hadn't been here in years. There
hadn't been a point.

No one greeted me when I'd arrived. It wasn't a
surprise. Only a skeleton staff of people my father
had deemed his most loyal—his most discreet—had
remained over the years. I paused, my hand on the
knob, and glanced over my shoulder. Georgia and
Norris remained at the other end of the corridor. For
a second, I recalled the last time I'd come here. I'd left
and gone to Georgia. I'd whipped her back until it
was raw. Darkness had taken hold of me that day,
when I faced what I'd done, the monster I'd become.
Standing here now, I knew I'd never freed myself
from it. It was always waiting, one door away, ready
to consume me and everything I loved.

I chose to walk away from this, and instead to the light that Clara offered. Now she was here. I had no choice but to face the darkness once again. I opened the door and stepped inside.

The monitors were off, no longer necessary after the impossible had happened. Clara didn't look towards me, her eyes were on the bed.

"It's a miracle," the nurse, whose name I'd long ago forgotten, said as she met me at the door.

I didn't tell her I'd stopped believing in miracles. After all, I did believe in Clara, and Clara was here. Had she led her out of darkness like she'd done for me?

"You didn't tell us anyone was coming," the nurse added under her breath. I didn't miss the edge of accusation there.

My gaze stayed on my wife, who was sitting, trying to process the family secret I'd guarded with my own life.

"We weren't informed your wife knew about—" the nurse continued before I cut her off.

"I don't have any secrets from Clara."

Not anymore.

The love story continues...
A shocking revelation and an unexpected miracle bring darkness to the Royal family's doorstep in Claim Me, the second volume in the Royal World.

Read Claim Me now!

Keep reading for a sneak peek of
Claim Me!

Want updates, exclusive bonus content, including
the newsletter first book: *X* (Alexander's story)?
Become a VIP:
http://www.genevalee.com/vip

Love all things royal? Join my private reader group on
facebook:
Geneva Lee's Loves

AND NOW A SNEAK PEEK AT CLAIM ME:

The creak of the door alerted the nurse to
Alexander's presence, but I'd felt him coming long
before that. I'd known he would come. An hour ago,
I'd felt a prickle along my skin. Moments ago, goose-
bumps had broken out on my arms. Before the door
opened, a shiver ran up my neck. My body responded
to him like air surging before an approaching storm.

But today Alexander wasn't the reckoning.

I was.

I didn't turn. It wasn't that I couldn't face him,
but rather that I refused to look at him. Instead, my
eyes stayed on hers, briefly closing when I heard him
speak.

"I don't have any secrets from my wife."

I would have laughed if I'd had it in me. Another lie. It was getting harder to decide which I hated more, the lies or the secrets, although it didn't seem like there was much difference between the two.

She glanced up, drinking in Alexander's words before her eyes darted back to me. Now she was piecing it together. I hadn't explained who I was. It felt wrong, somehow, to be the one to tell her. She had missed so much of Alexander's life. How was I supposed to tell her that I was his wife? That we had a child together? That I was expecting another? There were years of information to relay, and I had started my relationship with her by keeping secrets.

Maybe my husband and I weren't so different after all.

There hadn't been much time to tell her anything before Alexander arrived, anyway. First, the nurse panicked and checked all her vitals. I remained off to the side, largely unnoticed. Then the doctor had arrived. I was only alone with her for a few minutes. She had only asked one question.

"Where is my family?"

I'd told her he was on his way. I had known he would find me. It was one way he never let me down. After that, the uncomfortable silence set in. I'd offered her my name and told her I was a friend.

When Alexander clarified who I really was, she continued to stare at me.

"Wife?" Her voice was still weak, feeble from

years of silence, but the tremble of pain in that one word had nothing to do with it. I couldn't bring myself to meet her eyes and look into their shadowed, blank depths.

I only nodded. I couldn't do this. He had kept this from me for a reason. Later, I would make him explain why. Now? I didn't want to be here. I had no place in this family reunion. She was as much a stranger to me as I was to her. Alexander had seen to that.

Rising to my feet, I forced a small smile. "Excuse me."

I moved quickly, refusing to allow myself time to reconsider. I needed to get away from her. I needed to be away from him. I needed to be able to think.

Alexander reached for me as I passed, but I skirted away, shaking my head. Even now, my body fought against me, tempting me toward him like a bee to honey. He'd thrown on jeans and a t-shirt that hugged his powerful body, stubble peppered his jawline, and his black hair was a chaotic mess. Apart from the clothing, this was the man I would have woken up to if I had stayed in bed. We would have made love. I could almost feel the scratch of his stubble on my thighs. I'd come here instead, lured into the darkness of his past and the mistakes we couldn't seem to escape. It's what kept me from going to him now—even a bee could drown in honey.

"Clara," he said in a hollow voice, his blue eyes

flashing with regret. He didn't speak again as I reached the door. He didn't try to stop me.

We both knew it wouldn't matter. There was nothing he could say. I thought he'd given me all of him — body, heart, soul. I was wrong.

Claim Me is available now!

SOMETHING WICKED THIS WAY
COMES...

Our love has become poison and it's killing us slowly.

I hate how I can't control myself around him. I hate how I always forgive him. I hate that he consumes me. Because Alexander is in my blood. His heart beats in my chest.

He owns me.

But I can't see past his betrayal and his lies. Not this time. I don't know if our love can survive this, because I'm not the girl that fell in love with him anymore. I'm a queen and everyone, even him, will bow to me.

Every family has its secrets. The Royals more than most. The next seductive chapter in the Royal World is hotter, darker, and wilder than ever.

CLAIM ME
AVAILABLE NOW

ACKNOWLEDGMENTS

There are so many people who made this book a reality. First of all to every reader who's asked for more Royals at signings, over emails, online, thank you for loving these characters as much as I do! This book is for you!

To Louise Fury, thank you for standing by me through the last few years as I've navigated new waters. I couldn't ask for a better business partner. A big shout out to Victoria Capello and the team at The Bent Agency for all their hard work. Thank you to my foreign agents for helping bring my words to readers all over the world!

This book wouldn't be here without the support, encouragement and friendship of Audrey Carlan. Thank you for helping me trust the journey even when the road got dark. Brighter days are ahead for us, my friend.

There are a lot of people who have helped lift me

up over the course of writing this book and the last few years. I'm not going to get them all but I want to say a special thanks to Jeananna Goodall, Jessica Laws, Selina Washington, Camille Newman, Kimberly Newman, Christina Brame, Shana Gray, and Trish L. McHugh. Thank you to Elsi Gabrielsen for giving me the stars!

To my author friends—there are too many of you to name—a thanks. Some of you are about to see your first movies come to the screen, others of you are just getting started. You are ALL an inspiration to me with your words and your stories. I am so blessed to know you and learn from you. Thank you

It takes a village to write a book and to keep me sane, thank you to my family and friends for understanding when I miss a call because "I'm in London." But a village needs leaders and mine wouldn't function at all without Elise Lee. You are my best friend, my business partner, my sister. I see more wild adventures ahead!

Thank you to my editor Tamara Mataya for gleefully converting Alexander's chapters to British English. You are the best.

To the kids, thank you for sharing your mother with her other family—and for learning how to load the dishwasher.

And to Josh, thank you for always reading, for always taking Clara's side, for always being there. In other words, for always.

ABOUT THE AUTHOR

Geneva Lee is the *New York Times*, *USA Today*, and internationally bestselling author of eighteen novels. Her bestselling Royals Saga has sold nearly two million copies worldwide. She is the co-owner of Away With Words, a destination bookstore in Poulsbo, Washington where she lives with her family. When she isn't traveling, she can usually be found writing, reading, or buying another pair of shoes.

Learn more about Geneva Lee at:
www.GenevaLee.com

Made in the USA
Las Vegas, NV
24 April 2023

71026975R00218